KEEPER OF THE LIGHT

Leanne Lovegrove

www.BOROUGHSPUBLISHINGGROUP.com

KEEPER OF THE LIGHT
Copyright © 2020 Leanne Lovegrove

ISBN: 978-1-953810-01-4

Dear Eloise, you brighten up every day, I love you, Mum

ACKNOWLEDGMENTS

My sincere thanks to you, the reader, for choosing *Keeper of the Light*. I loved writing the story so much and visiting Bruny Island and the lighthouse which provided the inspiration for the novel.

Foremost, to my first reader and greatest support, my husband Justin, and to the three teenagers who tolerate their mother reading and writing ALL the time. My love and thanks to all of you.

Many people have assisted bring this novel to life, special thanks to my writing friend and mentor, Annie Seaton, my writing group pals, and especially Sue, my neighbour, Liana, for the endless enthusiasm about my work, and to all of the fabulous authors I have met and everyone else who has supported me along the way.

KEEPER OF THE LIGHT

Chapter One

May 1952

Esther heard it first in her dreams. A loud, sharp crack. The hairs on her arms stood with a rush of goose bumps as crisp morning air kissed her bare arms.

What was it?

She opened an eye to search for her blankets and felt the glare of bright, dawn light as it crept into her bedroom. The covers hung from the bedframe and she reached to wrap them around her body.

Please don't let it be daytime yet. That damn storm.

Thunder had echoed on the horizon and rain had pelted against the windowpanes throughout the whole night. With each rumble, she'd woken. And that had meant a fitful sleep.

The day hadn't even begun—and there'd be plenty to do when it did. It was no longer raining, but she heard the wind. There'd be a mess to clean up this morning. Already, she dreaded the hours ahead.

Rolling over, she tugged the blankets with her, warm and snuggly now, and willed sleep to return. Instead, *bang*, there it was again.

Fully awake now, she waited, she listened. The world on Cape Bruny was not yet stirring, but something disturbed her.

A clapping noise.

She sat upright. Her heart jumped in her chest.

A shutter. It was slapping in the wind. Squeezing her eyes shut, she lay back down and threw the covers over her face. Was the mail due today? Would she have the next edition of her *Australian Women's Weekly* to drool over when the chores were done? She sure hoped so.

Once, twice more, the shutter struck, mocking her and her desire for sleep.

She tuned in for the sound of footsteps within the small cottage.

"Damn it," she cussed as the shutter slapped again. Couldn't anyone else hear it? Instead, her father's melodic snoring reverberated around the quiet rooms. What of her brother, Charles? Surely he would rise and stop the din? Thirty seconds passed and no one stirred.

Esther sighed, threw back her blankets, and searched for the slippers under her bed. She pulled on her well-worn robe and crossed the bedroom she shared with her sister, Margaret.

Oh, to be a child and sleep through this racket.

The force of the squall drove her backwards as she swung open the front door. Arms straining, she managed to yank it shut behind her.

Outside, the wind howled, whipping strands of hair against her cheeks and stinging them. It shook all sleepiness away. Esther tasted salt on her tongue, whisked up from the ocean below. At the southern edge of South Bruny Island, Tasmania, a breeze always blew, but today it was turbulent. The steep surrounding cliffs did little to protect the community perched at the apex. She'd grown used to the whims of the weather on the island. Today it was wind…better than rain.

She rounded the cottage perimeter to search for the shutter. It released once more and slammed back against its casings.

Esther reached for it and latched it back in place. With one last look around, she turned back towards the house. Her mother would be proud that she'd alleviated the problem without fuss. Maybe she wouldn't be accused of daydreaming today.

Pleased with herself, she walked faster now, picturing her warm bed. She almost stumbled as a strong gust rose over the cliff edge. With it came a muffled groan.

It sounded like a cry for help. Listening, she heard it again. No mistake. A moan. She paused. Something was out there. Had the cow gone into calf? Perhaps a wounded animal? There were so many rabbits in these parts that one could have been attacked by a fox or feral cat…. But a poor little rabbit wasn't likely to moan.

Sighing? A whimper perhaps? Was it Lady, their dog, caught outdoors?

The wind rattled in Esther's ears and made it impossible to pick the direction of the noise. Common sense steered her towards the far rise, above the bay. Fallen tree branches were in her path and she was forced to clamber over them. Leaves swirled past in the wind, dancing wildly. The chill crept into her bones, and her arms and legs trembled.

Another cry, this one louder. Her heart hammered hard against her chest and her breath became short.

Esther gazed across the thick foliage around her feet and the nearby verge where the hill descended to the beach.

Why would anyone be here? And, more importantly, who could it possibly be?

The path was steep and rocky, and unlike her brothers, who raced along the well-trodden paths, she rarely ventured south, preferring the safety of the summit. Forgetting that now, she stepped forward.

A twig cracked behind her and Esther spun on the spot. Her hand clutched her throat as her eyes darted left and right, searching. She forced herself to swallow to moisten her dry mouth as the grass crunched under her feet. She fought the urge to flee.

Three gulls flew low, heading straight for her so she had no choice but to duck. They squawked and zoomed in a frenzied state. Bent over, she glimpsed a shot of red in the grass. A face rose and stared at her. A man. She screamed, but her voice was swallowed by the wind.

***

"Father," Esther shrieked, letting the door slam shut this time before she skidded down the hallway on her heels.

"Father." She thumped her fist on her parents' bedroom door. Inside, she heard her mother mutter.

"Come in," said her father. His head poked up from his pillow, his grey hair tousled from sleep. Mary Anderson scowled, as usual.

"There's a man out on the rise. A broken shutter woke me, smashing against the windows, and I couldn't stand the noise because it prevented me from sleeping, so I thought I would let everyone else rest and go and fix it. But when I was out there, I heard noises and it sounded like a person or maybe an injured animal—"

"Esther." Her mother's voice was stern. Her father put his hand on her mother's arm. Esther was rambling and her hands shook. She must look a fright, too.

John Anderson, keeper of the lighthouse on Cape Bruny, got up. "Go and wake your brother."

Esther raced to the front bedroom that her eldest brother, Charles, who was twenty-one, shared with twelve-year-old Tommy. Both were fast asleep in their bunks, their mouths open in blissful slumber.

"Charles, wake up." She grabbed his shoulders and shook him. His head tilted sideways towards her voice and his mouth shut and swallowed. He settled back for further rest. "Charles." she spoke louder and rustled him for good measure.

Keeping his eyes squeezed shut, he said, "What is it, Esther?"

He wasn't taking her seriously. Well, he would.

"There's a man on the cliff. He's hurt…"

Charles opened his eyes.

"Father said you have to come."

He jumped from his bed and reached for his clothes.

Their father stood in the doorway, pulling on his heavy jacket. He must have dressed in haste, but like always, his clothes were impeccable. Father was notorious for wearing his suspender belt with tweed trousers and matching jacket. Everyone in the family thought it ludicrous given their isolation, but Father maintained how you dressed determined your attitude for the day. As a flashback from his military days, it also meant a well-structured day spent in productive engagement. Perhaps that was why Esther screamed around like a banshee dressed only in her nightgown and slippers, her hair a tangled mess.

Standing next to her father and brother, she whispered, "I think he's a foreigner."

The man was unlike any she'd seen before. Not that she'd met many men, having lived on the Cape for the previous five years. This man was dark, though not of skin; his hair was jet black, with bushy, thick eyebrows and eyes like midnight. His hair was long. Elongated fingers had reached for her and, at that, she'd collapsed back onto her bottom. He spoke in an unfamiliar tongue. At the sight of blood on his cheek and the way he'd clutched at his arm, she'd jumped up and sprinted back to the cottage. Her lungs had stung as the cold bit at her skin and snatched away her short breaths on the mad dash from the cliff.

She bolted ahead of her family. This man was different than her father, who'd been prematurely grey for ages, well advanced of his forty-five years. She'd always thought it made him look distinguished, as if he could have appeared on one of the pages of her *Women's Weekly*. If her father's hair had ever been dark, she couldn't remember it in her eighteen years of life.

Esther couldn't hear any moaning as they strode back along the path. She searched for his bright red jacket, but before she found it, she saw the shock of black hair.

Trailing behind, her father remained silent; he never spoke without purpose. It was as though it would evaporate useful energy if he prattled on unnecessarily. This was one trait Esther had not inherited. As her father reached the man, he bent low and spoke calmly. The man responded in broken English. Esther clapped her hands together before he wailed as her father checked his injuries. His arm rested at an odd angle, turning sideways when it shouldn't. Instinctively, she cradled her own arm.

"Esther, return to the cottage. Fetch the medicine kit and prepare the sofa in the front room."

She nodded but her feet seemed cemented to the spot.

"Go now, hurry."

She raced back along the track. Albert Hawkins, assistant lightkeeper, came outside and blocked her path.

"Urgh," she said as her bare skin touched his body.

"What's going on?" he asked. Esther went to move around him, but he grasped her arm. She attempted to shake it free, but he held fast, wanting an answer.

"Go see for yourself."

He shoved past her.

Esther entered the cottage and her mother held up her flat palm. "Calm yourself, Esther. Tell me plainly without any dramatics what is to be done."

Chastened, Esther rose taller, squared her shoulders, and gulped down two deep breaths. Mother was always one for propriety, and Esther wondered what situation would cause her mother's slick bun to become dishevelled. In the few short minutes they'd been gone, her mother had dressed for the day ahead. Her trademark bun was perfectly smooth and in position. Unlike her father, Mother didn't dress to match her attitude; it was all about decency and *doing the right thing*.

Only when she was the recipient of an admonishing stare did Esther continue. "Father says to retrieve the medical kit and prepare the sofa in the front room."

Her mother nodded so Esther bit back the rest of her words. She was desperate to describe the blood that oozed from the stranger's gaping wounds.

The front door opened. She dashed down the short hall and watched her father and Charles; their backs buckled under the weight of the man, who was struggling to stay upright. His face was scrunched in pain.

That is a good sign, surely? But a sign of what, she wasn't sure.

As they shuffled in, her mother placed a sheet over the settee.

Albert Hawkins followed like a lost puppy behind them. He blocked Esther's view and she shifted from foot to foot to gain a better vantage.

The stranger's eyes were squeezed shut, his face clenched in agony as he was placed on the sofa. His ripped shirt hung open, revealing bare flesh. She fixated on the mass of black hair covering his chest and her gaze roamed over his body. A sudden rush of warmth flooded her, and the air around her became electrified. He was beautiful, and Esther surged with an immediate, overwhelming attraction.

And then she couldn't see as Mother peered into her face.

"For goodness sake, Esther, get dressed. And stoke the fire before putting the kettle on for tea." Her mother didn't shift until Esther, wide-eyed, skulked from the room.

Chapter Two

Esther yanked on yesterday's dress and dragged a brush through her hair. She found her sensible house shoes and slipped them on her chilled feet. Within minutes, she smoothed down her hair as she re-entered the front room.

Three heads were bent over the man.

Where should she stand? She shuffled to get a better view. He moaned. Damn it, she wanted to see him, but didn't want to get in the way, particularly in her mother's way.

Oh no. What were her mother's directions? Was it to fetch clean towels? Oh well, she watched instead. The air smelled of murky water and grime, as though the outdoors had entered the house.

"Charles," her father said. "Radio for the doctor."

Her brother hurried from the room.

Father then turned to Albert. "Please alert the authorities to commence a search."

Unlike her brother, Albert hobbled away.

For once, Mother was preoccupied as well. She didn't bark at Esther to get on with it—whatever *it* was, she couldn't remember. Mary administered pain relief. At least that might stop the man's distressing groans. Even when her younger siblings had hurt themselves, they never released such agonizing growls.

With the room emptying, Esther had a clear view. The man's head lolled sideways on the worn armrest. She reached for a cushion and put it forward, once, twice and paused. She'd never touched a man before. Her mother seized the pillow and placed it under his head, regarding her with raised eyebrows, as though she hadn't seen her daughter as a young woman before.

"Fetch a bowl of hot water, please, Esther. His grazes and cuts need cleaning."

"Yes, Mother."

As the water boiled, she remembered the tea and placed leaves into the pot to brew. And the fire, darn it. They'd all be freezing soon. Where was Tommy?

"Tommy," she called out as she raced to his room. He was still in bed, dead to the world. "Tommy. Wake up. How can you sleep through all this commotion?" she said as she shook him awake. "Tommy, I need your help. A man is injured in the front parlour. We need firewood. Can you collect some, please?"

Her brother opened his eyes and yanked off the sheets and placed his feet over the edge of the bed, alert and already searching for his clothes.

"Quickly, I'm helping with his wounds, can you get the wood and stoke the fire?"

Her young brother nodded.

Esther returned with a tray holding the teapot, cups and saucers, and a bowl of tepid water.

The man was speaking what sounded like gibberish to her. What on earth had happened to him? Esther wanted to ask her father a thousand questions.

As if her mother sensed her curiosity, she glared at her. That's all it took, and her mouth clamped shut.

Instead, she watched as her mother gently wiped away the grime and pebbles that had collected in his grazes. He was so tall. And more of that curly hair sprang from his calves, lessening as it moved up his legs.

"Help me, Esther, please. Like this." Her mother applied careful strokes. The man writhed as she sponged into the deep folds of skin. As he moved, his chest was exposed once more, and Esther's gaze transfixed on his torso. His chest rose and fell with his pained breaths. Her fingers itched to reach out, to run them through his coarse chest hair, even though she knew she'd never be brave or bold enough to do so.

Still, the temptation.

Her mother's eagle eye felt like it burned her skin.

"If you're not going to help, get your father a cup of tea. He hasn't had a drink since he woke."

Neither have I. Esther bit her tongue.

She served her parents and noticed the moaning had stopped. The man no longer wriggled in agony. Thank goodness the Bex had worked. Her father had performed his handiwork on the man's forearm, and it was now secured in a splint using a short plank of timber and wrapped in a bandage.

He'd completed such intricate work in a short space of time. Her chest puffed out a little in admiration of her father.

Tommy slid into the room on his socks and almost toppled the timber he cradled in his arms.

"*Tommy*," their mother admonished harshly.

"Sorry, Mother."

Tommy kneeled at the grate and worked on building the fire. Glad of the disruption, Esther turned away. She soaked the cloth in the water and squeezed out the excess before starting to clean the man's feet.

She could do it.

Her parents drifted into the kitchen. Esther's mouth watered as the smell of fresh bread toasting wafted into the room. The kettle boiled with a whistle before she heard the clink of china.

"That's a beauty," Esther said, nodding towards the raging fire. "I feel warmer already."

"What do you think happened to him?"

"Who knows? I can't imagine how anyone would end up here. And on the cliff, of all places. As far as isolation goes, we top the list, don't we, Tommy? There's a mighty stretch of sea across the Tasman from Hobart. And he had to have come by boat. I can't imagine he travelled by road. What a mystery."

They paused and considered the man sprawled out before them. At present, quiet and hopefully comfortable.

"I'm guessing he's had an adventure and I can't wait to hear it." Tommy said, and he left the room too.

Esther brushed the cloth between the man's narrow toes and around the long, smooth-lined soles. He even had sprinkles of hair on each knuckle. Her hands shook a little as she worked, but her strength garnered when he didn't move.

Her heart raced and her breaths came short and fast as her hands moved up to his chest. Most of his scrapes were on his torso, and there was a nasty gash to his head. Her mother had tended to that earlier. She was certain the man would wake due to the sound of her thudding heart.

Was it a sin to enjoy touching him so much? Gertrude, her friend and the postman's daughter, would call her a baby, but she wasn't a scaredy-cat.

Esther's hands hovered before she connected with a gash on his chest, below his left nipple. Instead of cleaning the cut, she couldn't tear her gaze away from the dark pink circle.

Flustered, her hands tremored as she worked her way across his shoulders. She touched bare, olive skin.

She leaned in close, examining his features, and his breath brushed her cheek. A short beard lined his face.

Gathering further courage, she applied the washer to his face. His eyebrows glistened after a few gentle wipes and he almost looked fresh. Excepting, of course, the gash to his forehead. The blood had soaked through, turning the white compress a nasty shade of brown. Esther pulled away the dirty dressing. Fresh blood oozed from the wound. It was wide and open, and she saw the little blisters of skin under the surface.

This cut needed stitches. Where was the doctor?

She didn't hear her mother enter.

"Esther?"

"Mm?" she murmured, not looking up.

"It's lunchtime. Have you left his bedside since this morning?"

"No, but that's okay. I wanted to clean his wounds so he might feel better. Why is the doctor taking so long?"

"Charles called for him first thing, but he was with another patient. He knows we need him and he'll come as soon as he can. All we can do is keep him comfortable until then. You need to take a break and eat something. Plus, there's work to be done."

"Yes, Mother."

Her time was up. Esther sighed, sloshed the cloth into the bowl and looked at the sleeping giant. Her hands felt cold now they'd left his skin. They twitched to be touching him again. Why did it feel so exciting to be near him—a man she didn't know? Why did she long to keep touching him? Was it because her own skin came alive and a tingle developed deep down inside? It was a funny feeling, one she'd not experienced before. Not quite excitement or nerves, but something in between. One thing she did know was that she wanted to stay by his side. Something pulled her to him. She vowed to come back as soon as she could.

Her mother kept Esther engaged that long afternoon. The door to the front room remained shut. It was as if a strange man wasn't taking up space in their sitting room.

Outside, Esther drank in the fresh ocean air. After the fetid air filled with filth and antiseptic, it was a welcome reprieve. The gushing winds had died down and the world smelled fresh and cleansed after the downpour of last night. The sky gave everything a yellow flush.

"How is he, Esther?" Margaret asked as Esther approached the pigpen. "Mother hasn't allowed me anywhere near at all. It's so unfair." Margaret paused to pull a face and Esther shot her a distracted smile. "I've fed all the animals and milked the cows."

"Thanks, Margaret. He's sleeping. Has a rather bad arm, but we're waiting on Doctor Collins to know more. I feel so sorry for him. Can you imagine what's happened to him?"

Margaret shrugged and turned towards the house, shouting over her shoulder, "I've done enough jobs. I'll leave the washing for you. I'm sixteen after all, not the maid of this house."

Esther would usually scoff. The washing wasn't her chore, but today she needed to be occupied. Most likely, Margaret would hole up somewhere and check her nail polish hadn't chipped. Esther couldn't lecture. If her magazine arrived today, she'd be hiding somewhere, too—perhaps on one of the faraway boulders lining the cliff—reading it from cover to cover.

Esther checked the pigs, ensured the cows were happy, the chickens had seed, and the goats weren't eating her vegetable patch.

Oh, her garden. The storm had ravaged it, having no mercy for her broad beans or broccoli or lettuce. They were shredded. Esther collected the bruised tomatoes—those, at least, could be boiled up for a tasty sauce. She tided the mess as best she could. The rest would have to wait until tomorrow.

Her gaze caught the vastness of the ocean. It engulfed her, this sense of place. She knew a world existed across the waters, outside their little community. But that world had entered their domain today and delivered them an exotic package. This dark man with his foreign accent represented a world she'd never seen. What was out there? Was it anything like she imagined from her magazines?

Albert shuffled along the path towards the lighthouse, his customary scowl prominent. He always appeared as if he wanted to walk faster and unaided. Little was known of his injury and sudden discharge from the army, but he and his bung leg and bad mood had become a permanent and unwelcome fixture at the lighthouse. She darted into the laundry room to avoid him, but she wasn't fast enough.

Albert sidled up, his body touching hers.

Esther decided to play nice. "Hello, Albert."

A sly grin spread across his face, revealing his missing front tooth. He wore an odour of stale alcohol. Unable to place too much weight on his leg, he steadied his balance, pushing against her. Esther's stomach clenched and she gagged, his touch repulsive. His hand found her thigh. She stepped sideways but couldn't escape.

"Take your hand off me," she said.

He laughed and the blood froze in her veins. The back door opened and shut. If the person stepped into the yard, they'd have a direct view of Hawkins and his wandering hand. He was too smart for that and he dropped it.

It was times like this the serenity of the lighthouse became tainted. Its isolation like a rope around her, tethering her to it, preventing escape. How could a place be filled with such beauty and wonder and yet have Hawkins contaminate it? Did the man inside treat women that way? Was it normal to claw at them and leer in their face? Treat them like a possession? Esther didn't know much, but the movie stars she read about didn't look like they'd let a man treat them like that. She didn't think their stranger would either.

Chapter Three

That night, Esther should have slipped into a dreamless sleep. But she didn't. All she could think about was *him.*

When she eventually drifted off, even her dreams were filled with the dark stranger who spoke in a foreign tongue. The words that frightened her at the time now sounded like expressions of love. The verses replayed in her head, as beautiful as poetry, and she curled her lips into a smile as she dozed. As he leaned in to kiss her, she woke. Her skin was moist and her heart raced faster than it should during sleep.

In the early hours, after the visions disappeared and she'd fought with her bed covers for too long, Esther gave up on sleeping. She had to see him and reassure herself he was real. Her mother regularly reminded her that she was not sufficiently self-disciplined. She didn't care, though. Her urge to see him was strong and, quite frankly, not something she wanted to ignore. The feelings were all the more severe as her mother had refused to let her see him after dinner. She'd longed to check on his cuts and wipe his brow of sweat. Or simply gaze at him.

"You've done quite enough today," Mother had said. "Get along and do something useful. Finish your cross-stitch." She might as well have directed her to butcher the cow for supper, such was her hatred of boring old cross-stitch. Instead, Esther had slunk to her room. Her stomach had had a hundred little butterflies playing games. Occasionally, those beautiful butterflies turned into grey moths fighting for space and attacking each other. Esther didn't understand these feelings, but she knew life at the lighthouse had irretrievably changed. That thought both exhilarated her and made her sick.

Enough. She got up and snuck into the front room. The door was ajar, and she pulled it closed behind her. She was alone with him once more. Her heart gave an extra-strong beat and all those moths disappeared.

The air smelled stale. Despite the cooler temperature, he would surely need fresh air, wouldn't he? A swift breeze off the ocean would do him the world of good, as her mother would say. Esther only opened the window an inch. She wasn't sure about him, but she felt immediately invigorated.

The world outside was still dark and eerie. Almost every ten seconds the beam of the lighthouse light swept across the room, engulfing it in brightness. She switched on the lamp in the corner near the sofa. It clicked and she froze as he stirred and shifted onto his side. After a few seconds, her pulse slowed and she moved closer. His face was free of creases and his forehead clear. She was unsure whether he was unconscious or merely asleep, but he looked peaceful nonetheless. Blankets now covered his torso, his body tucked within its confines. Esther patted down the sides to keep him warm. Again, he didn't fuss.

Checking on the handsome visitor had to be a valid excuse to be in the room with him. And he *was* handsome, wasn't he? If the men in her magazines were any example, he looked like he'd walked off their pages. His lanky frame would fit the suave suits of the day. One with pinstripes, she imagined. And a hat. Definitely a black felt bowler hat. Goodness knows why, it would be ridiculously unsuitable.

He sure had slept a long time. She leaned over and felt his warm breath in the guise of checking if he was alive. She breathed him in. He had a manly smell: spicy and woody. Such a different scent than her father and brothers, who smelled of oil and grease.

His eyes were closed, and his hands lay atop the blanket. The skin was tanned and blemish-free, but his nails were dirty—the only evidence of his travails from yesterday. Smudges of mud lined his fingers. Damn, she hadn't wiped his hands.

His splint rested on his body. With one finger she traced along his knuckles and across his fingertips. Her breath caught in her throat, but not in an unpleasant way, such as when she ran too fast along the beach or like a loud laugh that might bubble out of you, filling you up with happiness. She had no words to describe the feeling. Standing close to him, her nerve endings tingled but her stomach quivered; it was an odd sensation, but she already knew she liked it and wanted to experience it over and over again.

Would his personality be dark? Was he a bleak, callous man like ghastly Hawkins? She couldn't believe he would be.

Esther wanted him to wake. Sleep was lost to her now and there was no way she'd leave him. She settled in the armchair and pulled a magazine from the rack. Its pages were dog-eared and worn. She knew every page. Reading material was scarce on the Cape and she'd read her few books and her beloved magazines until she'd memorised the words.

A sharp tug to her arm and the magazine dropped from her lap, waking her. A twinge shot up her neck from its crooked position on the arm of the chair. Rays of sunshine snuck through the cracks in the curtains and lit up the room.

Another harder pull to her arm.

"Where am I?" The voice was raspy.

The man leaned in, peering perilously close. His brow was creased and his eyebrows raised in question.

"Oh, you're awake," she stammered. She tried to increase the distance between them, but he didn't release her.

"Where is this?" He indicated a wide arc with his injured arm before placing it back down. Tears pooled in the corners of his eyes.

"Don't move. You're hurt." Esther pointed to his splint and inched forward. "The doctor is coming."

The blankets tipped to reveal his body. His left hand roamed over his legs, his face scrunching up as he hit bumpy abrasions. Fear radiated from him and he talked fast in that strange language. Suddenly it sounded vulgar.

"You're on Cape Bruny, at the lighthouse. I found you…"

He turned towards her and stared hard, straight into her eyes, and held her gaze. He shuffled his feet to stand, and when that didn't work, he supported his body weight on the armrest but fell sideways at the first attempt. He yelled and pumped his fist against the cushions. His eyes bulged so she saw the whites. He reached for her to help lift himself upwards. His grip was tight and she grimaced.

"No, you mustn't, shouldn't move—"

Ignoring her, he didn't notice as he slipped from the settee. His splint connected with the lamp next to Esther's chair. It smashed to the ground, lime green shards shattering across the floor. As the glass bounced off the ground, Esther landed with a thump and they toppled together. She closed her eyes as glass scattered onto her nightdress. His body struck the hard floor and his leg straddled her lap, pinning her to the spot.

She screamed.

The door slammed open. Her parents rushed in.

"Esther. Get up this instant," her mother ordered.

Shock had locked her jaws shut. She fumbled wildly, pushing at him to get off, but instead, brushed his hairy leg and felt the curve of his bottom.

Her mother yanked at her arms uselessly, but she couldn't move.

"Mary, get Charles."

Mother rushed from the room. Esther calmed her breathing. The man was on top of her. At the feel of his body against her, a red-hot flush crept up her neck. With her fingers, she drew together the gaping neckline of her night dress and clasped her hands there. Where else could she put them? Anywhere else and she'd touch the stranger in places that would make her hands shake.

Charles arrived and they pulled the fellow to his feet and placed him back on the couch. As he was lowered, his eyes connected with Esther's. She'd remembered right, those eyes were dark. His forehead cleared and his mouth opened slightly.

Oh my.

Once the man was settled, her father assisted her back on her feet. Her mother bustled in, crunching over the broken glass.

"What on earth, Esther? What were you doing in here, alone?"

"I-I, um, came to check on him, Mother. See if he needed anything."

"And why was he moving?"

"I don't know. I think I fell asleep and he woke and became frightened." She turned to look at him again. "He was unsure where he was." He was watching her lips move.

Father sat down beside him and placed one hand on his knee. It calmed the man instantly. Father gestured with his hands to his mouth, like you would to an infant. Food. Of course, he must be starving. Esther was annoyed she hadn't thought of that.

The man answered, *"Si."*

Her parents turned to one another. Esther gasped.

"Is that Italian?" she asked. Her father nodded.

"Hurt." He cradled his arm.

Her father nodded. "Yes, you're hurt. You've injured your arm and head."

The man touched his forehead. As he took his hand away, he considered it, like it might be bloody. It was clear.

Father turned to Mary. "He must need more pain relief. Let's fetch that and some food. And maybe change his dressings, too."

"Esther, come with me, please," Mary said.

Esther rose and cast a sidelong glance at the stranger. *Italian. Fancy that.* A real live Italian man in their cottage. He followed her with his gaze, his stare boring deep into her, steadfast and locked. Her heart raced. No one had ever looked at her like that. It seared into her, entering her soul and massaging her heart. Did he know she'd touched his naked body, admired him as he slept, and leaned in close when she shouldn't have?

Esther scurried away to avoid his scrutiny.

***

"Nope, he won't eat for me either," Margaret said as she entered the kitchen and placed the untouched plate of food on the table with a clatter. "But," she continued, "he told me he's twenty-two."

Margaret placed her hands on her hips, as if to say, so there, she'd succeeded. She could be such a little upstart at times.

"He was ever so nice about it, politely refusing to eat. Speaking in Italian. He said he has sisters, one named Sofia and another named Anna."

Deep down, a longing tugged in Esther's stomach. She'd wanted to be the one to speak with him and extract his story.

Her mother and father exchanged a glance.

"Well, he needs to eat, otherwise he won't heal," said her father. "But, moreover, I need to know what happened to assist the search. If he doesn't eat or doesn't speak, we'll be in a right pickle." He shook his head. "Charles, you try. Might help being man to man."

Charles's look conveyed that he doubted it, but nonetheless he obeyed and snatched up the plate.

Fifteen minutes later, Charles returned with a still-full plate and shook his head. "No words and no food. Maybe he doesn't like it? They do eat different foods in Italy." This hadn't occurred to anyone.

Mother had made a typical sandwich of leftover corned beef and mustard on thick wholemeal slices. "He probably wants cheeses and salamis and crackers with olives."

"Did he say that?" she asked.

"He said, no, *grazie,* and shook his head." Charles bit into the sandwich and shrugged. "No point it going to waste."

Margaret opened various cupboards and rifled through the contents. Eventually, she collected an assortment of salted crackers, some ham, and a few cubes of cheese. "Worth a try," she said. Esther reached for the tray but Tommy snatched it away.

"My turn," he squealed and ran off, almost spilling the food.

Esther tapped her foot, her mother and father shared yet another cup of tea, her brother and sister bickered, and together, they all kept checking the clock.

"Boy, he's interesting," Tommy said as he raced back into the kitchen. The boy never walked when he could run. "His name is Luca and his family live in some long-sounding place that I can't pronounce, but starts with an M, which apparently is in a part of Italy called Tuscany. He tried a cracker with the ham and cheese but screwed up his face. He started talking about wine, I think." Tommy laughed. "Do you think he'd like a beer?"

"So, he can speak English well, then?" her father asked, ignoring the part about the beer.

"Well, it was a bit funny. Some words were out of order, and he says everything with a twang, but I could understand him."

"Luca," Esther whispered.

The unmistakable rumble of a car engine drifted in through the windows, rattling on their unsealed road. Quickly thereafter, there was the clunk of a handbrake.

"The doctor. Thank goodness." Her father rose to welcome Dr Collins. Tommy tore out after him, yelling to the doctor all the minute detail he'd discovered about the man in their front room.

Where had the day disappeared? The sun had already started its slow descent and the mild temperature of the day dropped a few more degrees. Esther hugged her cardigan tighter and pulled an apron over her head. She'd make a start on dinner.

As she sliced a carrot, a piercing scream filled the air. Esther dropped the knife, narrowly missing her toes as it clattered to the floor. "What is Dr Collins doing?" she asked her mother.

"Doing what he must, I imagine," her mother said as if it was of no concern. Further moans drifted down the hall.

Esther abandoned dinner preparation and hovered outside the open door. Dr Collins held Luca's injured arm as he applied a white floury-like substance. With each application, the man squalled and rolled in upon himself.

Esther entered and approached Dr Collins. "Doctor, would you like me to fetch the Bex?"

Dr Collins had white hair and a Santa Claus beard, and appeared much older than his sixty years. He regarded her over his half-moon spectacles.

"No, thank you, Esther, I have everything I need for the patient. Best you wait outside."

She chanced a glance at her father, who turned away. Luca's face was scrunched into a grimace, his jaw locked tight. She wished she hadn't looked. Yes, Luca had everything he needed except pain relief, it appeared.

Exiting, she slammed the door shut behind her. Hopefully that would block out the groans of discomfort. Someone needed to remind Dr Collins it was 1952 and women could be quite helpful in most situations. And might do better than some men.

Chastised, she continued with her women's work of preparing the evening meal. Soup. Perhaps she could convince Luca to try some.

The soup was boiling on the stove by the time the doctor drove away and her father returned to the kitchen. Esther cut the fresh bread she'd made that day to accompany it. Her tummy rumbled. She hadn't eaten since lunch. Her mother was busy convincing Tommy to have a bath before dinner so Esther filled a bowl with the steaming soup, arranged a large slice of bread on the plate, topped it with a generous slather of salty butter, and stole away with it into the front room.

Chapter Four

Esther balanced the tray of food in the crook of her elbow and rapped on the door. The knock was soft, tentative, and exactly how she felt about seeing Luca again. Her stomach did somersaults as she waited for a response. None came. She nudged the door with her foot and glanced inside. Luca lay prone on the sofa. He faced away from the door so she couldn't tell if he was asleep or not. She inched inside and loudly cleared her throat. His head turned, his eyes widened, and he sat up straight.

Those somersaults turned into an acrobatics show.

Should she be scared of him after their last encounter? She wasn't. He'd been agitated, that's all. Who wouldn't be?

"I've brought you some more food. You really do need to eat."

Hollow eyes looked up at her.

"Smells good. What is it?" His accented voice sounded like music: deep and masculine, yet melodic. Esther wanted to listen to it all day.

The tray grew heavy and she set it down on the coffee table. Luca swung his feet off the couch and landed them square on the floor. He leaned in and inhaled, closing his eyes.

"Meat?"

Esther nodded. "Yes, mutton."

"Mutton?" His face creased in question.

"Yes, um, lamb or sheep."

"*Si*. You Australians like sheep."

Esther perched on the armchair adjacent to him. "Yes, we do. We have many sheep. Lamb is tasty."

"This is, what you call it?" He waved his good arm around the bowl.

"Soup."

"Mutton soup."

"Yes, exactly. Are you hungry?"

Luca's gaze roamed up and down her body and a smile curled at the corner of his lips. He lifted his hand and she flinched. Had she misread him? Was he going to overreact again, like yesterday?

He reached for the bread and bit into it. No, she wasn't a fool, his intentions were good. A wave of regret washed over her. How could she have doubted him? She exhaled and her stomach did a funny flip.

His movement was clumsy and Esther remembered his right arm was in the cast. Was he right-handed? Was that why he hadn't eaten? Had it been too hard and he needed assistance but couldn't ask? Her eyes pooled with tears. They all needed to remember he was an invalid.

Luca closed his eyes, seeming to savour the food. He was enjoying her bread. And he was eating. No one else had achieved that feat. She'd showed up Margaret nicely. Buoyed, she moved across and sat next to him on the sofa.

"Perhaps I can help you?" Esther collected the bowl and dipped in the spoon. She blew on it to cool and then offered it to him, holding it to his dry lips.

He sipped and murmured. A deep rumble low in his throat.

"Slimy."

"Slimy?" Esther queried. "Oh, do you mean fatty? Yes, mutton is fatty. It adds to the flavour of the soup."

She offered another spoonful, holding it to his mouth. His tongue darted across his lips to lick up the remnants. Luca accepted her help and she kept feeding him until the soup was finished. In between sips, he ate the bread and in the end he sloshed it around the bowl to soak up the remains.

Esther laughed.

Luca glanced up and smiled. It made his eyes sparkle. It was an unexpected surprise, and her stomach swooped. A droplet of soup dribbled down his chin and Esther reached for the cloth serviette and wiped it away. She concentrated her eyes on the spot, but when they lifted, they connected with his. The world around her slipped away and only they existed, in that room, together. The intimacy of it hit her square in the chest, stealing her breath away. Only her and Luca.

But then his grin dropped. Had she done the wrong thing? Should she not have treated him like a child and wiped his messy chin?

"I'm sorry," she muttered and dropped her hand to her lap.

Luca reached over and grasped it.

"*Grazie*," he said.

His slender hand was rough but warm. His touch ignited a spark and her body became hot like it was on fire. Her pulse rose out of her neck and bellowed in her ears.

"That's okay. I'm glad you've had something to eat. You'll feel much better. Would you like some more?"

He shook his head but removed his hand and took another slice of bread. She watched his jaw move as he chewed. She enjoyed seeing him finally eat something, of course, but Esther wanted his touch back on her. All of a sudden, the room became stifled, as if the oxygen had been sucked right out.

"Your name?"

"Um, my name?"

Pull yourself together, Esther.

But her fingers still tingled, and jolts of electricity sizzled up her body. The sensations distracted her. She placed her hand to her chest. "My name is Esther."

"Esther," he repeated. "Esther." He nodded. "*Bellissimo.*"

His gaze sent those electric jolts crazy, and when he spoke her name with his accent, she went lightheaded. She stood quickly, demanding her body obey.

"Tea?"

Luca laughed. "I must be sick. Italians"—he pointed to himself—"We drink tea when we are sick."

Esther plonked herself back down again. "Sick. Oh, we drink tea all the time. All day and night." She giggled and poured them both a cup from the teapot. Esther drank her tea with milk and poured a drop into Luca's cup. She passed it to him and he held the cup and smelled it. He screwed up his nose and took a tiny sip. He clinked the cup back into its saucer.

"I am not dying. Therefore, I do not drink tea. Coffee?"

Esther took a sizeable gulp from her own cup and laughed. "We don't have any coffee. In fact, I've never tried it."

He sat back. "No coffee?"

Esther shook her head so that her shoulder-length hair fanned her face. Luca reached out and felt the tips of it where it stroked her collarbone. He curled a tendril around one finger.

"So light. So pretty."

"Esther?" Her mother entered.

She sprang out of her seat, almost toppling the hot tea. "Mother, Luca has finally eaten. He's had an entire bowl of the mutton soup I've prepared for dinner," Esther rambled, and a flush overcame her cheeks. She placed her cup down and avoided her mother's eye. She didn't look at Luca, either. Placing one hand to her cheek, she tried to hide its pink tinge.

"Well, that's wonderful," Mary said flatly. "Did you enjoy it?" she addressed Luca.

He gave her mother a bright smile. *"Si,* very much. It was slimy."

Her mother looked at her, but she didn't respond. "Thank you, Esther. I'll look after Luca for the moment. You run along."

Disappointment hit her like a punch to the stomach and her body went limp. Damn her mother for being so strict. She hadn't done anything wrong; in fact, she'd been helping. Her mother should be thanking her. She resisted stamping her foot. Moving away, she clasped her hands together, remembering his touch on her skin.

***

According to her parents, Luca slept the remainder of the evening. Each time Esther snuck out of her room, her parents were still awake. It was incredibly frustrating. She had no choice but to retire, punching her pillow as she did. How could she sleep when Luca was only feet away?

Esther was determined to get to him first the next day. Acting like Tommy, she raced through her morning chores and slunk away to the sitting room at the first moment it was respectable. She knocked and entered without waiting this time. The sofa was empty, the blankets strewn back in a messy heap. But she could smell his scent. Luca was pacing back and forth in front of the window, muttering to himself. He spoke quickly and his good hand gesticulated wildly.

"Luca? Are you well?"

"Esther." He raced over. "Where's my friend? From the boat?"

"Your friend from the boat?"

"Si." He waited for her response.

Oh no, this was exactly what her father feared.

"My friend," he repeated and grasped her forearm. "I must go."

He raced over to his pile of tattered clothes in the corner of the room. Esther was surprised her mother hadn't thrown them in the fire. Luca rummaged through them and pulled on a jumper. He searched the floor, crouched low to sweep his hand under the couch. He pointed to his bare feet. "Shoes?"

"No, Luca, you cannot go outside, you must rest. The doctor said so. You have to stay here."

"Cannot. I must find my friend. Show me where to go." He headed for the door.

"Father," Esther cried out.

Her mother rushed in. "What is it, Esther?" Then she saw Luca with his stiff movements and flying, agitated hands. "Tommy. Run and fetch your father. He's at the lighthouse."

Her mother stood before Luca and placed her hand on his arm. She tried to guide him away from the door and to sit down. Luca might be slight of weight given what he'd been through, but he had double the strength of her mother. He wrenched his arm back and out of her reach.

Her mother tsked. "Don't be like that. Come along and tell me what's wrong."

"Mother, he's remembered what happened and that he was with someone when he washed up on the beach. He's rambling about a friend and a boat."

"That happens, after the shock wears off," Mary murmured. "Luca, tell me about your friend. When did you last see him?"

It worked. He breathed out all the air he'd been holding. He sat with a thump in the armchair facing her mother.

"Antonio."

"Yes, Antonio. Is he your friend?"

"Yes. Antonio worked with me. We had a day off and he had a boat. His brother's boat. First time. Big wave, storm coming, and boat…" He gestured with his hand in a rolling motion.

Esther clutched her hands to her chest. Her mother leaned in closer to Luca.

"Did he fall out of the boat with you?"

"I don't know. After I fell, I couldn't see anything."

"Of course," she said, her face a web of frowns. "Luca…" She grasped his hand. "People have searched but found nothing. We'll tell Mr Anderson and he'll arrange a further search to find your friend and the boat."

Her father entered and her mother advised him of the news.

"What was the name of the boat, Luca?" he asked.

"Um, *Enchanted Lady*. Funny English name."

Her father extracted a notebook from his breast pocket and took notes. He asked further questions until he was satisfied. "Luca, you need to rest. Stay here. We will find Antonio and the *Enchanted Lady*."

Luca had sat back in the chair, but at those words leapt forward immediately. "You will find Antonio?"

"Yes, Luca. I promise we will try." Her father's words were calm and reassuring. "Esther and Mary will look after you. Make you breakfast, tea."

Luca glanced at Esther, a smile playing across his lips. "No, no tea."

"He drinks only coffee," Esther interjected.

"Well, la di da," her mother said patronisingly. "We'll get some delivered given he'll be staying with us until his health improves."

Esther's heart skipped a beat. He would be *staying*.

Hawkins hobbled into the room, too late to be of any assistance and wiping his sleeved arm across his mouth.

"What's all the ruckus?"

"We have more information about possible survivors and the boat that washed Luca ashore. I'll alert the coastguard and then we'll organise some locals to perform another ground search. Albert, can you please spread the word?"

Albert gazed at Esther instead of her father. Disgust swelled up like bile in her throat as he licked his tongue across his lips. Esther looked away, towards Luca, who was watching her. He then turned his attention to Albert.

Luca stood suddenly and cried, "*Mamma mia, Antonio.*" and a sob escaped.

Esther rushed to his side and clutched his elbow. "Luca, come and sit. I will fetch some water and food. Father will find your friend and he'll be safe and well." She avoided her father's gaze, aware of the weight of it in her direction. He was an honest man and wouldn't make false promises.

"Pull yourself together, man. Crying like a baby won't help." Albert chortled.

"Move along, Mr Hawkins, you've a job to do." She'd pay for that later, for sure. But he didn't dare talk back in front of her parents.

There was a rush of activity and everyone left the room. Luca collapsed, sobbing into the folds of the couch. Esther had never seen a man cry before. But as she was quickly realising, this man was something different.

"I should be dead. Have died—me, not Antonio. Not fair. He is good man."

He rambled on, crying out in despair. How could she console him? She did what she knew and cradled him like she would an injured child. Esther could barely breathe as she pulled him in close to her breast. Her head rested upon his and she smelled his hair, the antiseptic that lingered on his skin. She could feel his heart racing against her arm. After a time, his cries lessened and he leaned into her and became heavy. Not long after, he fell silent.

When her arm went numb, she gently eased him back against the sofa. He remained asleep. She didn't want to leave him. What if he woke and needed her? Esther had never felt so useful before. She snuck out and prepared food and a pot of tea and returned to sit with him as quickly as she could. As she drank her tea, she gazed out at the crystal-clear day. There was no hint of a storm. No sign of the destruction that had upended Luca's boat.

What had happened to his friend? It was hard to imagine the world outside, with the birds chirping and the wildflowers blossoming over the nearby hills, to be anything but serene. Ironic really, given that they were the caretakers of these cliffs, her father the light to guide them all to safety. Not Luca, though, and perhaps not his friend. She'd always viewed their home, the Cape, as a haven, but she'd never met someone who'd been wrecked against the shores before. She'd never met anyone like Luca before.

Esther wandered over to the bookshelf and pulled down their copy of *The Lion, the Witch and the Wardrobe*. They'd been so excited when the mailman had delivered the book. It was only released two years ago, and they'd all read it at least twice over. Opening the front cover, she started to read aloud.

Chapter Five

"Esther," Luca pounced the moment she entered his room. "There must be news. It's been two days."

Yes, she knew. Four days since they'd found Luca and a further two since they'd ramped up the search. For two long days no one had slept. Both the land and the sea were congested with search parties. The lightkeeper's cottage became operation central as local volunteers came and went.

Esther's heart twisted like it was being squeezed too tight. She gazed out the window, at the floor, anywhere but at him. One glance at his face with its deep crevices of worry and baggy dark circles under his eyes and she'd be lost. She wanted Antonio found more than anything she'd wanted in her short life. She wanted it for Luca.

Like him, she'd pestered her father for news, until he'd told her—nicely, mind—that he'd report if the search was successful. But his demeanour told her what his words didn't: they'd found nothing so far and that could only mean the worst. At best, she knew they were hoping to recover a body.

"Everyone is still looking."

Luca flopped into the chair, the air rushing out of him in defeat.

"All is lost."

"No, it isn't, Luca. You mustn't talk like that. You survived, Antonio can, too. If he's as tough as you are." Her attempt at humour didn't work on Luca, who stared into the distance.

"No." He shook his head. "You don't understand. It should have been me. I should be dead. Kaput. No longer here. Antonio… he…" Luca's voice cracked. "He has wife, little baby. We should never have been on the water." He hung his head.

"Luca, it's not your fault. You cannot prevent a storm."

He kept his head low and didn't respond.

"Father will…"

"Leave me, Esther. You cannot understand."

An ache zoomed through her chest like he'd punched her.

"Fine. I have plenty of chores that I've neglected." Esther walked with a confident step, but slowed her pace as she neared the door, praying he'd call her back.

He didn't.

***

Esther gathered the pile of darning close to her and sighed. Three more socks with holes, one pair of pants with a loose hem and four missing buttons waiting to be returned to their owners. She closed her eyes, soaking in the sun and catching the slight breeze. The only positive about this task was being outside. Any mind-numbing task was better in the fresh air.

The sea eagles soared above with a whoosh contrasting with the violent crash of waves against the cliffs below. Esther had chosen to sit on a flat rock amongst a carpet of wild purple daisies. They grew like weeds but brightened up the most drab of days. Esther pulled one out from its roots and held it to her nose. She inhaled the smell deep into her lungs, enjoying the light, summery scent.

Before Luca arrived, these moments were the ones that kept her going. Insignificant, precious occasions of beauty. Her mother accused her of being a daydreamer, but she wasn't. She simply longed for *more*—of what exactly, she didn't know. But that longing had worsened with Luca's arrival. He represented more.

Soon enough he'd be gone, headed back to wherever he came from. She bit her lip until she tasted blood, wishing that day might never arrive. She felt like a small child once more, not the woman she'd become in only a few short days. Melancholy sat on her shoulders like a cloak.

"Not out helping the search?" she asked as Hawkins hurried past, making him pause his step.

"If you are fool enough to get yourself shipwrecked in these parts, then I'm not the fool to be looking for ya. Besides, he'll be dead by now."

Esther wished she hadn't asked.

"Esther."

She turned at Tommy's voice. Walking towards her, Tommy was supporting Luca, who leaned one arm onto the boy's shoulder. Margaret followed behind.

"What are you doing? Luca needs to rest," she scolded.

"Yes, Mummy," he mocked. "Mother said we were to take him outside to help him get out of his funk. What's a funk?"

Esther's mouth hung open as she rushed over to assist, taking some of his weight. Mother must have thought he needed cheering up.

Margaret carried the plaid picnic blanket, which she set out over the daisies. Once Luca sat cross-legged, Margaret reached into the basket and retrieved their lunch.

"Mother permitted you to take all of this from the pantry?"

"Uh-huh. I know. Thank goodness for Luca. It's our own little picnic. Usually she'd kill us if we touched this stuff." Tommy rubbed his hands together in glee and couldn't wait; he dove straight in.

"Manners, Tommy. Luca is our guest, let him help himself first."

Tommy obediently handed Luca a square of nougat. The slim log had been a present last Christmas in a hamper filled with luxurious foods they rarely received on the Cape. Little by little they'd been working their way through the products, at their mother's discretion.

Luca's eyes lit up. Esther's breath hitched.

"Ah, nougat, *si*. Nice." He bit into the deliciously sticky treat. No one spoke as they nibbled until the log had disappeared.

"I hope Mother wasn't expecting us to bring back any leftovers." Esther giggled.

"What food do you enjoy in Italy?" Margaret asked Luca. "Lots of pasta?"

"*Si*. But we eat pasta first, um, before a meal. Then we eat meat—veal, chicken or maybe fish. Always the wine." He smiled and held up his tumbler of water. "And lots of olives and cheeses and cured meats."

"And gelato," Esther added.

"Yes, Esther. Gelato, how you hear about it?"

Her cheeks turned pink. "A magazine."

"She reads girlie magazines." Tommy cried.

Luca looked aghast. His forehead pulled high. "Girlie. With no clothes on?"

"What? No." Esther flicked one of her darned socks at Tommy, stinging his bare flesh. "It's a social magazine. Popular stories of the day. Events, and the like."

Luca understood. "This is beautiful place. If my friend die, good place to die. Here is good for the soul."

***

Was this place for real?

Luca sat on an isolated craggy outcrop of land. He knew about lighthouses, of course, they were scattered throughout the world, but this was something else. It felt like he was at the top of the world. Instead, he sat at the top of a summit, one hundred feet or so from the family's cottage. Their backyard was a steep rise that rolled away to a sandy beach where the waves rolled in, small by the time they reached the cove. Next to it was a steep incline of rocks where the waves didn't roll, they exploded. The broad sky was a tapestry roof above him, clouds flowing quickly past. Birds hovered and squawked, the grass bristled under his feet, and the air tasted of salt. Even though the day was calm, a breeze kissed his cheeks.

It was idyllic. A scene of a postcard he would send his parents. This could be a place to heal. And he wasn't thinking of his physical injuries.

Tommy joked with his sisters. Esther laughed.

"Luca, how is your arm?" Margaret enquired.

He turned to gaze upon it and lifted it as if searching for the answer. "It is better, not so hurt anymore. But this is heavy and hot." He indicated the plaster that covered from his fingertips to his elbow.

"Luca, are you on holidays?" the boy asked.

"No, I live in Australia now. I came on a boat—a much more large boat." He indicated the dimensions with his hands. "All the way from Italy. Your country offers work to people from around the world. I am, what you say, displaced person."

Tommy and Margaret frowned.

"Yes, I heard the government had a program in place. It's fantastic. We welcome migrants because they make jobs. Lots of foreigners are coming," Esther said.

Luca nodded, impressed. "I am hydroelectric scheme. I dig, how you say, holes? No, long holes?"

"Oh, you mean like a tunnel?"

"*Si,* Tommy. Hard work."

"How interesting," Esther murmured. "Did you leave your family in Italy?"

He paused and didn't meet her eye. "Yes, my papa, mamma, *nonna*, and sisters. Big family. Nice family." He forced a tight smile.

"That must have been hard."

Always the same knot coiled in his tummy at talk of home, his family. God, he missed them. It had been hard, but here, he could be Luca Moretti with no past and make his own future. One he was in control of. He knew his family understood. They agreed it was for the best. Even if he'd had the English words, he couldn't explain to his new friends what he'd fled, make them understand. And would he even want to?

"Here, Luca, this is for you." Margaret placed a daisy chain she'd made on top of his head like a crown.

He laughed and shook it free. Then he lifted it and placed it onto Esther's head. He gazed at her as he shifted it into position. "A crown needs a princess."

Esther blushed and he tried not to notice. It was becoming more difficult to avoid how beautiful Esther was. At first, he thought she was young and sweet, fussing over him. But when the darkness descended, it was she who made the room bright again. Her smile that lit him up with her beauty and innocence—and, yes, she was all innocence. He loved that. He tried to look away but couldn't avoid the soft curve of her breasts under her blouse.

She nibbled a slice of apple and lifted her face, regarding him over her lashes. He tingled all over and didn't want to. She couldn't, shouldn't like him.

"I'd like to take you for gelato one day."

She stared at him as if he'd spoken in Italian. Had he said it wrong? No. Her blush crept up her neck and she moved strands of hair off her face.

"I'd like that, too."

His heart swelled to fill his chest cavity. Ah, he could not resist her. He smiled too broadly and winced. The gash on his forehead wasn't bad, but it hurt when his skin stretched tight. Tommy and Margaret rose to chase a butterfly and Luca placed his hand on Esther's thigh.

"I want you show me your magazine."

A tinkle of a laugh escaped from her. He lifted her hand and kissed it, his lips lingering on her smooth skin. As he lowered it, he brushed his thumb along her palm.

"Esther. Luca." Charles's voice rang out. "Father has news, come quick."

Luca dropped her hand and swivelled too fast in an effort to stand. Esther came to his aid and leaned in close. He smelled her floral scent, so like the flowers he'd placed on her head. The daisy crown fell to the grass and stayed where it landed.

"I'll help you back to the house."

***

A small crowd had gathered on the lawns of the lightkeeper's cottage. Theirs was the third house in the row and also the largest. A picket fence enclosed trimmed grass, in deep contrast to the scrubby bushlands around it. On the wraparound veranda that skirted the house there was a view of the Cape in every direction. Along one edge, protected from the force of the winds, was her mother's garden. A kaleidoscope of colour burst from rose bushes that smelled as good as they looked. A few pale pink petals strewn on the path lifted in the breeze.

The men had spent the last few days searching the hills by foot and the ocean in rescue boats. Her mother and Margaret stood to the rear of the group. Esther joined them and held Margaret's hand.

Luca went straight to her father. He flipped off his hat and grasped it until his knuckles turned white.

"Luca, come sit." Her father guided him by the elbow to an outdoor table and chair. After Luca was settled, he crouched at eye level in front of him. "We found the boat, the *Enchanted Lady*. She washed up on the shore about sixty miles from here. A rugged stretch of land. She was perched on top a layer of rocks. As far as wreckage goes, she was pretty intact." Her father paused, smiled. "That's good news. The boat can be returned to whomever it belongs and be repaired."

"Antonio?"

John Anderson lowered his head before he spoke. "There was no sign of your friend. He must have escaped the boat or at least been toppled over, like you. Many men have searched." He swept his arm around to encompass the group. "It is unlikely he'll be found. If he didn't wash ashore like you, he most likely has drowned. I'm sorry." He shrugged and placed his hand upon Luca's knee. This shocked Esther. Her father wasn't a shrugging kind of man. He always had an answer, even if it wasn't the one you wanted. That had always been reassuring about him.

Now, he reached into his pocket and retrieved a small card. "We did find this, stuck like glue to the inside of the cabin. Is it yours?"

Luca observed the card and moaned. Tears rolled down his cheeks and he held the square up to the light. Esther saw it was a small black-and-white photograph. He leaned over and embraced her father. Luca circled her father's shoulders, his eyes closed. John patted him on the back and didn't pull away.

Soon enough, they moved apart. Luca glanced at the photograph again, brought it to his lips, and kissed it before placing it against his breast. Then he rose. Esther feared he might run, escape from his own grief, or worse, collapse in a heap. Instead, he turned to each individual man and shook their hand and slapped them on the back. In his fluster, he spoke in Italian. The men took steps backwards. Esther watched their quizzical expressions. Despite what she'd heard on the news and told Luca earlier, foreigners were still strange to many people. Of course, on Bruny Island they'd had little opportunity to meet any. She'd heard from her friend, Gertrude, that some Italians worked on the berry farms on the north of the island, but Esther had had no reason to venture there. Naturally, many more were in the capital city of Hobart, but she rarely went there, either.

Luca realised his mistake and adopted his broadest Australian accent. Esther smiled; it was terrible, but the men recognised his effort to be like them.

Albert lurked amongst the rescue volunteers. Luca stood in front of him and reached out to express his thanks. The men around them dispersed and moved towards the refreshment table her mother had set up with sandwiches and tea.

Albert stood ramrod stiff and unwelcoming and left Luca's arm hanging. Esther's stomach knotted. Luca's face wavered with uncertainty before he dropped his hand. She walked over to hear the tail end of Albert's words.

"...we don't need dagos here. Go back to where you came from."

The moment she reached them, Albert paused and squared his eyes at Esther, challenging her.

"It might be time for our new friend to head back to Hobart where he can recuperate amongst his own kind."

"What on earth..." Esther started to say but Albert continued.

"Yes, I'll arrange your passage back to Hobart myself."

How dare he. "Mr Hawkins," she stammered, but Luca held her elbow and guided her away.

"Luca, he can't talk to you that way. I want to tear strips off him. He thinks he can do whatever he likes, but he can't. I'll tell Father."

Luca didn't respond.

A gulf of shame overcame her. Yes, she was so tough—planning to run off to her father to tell tales. If Luca could be insulted and not respond, who was she to carry on like a duffer?

"It is hard for Australians. We're different." He waved his hands up and down his body. "We look different, sound strange and particularly, with your men, we are... what you say, emotional? We express our feelings. Australian men, they lift up their chin and carry on, or they talk with their fists. He can't help it if he is racist."

Esther stared. Racist? She'd thought Hawkins many things before, but never racist. Is this the treatment foreigners like Luca were receiving in their country? Taunts instead of acceptance of their differences? Why did the government allow them to arrive to such hostility? Her magazine didn't report on such things.

Turning away from the few men still on their lawn, Luca placed the lightest of touches to her hand and held her gaze. "None of that matters. Antonio is dead and it's all my fault."

Words wanted to burst off Esther's tongue—in comfort or denial, she wasn't sure—but Charles joined them, offering snacks, and she fell silent.

"I'm sorry about your friend. Terrible business."

And with that, Esther became the observer in a conversation she wanted to lead.

Chapter Six

"Leave him be, Esther. After the shock of yesterday, he'll want to be alone." Her mother's stout frame barred her path.

As if he'd want to be alone.

"Have you checked him this morning?" she asked.

Mary shook her head.

"I'll check on him, Mother. See if he's hungry and then leave him be, as you say. I'll attend to my chores." Esther didn't wait for her mother's approval and instead simply brushed past and entered the front room.

It was empty. Esther opened the door wider, but Luca wasn't there.

"Mother," she shouted. "He's not here. Did you see him leave?"

Her knotted eyebrows confirmed she wasn't tricking and attempting to keep the two of them apart. Mary entered the room to check for herself.

Esther didn't wait for confirmation of what she already knew. She raced out the front door and up the lighthouse path to the apex of the cliff. Her legs moved fast. Intuition called her to the rocky ledge. Where else would someone go to be alone?

As she drew closer, she saw him. Her stomach swooped with relief. All she wanted to do was embrace him and never let go. She strode quickly.

"Luca."

He didn't turn.

"Luca," she screamed so loud her throat went raspy.

He cut a solitary figure, standing at the edge of the world as he was. The luminous blue sky surrounded him with the dim light casting him in a pale glow.

The cliff face before which he stood was steep, but it gave way in gradual platforms to a bramble patch of shrubs before lending itself to the treacherous waves below. If he took one step forward, he might stumble. She had to gulp down her rising panic.

Reaching beside him, she bent at her waist to catch her breath.

"Go away and leave me alone, Esther." The way he pronounced her name, it made her insides quiver despite the words he spat at her. Even his angry voice was sensual.

"I am, what you say, bad luck. Antonio is dead. Serafina dead. My country is ravaged after the war. If anyone is to die, it should be me. You should not be my friend. Bad things will happen if we are friends." Unexpectedly he moved and she rushed into his path. His left arm rose as if to ward her off, but then it sank back to his side.

What was wrong with him? It was her, Esther. The creases in his face had deepened overnight, his lips firmed. It looked as if grief was a living thing and had devastated him. A deep sadness welled up inside of her, but also a fierce determination. She could help him.

Esther spoke softly. "What are you talking about?"

He gazed at her then. He was good at that. Good at staring so hard she forgot herself. Esther didn't hear the birds chirping or the waves crashing against the rocks or the steady hum of life on the Cape waking up to the morning. She could only hear his intake of breath as he dragged air into his lungs and steadied himself on his two feet.

"Who is Serafina?"

But he'd lost his tongue. He kept staring, now turning his eyes far away, to another time and another place, searching the blue reaches of the horizon for answers.

Esther wouldn't stop. "Was she someone from home?"

He nodded. "My cousin. She drowned—because of me. I should have been watching her, should have been paying attention. But I wasn't and she's gone." His voice hitched on the last words. "And now, Antonio too. I should have done more."

A foghorn echoed in the wind. Esther turned to see a fishing boat rising and falling with the waves. Instinctively, Esther lifted her hand to wave, but stopped as soon as she started. The movement felt wrong. Happy.

She turned back to Luca. "What are you doing up here?"

"Thinking."

She held both his hands in hers and held them to her chest. "Luca, you are alive. You survived for a reason. You are meant to be here. With me. You were meant to come to Bruny and meet me. We are friends." She tightened her grip. The tips of his fingers were cold and thawed the heat building in her tummy. The sensation of skin on skin nearly drove her wild.

"You're too good for me," Luca said.

"Stop that. How old was your cousin when she drowned?"

"Five."

"I don't know what happened, but I'm sure it was an accident. It wasn't your fault. And you can't be blamed for the condition of your country. That's silly."

Now he wouldn't look at her, focusing only on the vast skyline where the light blue of the sky met the deepest aqua of the ocean. A wave of pain crossed his features. Esther's desire to ease that agony was overwhelming. Her words weren't working. She had to try harder.

"Your family loves you. They must miss you terribly. My family will miss you when you return to Hobart." She tried to muster a smile but didn't quite make it. "Antonio was your friend and I'm sure you've made other Australian friends. Your life needs you, Luca. Australia needs you. I need you." Esther whispered those last words.

His left eye twitched but a spark of light returned to his dark eyes. He'd heard her.

"Everything seems to have gone wrong," he said. His words made her want to weep. In usual Esther style, she forged on, desperate to get him away from the cliff.

"It's cold, come away from here. You need to eat breakfast and rest. Keep up your strength and make sure you become well again. That's the only way matters will improve."

She tugged Luca's elbow, and he turned from the edge and gradually moved with her towards the path.

"Will you try some more tea?"

He laughed and the tension broke. "No, no tea."

***

"Mail." An hour later Esther dashed back into the house. She dumped the pile of envelopes, books, and packages onto the kitchen table. "Is Father back yet?" she asked Tommy, who sat with his schoolbooks open and his tongue hanging out of his mouth in concentration. "Tommy?"

"Um, no, not yet."

Esther hugged her latest edition of the *Women's Weekly* to her chest, and another parcel too. The package meant she hadn't opened her magazine yet. Usually, she'd dive straight inside those pages. Instead, she clasped this other package tight and rushed back out the door and past the other cottages. She passed Albert's house especially fast, hoping he wouldn't spot her. As she climbed the pebbled path to the lighthouse, she paused to pick a solitary flame-orange wattle and place it behind her ear. Since she'd talked Luca back from the cliff, the morning had improved. She hummed as she ascended, her breaths becoming shallower with each step. She was jealous of her brother's agility to race up this hill. But the brief walk didn't take long. Outside the tall white lighthouse, she caught her breath. They were never allowed inside without permission. Esther pushed open the heavy door and sang out, her voice echoing around the circular dome and bouncing off the walls.

"Be down in a minute," her father called. Soon his heavy footsteps made the steel wraparound staircase vibrate. She loved staring upwards inside the lighthouse, from its base towards the sky, and admiring the curve of the staircase, replicating a snail's shell. Its architecture never ceased to amaze her.

"What is it, Esther? I'm due to have smoko soon."

"Sorry, Father, but this arrived addressed to you, and Mr Davies said it was a special delivery. I thought it might be important."

Her father wiped his brow with a starched white handkerchief, then took the package. Reading the label, he turned it this way and that. Then realisation hit. "Yes, it is important, for our guest anyway. I ordered coffee. Apparently, espresso coffee is becoming popular in Hobart nowadays. Thought it might cheer the poor fellow up."

Esther squealed and jumped up and down like a five-year-old. "Father. He'll love it. He hates tea. And especially after yesterday this will make him feel immeasurably better." She hugged her father. An aroma drifted up escaping from the box. "Argh, Father, it smells, um, rather disgusting, like dirt."

He chuckled, deep and low. "Let's walk down to the house together. I'll take my break now."

***

"What is that smell?" Margaret grimaced.

Esther shrugged. "It's coffee."

"It stinks," Charles grunted.

"I'm getting quite used to it," she said, but that wasn't at all true. How could Luca, or anyone for that matter, drink this stuff? It was the colour of chocolate, but didn't have an inviting, sweet scent. It reminded her of the smell of earth after rainfall, or of the odour that remained on her fingers after touching the small nut seeds on some of the low-lying bushes in the forest.

Her siblings guffawed and acted as if they were choking. It only spurred her on. To show them, she filled a cup with the black syrup and took a big gulp.

"Have I arrived in heaven?" Luca entered the kitchen.

Esther's tongue rebuked the flavour and she slopped the liquid around her mouth until her cheeks filled. She wanted to spit it out and rid her mouth of the bitter taste. Instead, she offered Luca a lopsided grin and swallowed it in one guzzle and kept her mouth wide open to help the taste evaporate.

"Luca, we have coffee for you." The children held hands and danced around him.

***

The strong aroma of roasted beans wafted through the house, piercing the fog that had hung over him since yesterday. The odour wasn't as rich or smooth as he was used to, but one sniff and he'd sat upright. It reinvigorated his soul and he chased that smell like a dog after a bone. He needed it. Only one thing could be better: a glass of chilled Chianti.

He slapped his hands together in a thunderous clap. "Please, can I have some?" His mouth watered. It had been too long. Moving close to the stovetop, he lifted Esther's empty cup and inhaled, relishing the aroma.

Tommy and Margaret burst into laughter, the sound filling the kitchen. "You Australians are so uncultured. Esther, did you try?"

She nodded.

"Did you like?"

"It was rather strong."

"How did you have it? With cream and sugar?"

Another head shake.

"Here, you let me make it. Where's your mama and papa? They have some, too."

"Do you make it in a pot?" Esther asked innocently.

A laugh rumbled deep in his belly. Tommy poked him in the ribs. It tickled. Charles joined in by play-punching and teasing him until Luca wrestled each of them under one arm, shaking them about and attempting to tickle them back.

"Enough," he said after a minute, "I need to drink my coffee." And he proceeded to make a show of pouring himself a cup.

"What on earth?" Mary uttered as she entered.

***

Night descended, blanketing the Cape in its clutches, the last rays of sun angling into the dining room where the family, joined by Luca for the first time, ate dinner. Luca sipped the remnants of his third cup of coffee before accepting a glass of red wine.

"You drink wine?"

"You sound surprised," John commented.

Luca flashed his smile.

"Mary and I enjoy an odd drink, usually on Sundays. And only one or two glasses, mind. Is this any good? Like you have back home?"

Making a show of it, Luca swirled the liquid in his long-stemmed glass and shoved it under his nose. He peeked over the rim, aware everyone was watching him. He inhaled deeply, closing his eyes and murmuring. With exaggerated movements, he sipped, only the tiniest of drops. Then he swirled it around his mouth before swallowing. "*Si*, is good, but my Italian wine better."

"Do you drink more often at home?" Margaret enquired.

"Oh, yes. I love wine. My family love wine, is family business. But it is also Italian custom to have a glass of wine with each meal, lunch and dinner."

"Your family make wine?" Tommy asked.

"*Si*, yes. *La Famiglia*. It is family vineyard. We make and sell wine. I grew up drinking wine. It is, what you say, passion for me?"

As he pointed to his chest, his joviality disappeared, his smile slipping.

"Well, we do make some wonderful Australian wines," said John, "but I'm sure they will not compete with your quality. We are more influenced by the English here. Like this Sunday roast. We like to gather together as a family on a Sunday with roasted meat and vegetables."

"My family do this, too, but not with roast. Is this a usual meal?" Luca pointed to the leftovers on his plate.

Mary responded, "Yes. It's always roast beef, lamb, or sometimes chicken. If we are lucky, pork."

Luca sat back, fully sated, and observed the Australian family. It wasn't like at home where they were loud and rambunctious and all talking at once. Here, one person spoke and each person listened. Whilst his uncle or papa would have refilled their glasses four times over by now, they all enjoyed one small drop. No chance of misbehaving then.

Uncrossing his long legs under the table, his foot brushed Esther's, who sat to his right. Instead of retracting it, he rested it there. He noticed her shimmy forward in her seat and glance around the table. Emboldened by the combination of coffee and wine, he lifted his foot and curled his little toes until they covered hers. This time she took a sip of her wine, lowering the glass slowly.

Mary rose and took some plates to the kitchen. The children giggled over an anecdote their father told. Luca pushed his chair in until his chest touched the edge of the table. Whilst everyone was occupied, he placed his splinted right arm on Esther's thigh. Her body stiffened.

"Thank you for helping me this morning…and for the coffee," he said.

Her customary blush crept up her neck, making her skin glow. "It wasn't me, it was Father. He hoped it would make you feel better. He was right, wasn't he? The moment you smelled it, you almost ran out of your room. But, of course, you know it isn't proper espresso like they serve in cafes. It's for making at home. Sorry we couldn't get you the real thing."

"I love it. It worked, and yes, I feel much better now." He couldn't stop his broad smile. Was that from the glow of the coffee or because he felt the flimsy cotton of her dress and caressed her skin underneath with the tips of his fingers that poked out of the cast? Esther sat upright. Was she uncomfortable? Or nervous?

"My girlie magazine arrived today." She lowered her voice and leaned in close. Then her left hand crept below the table until it found his. Her fingers twitched as if restless. Even the loose entwining of their fingers sent a tingle right up his spine. He was so near to her, he could smell her—all feminine and floral and sweet with a mixture of talcum powder, light and feathery. So different than Italian girls. So innocent and untainted by the reality of the harsh world. She peered at him with those big wide eyes that always sparkled. His gaze fell onto the creamy expanse of her neck. He swallowed dryly, aching to touch her everywhere. Blood coursed through his veins, and he knew.

Chapter Seven

How quickly Esther's whole world changed in seven days.

Everything felt topsy-turvy and out of balance, though she somehow still bounced out of bed at the same time. What a contrast to other days on the Cape. If she thought about it for too long, it troubled her, this bubble of exhilaration that elevated her spirits, that made her so happy. Rather than worry about it, she was determined not to dwell on it, at all.

Esther usually dawdled through her chores, performing them methodically and without haste. Since Luca's arrival, and with no liberty to skive off her duties, she rushed as quickly as her hands would work.

Outside, she tugged her cardigan closer to her chest and clenched her jaw to prevent her teeth chattering. This far into autumn, the days had retained some warmth. But today, she was reminded that winter approached. Soon she'd need her heavier jacket. Was this cold to Luca? All the photos of Italy she'd ever seen showed bronze beaches and a dazzling hot sun.

Esther hummed as she washed her hands in the tub. She'd finished her jobs at last, and was busting to see Luca. The ice-cold water and her vigorous scrubbing with the Palmolive soap turned her hands red. After wiping them hastily on the cloth hanging nearby, she ran them down the front of her dress and made the short walk to the front room. With each step, her heartbeat sped up.

With a bright smile on her face, she popped her head through his doorway. Empty. His bed was unmade. He must be making coffee. She turned back towards the kitchen. Nope, empty again. She craned her neck and listened. Tucking a loose strand of blonde hair behind her ear, she heard muffled voices. She followed the sound, leading her outside. On the veranda Luca and her father sat in the bright sun.

"Good morning, Esther," Luca said.

"Good morning. Hello, Father." She leaned down and kissed his bearded cheek.

Her father had his trademark pipe in his mouth. "It must be morning tea, is it?" He stopped exactly at 10.30 a.m. each day to enjoy a cup of tea and usually a slice of homemade cake and a pipe. He had to sit outside, Mother's orders, otherwise the house smelled like tobacco.

Seated in the chair next to him, Luca released a plume of smoke.

"You smoke?" she asked. The cherrywood scent tickled her nose. It was a smell she would forever associate with her father. And now, perhaps, Luca.

"In Italy everyone smokes. But here, I haven't so much. This is nice though, better than stale tobacco from a cigarette. It is sweeter."

Her father nodded and they both put the dark brown pipes to their mouths and held them tight between their lips. Moments later, smoke dispersed from their mouths and noses, drifting upwards.

"Your mother is bringing more tea. I must be getting back to the lighthouse. Later, Esther, if Luca is feeling up to it, bring him up for a tour."

Esther nodded as he moved away.

"What have you got there?" Luca asked her.

Her excitement bubbled over and she skipped to take her father's seat. From under her arm she pulled out a magazine. "Ta da." she sang.

"Ah, the girlie magazine. I can't wait to read it." He snatched it out of her hands and flicked through the pages. "Oh, too many words. Hard for me to read."

"I will read it to you and that will help you learn, yes?"

Luca nodded. Her mother returned holding a tray with coffee for Luca and a fresh teapot.

"Mother, is that your lemon cake?" Esther drooled. She glanced at Luca. "Mother's lemon cake is delicious. You'll have some?"

"Thank you, Esther. I understand Luca has already had a slice, but perhaps with his next cup of coffee, he'll enjoy another. And when you're done, there will still be plenty of time to attend to all of the other jobs you've neglected." With that, Mary placed the tray onto the small wicker table and retreated.

"Sorry, she's always so dour. Mother doesn't smile a lot and doesn't waste time on emotion. It can be hard to understand sometimes. Plus, she's annoyed because I'm spending too much time with you and not doing my jobs." Her mother must appear a terrible bore.

Luca shook his head. Today he wore his long hair loose. "Is okay. She's kind to me. But I'm sorry she is angry with you. Soon, I can help with the chores?"

"No one expects you to be doing any work, Luca."

Esther reached out and touched the tips of his hair as it grazed his earlobes. It sat in unruly ringlets. Why was his hair so long? Wasn't it annoying? But she didn't ask those questions. Her fingers curled around the long dark strands; the hair was soft, not like the springy coils on his legs. With those thoughts, heat crept up her neck, threatening to flush her cheeks. Luca kept his head bowed. Reluctantly, she dropped her fingers and placed them in her lap.

"Show me your magazine." His voice was low and husky, and he did not meet her eye.

Esther held up the cover with a woman in a bright yellow raincoat and red plastic hat. She flipped it open. "I will read you the story, but we'll have a flick through first." Esther made an "oh" sound and held the pages up close to her face.

"What is it?"

Esther showed him the page. His face creased in question.

"Do you think me foolish and silly?" she asked. Luca shook his head. "You see, up here on the Cape, we get so little and there is so much on offer, out there." She spread her arm wide to encompass the world. "I only see many of those things from the pages of this magazine. But there are truly so many beautiful things…. This is face powder, for example. It's silly, I know. Even if we lived in Hobart, Mother probably wouldn't let me have it anyway." Esther shrugged. "But look at the cream and white floral case it comes in."

"I would buy you this *cipria*."

"What do you mean?"

"That is the Italian for face powder."

"Can you teach me Italian?" She waited expectantly on his answer.

"*Si,* of course."

"As we read, I'll tell you the English and you can teach me the Italian words. Is that okay?" she asked. Butterflies danced in her tummy. "Who would have ever thought I'd be learning Italian." Her feet performed a little dance. "You have introduced me to so many new things, Luca."

He placed his pipe on the tray and sipped the coffee and carefully placed the cup back in its saucer before responding. Had she said the wrong thing? She was only being honest. He mustn't feel the same way.

His eyes didn't sparkle now, they were black. "And you, for me," he said and shifted slightly in his seat. Just as Esther thought he was about to lean over and embrace her, Tommy raced past.

"Hey, you two." He waved wildly.

Bugger you, Tommy, Esther thought. When she looked back at Luca, his face was clearer, his pupils lighter and he sat up straight. The moment was lost. Would he have kissed her? The thought sent a spiral of exploding fireworks up her spine.

He could still kiss her, and she hoped he still might, but he turned away. Disappointed, Esther read the next few pages. "Aren't these cars amazing? They are called Morris Minor, and look at that colour. A bright red car. How fabulous," Esther said.

"*Si,* cars are popular now. My brother has one, he drives too fast around the tight corners. Car is *auto* in Italian, but proper word is *veicolo a motore*, say like a motor vehicle."

"*Veicolo a motore*," she repeated. Luca smiled.

"Did I get it wrong?"

"Say like me, *veicolo a motore*," he sang.

He said it a few more times before being satisfied she had it right.

"Luca, look at this. Lipstick that won't eat off, drink off, or kiss off…"

Her words trailed away and when she glanced up, Luca flicked his tongue across his dry mouth. An action she unconsciously followed. His eyes widened as he watched.

"What colour would you wear?"

"Red?" She shrugged.

"Nice against your pale skin, maybe deep *rosso*."

"*Rosso* is red?"

"*Si.*"

Esther gawped at the fashion pages. Luca leaned over and expressed how fabulous she would look in the blue strapless knee-length gown with the sparkly beading on the hem. She blushed. It was a revealing dress. Her mother would disapprove.

"It's beautiful," she whispered.

He whispered back and made her repeat, "*Bellissimo.*" She gave him a quizzical look, realising when he continued to stare at her that it didn't mean dress.

They laughed over the ridiculous cigarette advertisement depicting a policeman and a woman who looked like she was about to ride a horse, then they settled in and Esther read the short story.

"The story this week is called 'The Patient at Peacocks Hall.'" They burst into laughter.

"Me," Luca pointed to himself, "I am Italian at Cape Bruny Lighthouse."

Esther read to him, stopping and helping him when he stumbled over the English words. Occasionally, he'd break into Italian and she'd repeat the words over and over again. Or sometimes she simply listened to him. Esther couldn't get enough of the foreign dialect. Her heart skipped a beat each time Luca rolled his Rs and gurgled the words from his throat.

The clothes remained unwashed and her siblings did not have her attention that afternoon as they whiled away with their mathematics and history lessons. Luckily, Esther escaped her mother's wrath at her laziness, but her edition of *The Australian Women's Weekly* was read from front to back.

Chapter Eight

"This lighthouse has been operating for over one hundred and fourteen years. It has saved many boats navigating their way through these treacherous waters."

Luca bowed his head. "Not the *Enchanted Lady*."

"No," John agreed. "It's not possible to prevent every catastrophe, particularly when natural disasters lend a hand."

Luca nodded, his heart heavy like lead in his chest at the thought of his friend. When he couldn't sleep, he imagined his friend's lifeless body being eaten by a great white shark. Mixed in with his memories of Serafina and his homeland, he wondered whether he'd ever sleep soundly again.

"It was built by convicts from England?" he asked, turning his mind back to the present and standing behind Esther's father in the office at the base of the lighthouse.

"Yes. Free labour. Can you imagine how difficult it was to cart the building material to this summit through the scrub and bushland to this southern part of the island? There wasn't any road or means of transport."

"Brutal," Luca agreed.

"See here," John continued. "These are the maps, charts, and logbooks. Every incident, weather observation, and even passing sea traffic, I must record in here."

Luca ran his eyes over the pages laid out on a desk spanning the width of the narrow room. "You wrote about me in here?"

"Yes, of course," John said matter-of-factly.

Luca wanted to see the entry. What would it say? But he knew John wouldn't let him see the private entries of his work. Stupid anyway, he probably couldn't read the English. Luca kept silent.

"The lighthouse was revamped between 1901 and 1903. They replaced the original Wilkins lantern with a powerful new Chance

Bros catadioptric lantern …" John recited the history as they climbed the internal staircase to the top.

Luca heard the *tap, tap* on the cast-iron spiral stairs. Esther followed. "Seventy steps all up," she said, puffing as she arrived at the top.

Luca was interested but didn't understand everything John said. Esther would have realised he didn't comprehend and would have explained it to him. She'd stopped to sit on a small ledge overlooking the 360-degree panorama. In front he looked at the D'Entrecasteaux Channel and over to Southport. On this side, the mass of water stretched forever with no end. The middle of the sea appeared almost purple at its deepest. The waters against the beach grew paler, almost turquoise, but here, where the rocky outcrop sat feet below, the water remained dazzling.

There was land slightly to his left. The cottages sat below with a visible snake line of a road. It was a vast landmass scattered with idyllic coves. It was serene, but so rugged. So different than his homeland, where yellow fields dotted the landscape. Shivers raced up his spine as he watched the waves roll with force and the choppy white peaks form with each blow of the wind. He wasn't keen to be back in the water anytime soon.

Esther squealed and clutched her hand to her heart. Hawkins appeared in the window right before her, cloth in hand, scrubbing the glass pane. He worked outside on a narrow, high balcony. Below was another steel deck.

"Let's go outside," John invited Luca.

He clutched his hat as the wind gust almost toppled him. The salty air hit his face and he licked the taste from his lips. A fine spray of sea water flicked across his bare arms. He gripped the handrail as his steps became unsteady. The grated steel base was see-through, and the ground came up to meet him. The structure shifted under his feet. Funny, heights had never bothered him before.

Albert chuckled. He stood above, peering down at him.

"Afraid of heights, are ya?"

Luca didn't respond, instead only following John as he walked the circumference. All of a sudden, he felt vulnerable.

John paused, pointing. On the horizon a white blob slowly came into view. A boat. But it wasn't the boat John was showing him. "Look, there. A pod of dolphins."

"Ah, *delfini*. Esther," he shouted behind him. "Come look."

Esther smiled and his body came alive. She didn't hesitate and jumped up and raced out to the edge, not fearful like him. He placed his hand on her arm, "*Ci sono I delfini*. Dolphins."

At first, she didn't look seawards, only at him. She repeated the phrase. "*Delfini* is dolphin. The word is so similar."

"*Si.*"

"*Grazie*," she responded.

Luca felt two gazes upon them. A harsh burn into his back from Albert, who'd come down to their level. And another, from Esther's father. Esther seemed oblivious and kept repeating "*delfini*" over and over.

"Tell me the name of some other water animals," she asked innocently.

"Mr Anderson." Albert stepped forward into a gap between the trio. "I have arranged the passage for…" He paused, looked at Luca, and appeared to consider his words. "Luca," he said with a sneer, "to return to Hobart. The supply boat is due in five days."

Turning out of view from Esther's father, Albert scowled at him. His lopsided and scarred face crinkled and his eyes almost disappeared. His smirk made Luca's stomach crawl. Esther swirled so fast to face her father that her skirt spun out wide in an arc.

"Father, already? Is he able to travel yet? Didn't the doctor order him to rest?"

Luca winced at her pleading tone.

"Thank you, Albert. It's five days then."

Albert threw them a smirk.

"It's not up to us, Esther. Luca is part of the hydroelectric scheme. He has a job. A job that our government provided for him along with his passage to Australia. They want him back to classify his injuries and allow him to recuperate as necessary. It will have been over two weeks by then."

***

Esther bowed her head. Only five more days. An ache pierced her chest. Suddenly she lost her breath; it was caught by the wind and carried away. She couldn't risk a glance at Luca or her father. Her feelings at the prospect of Luca leaving would be scripted across her face.

Life had sped up and it made her giddy. She turned and reentered the lighthouse. Through the glass panelling, she could see her father's mouth moving, no doubt continuing his educational monologue on the lighthouse.

Albert walked a pace behind, his hands clasped, trailing like an unwanted stray dog. Oh, she could step on his toes, he was so menacing. Eventually, even her father tired of him and directed him onto another task. He was the assistant lightkeeper after all, and that meant he did the night shift whilst her father slept, and at other times, he was the general dogsbody, fixing this, cleaning that, and performing basic repair. Being a nuisance is how Esther would describe him. But he was more than that. The way he glared at her like she wore no clothes and drooled from his lips. A shudder ran through her at the thought.

She turned away as he scurried down the stairs. He stomped louder than necessary, making the cylinder vibrate with his steps.

Her breathing had calmed by the time her father and Luca returned.

"I can be a keeper of the light now, after everything your father has taught me," Luca joked.

How could he joke at a time like this? He obviously didn't care that they were about to be torn apart.

"Esther, I'll head home now. Stay a few more minutes and watch the sun sink into the horizon and wait for the light to twirl. Luca will like that."

"Okay. See you soon."

Esther listened to her father's echoing footsteps as she looked out to the reaches of the horizon, wishing it would gobble her up. Neither she nor Luca spoke until the lower door slammed shut.

Luca took her hand and held it in his lap. She turned to him then, unable to stem the tears pooling in her eyes.

"Don't you even care that you're leaving and we'll never see each other again?"

"Oh, *mia bella*. Of course I do. It cuts me in half. But your family saved me. I am grateful for what they've done. I cannot question your father's decisions. He is… honest man. If he says scheme wants me back, then I must go. For two years, I am not free man. I am committed to the scheme. That is part my agreement. I must work on the hydro scheme then maybe I am free to do something else. I'm not free right now."

"Me either. I'm stuck here on this island. I wish I could come with you." The tears escaped and rolled down her cheeks.

"Please, do not cry, *bella*. It makes me sad. I want you to be happy."

"I'm happy being with you."

"Me too," Luca whispered. He placed his hand to her cheek. It burned under her blush. He caressed her there, tracing from her creamy white lobe along her jawline to her lips with his thumb.

A strange flutter commenced down low. All her senses came alive and her heart beat like a drum in her chest. The diminishing sunlight danced along the top rim of the lighthouse, illuminating both of them in its glow. Luca moved closer so that she felt his warm breath on her neck as he nuzzled her hair. Her skin was on fire. His fingers' caress was like ice to a flame. He traced featherlight kisses up her neck.

Esther looked into his eyes and was lost. She wanted to gaze into those dark ink puddles forever, have them stare at her like they were now. She might be young, but she understood longing. And boy, did she feel it. A beast unravelled inside of her, unable to be controlled now that it sensed what was possible.

"Kiss me." She couldn't wait any longer.

"Are you sure?" he asked, but she wanted him to stop talking, stop thinking, and *kiss* her.

Esther moved her hand up to cradle his head. She clutched strands of his hair and applied pressure, forcing his head towards her. She watched his lips lower and as they were about to touch, she closed her eyes and devoured him. His lips were inviting, wet and open. She'd never been kissed before. At the touch of their mouths pressing together, an explosion of pleasure erupted in her belly and her body pulsed.

The world melted away and all she could taste and feel was Luca. The first kiss was fast and hungry, their lips desperate. She responded with reckless abandon, wanting more. But soon, the kisses slowed, Luca tantalising her with his tongue and his slow and gentle movements. When they pulled apart to gulp in shallow breaths, she cradled his neck with both hands, their foreheads touching. Neither spoke, but held each other warm and close, letting their heart rates gradually slow. At that moment, the giant orb light shone bright and commenced its journey round and round and round, blinding them on each circle. All they could do was close their eyes and hold each other tight.

They agreed to leave separately, with Luca leaving first.

Esther felt her swollen lips. His bristle had slightly chafed her skin. Would her family know when they saw her that she'd experienced something incredible and wonderful and unforgettable merely fleeting minutes ago? How would she explain the twinkle in her eye and her pink cheeks? Esther couldn't stop smiling. Luca said something about washing his face in icy cold water and dousing the flame. She wasn't quite sure what that meant.

Esther let the heavy lighthouse door slam behind her. The sun had disappeared now and the stars in the night sky sparkled like diamonds. Esther wanted to break into song, there was so much emotion bubbling inside her wanting to escape.

Instead, she gripped the door handle and tap-danced with her feet, but it felt silly. Pulling herself together, she walked on tiptoe, floating down the pebbled path. All was quiet. The path lined with shrubs on both sides was enveloped by darkness and only illuminated by the beam of the lighthouse. Lost in her bubble of happiness, she didn't hear anyone approach.

"So, you and lover boy, huh. What a nice couple." A rough hand gripped her elbow, yanking her back a step. She smelled him before she turned, and her stomach roiled. She'd forgotten about him, bloody Hawkins.

"Get your hand off me."

He laughed and leaned closer. "Like our Italian dago, do you? You like his dark hair and swanky accent? It's disgusting, that's what it is." He spat onto the path. "You have a little secret, I see, one that we now share. How wonderful. What would happen if your father found out you were getting closely acquainted with the foreigner?"

"He's more of a man than you'll ever be."

Albert leaned on his cane and peered into her face. His features remained obscured until the light illuminated them. Esther wanted to divert her gaze at the abhorrent sight.

"He'll be gone, I'll see to that, and then you'll want me. I won't care that you kissed a dago."

Lady arrived, barking furiously, like a guard dog and not at all like a lady. That dog always had a good sense of people. She growled at Albert, a rumble deep in her belly, and bared her teeth, her lips curled backwards. Lady stood at the base of his feet, nudging him and Esther apart. Albert paused, transfixed by the dog.

Esther took a step back and the dog followed. Lady could rip into a man's arm, no trouble about that, and maybe she should let her.

Lady growled again when he wobbled a step forward, perhaps sensing Esther's demeanour. "You bastard." She hadn't learned that word in her *Women's Weekly*.

Albert didn't blink. "Lover boy will leave on the next freight boat, I'll see to that. Then we can forget about him and your secret will be safe with me."

Albert kicked out with his steel-capped boot and struck Lady in the muzzle. The dog yelped. Esther leaned low and cradled the dog, hoping Albert would leave. Lady reared on her hind legs, eager to retaliate.

Albert retrieved his cane and left. Esther shook as she held the dog by its collar. She nuzzled into her head, petting the soft fur.

A sob escaped. Followed by a second, but then she refused to give away more. Who did he think he was? Fury uncurled in Esther and she worried about what she might do. For now, nothing. She wouldn't waste her time on a nasty racist. Hawkins sure was a disgusting man.

She walked back to the cottage, leaving the lighthouse behind and the moon shining on what should have otherwise been a perfect night.

Chapter Nine

Luca had grown fond of the Andersons. Unlike his own family in every way, they had accepted him and his strange customs and ideas. Like the family, nothing about this rugged and unrelenting landscape was familiar to home, but it was quickly becoming a place he wanted to be. Or perhaps it was the attraction of one woman.

They walked together most afternoons through his recuperation. Most frequently, they went to Lighthouse Bay, where he'd been washed ashore. Before they arrived at the sandy milk-white cove, they traversed through thick scrub peppered with white daisies and wattles.

"Is this where?"

Esther nodded. The day his life changed.

Holding hands, they strolled so that the sand itched between their toes and their feet disappeared at the wet edge. At each lap of a wave, Luca moved farther up the beach. On land, he was safe. And here, it felt like their own deserted island where they could be stranded alone together.

"The clouds are rolling in, Luca. See how dark and ominous they are out on the horizon? Bad weather is coming." Esther shivered as the wind howled wickedly.

Luca gazed straight ahead where the world was still perfect, only sunshine and pillow clouds. Behind him, the sombre black sky sat. The temperature dipped and goose bumps rose on his skin.

He searched the seas for boats. "Esther, are any ships out there? Will they be safe?"

"That's Father's job, Luca, to protect them, to operate the lighthouse if the world turns grey."

Luca nodded. "*Si*. Do you think my boat is out there, will it be stuck?"

She dipped her toes in and out of the pooling sand, creating divots. "It's due tomorrow, so maybe."

Luca held her hand and pulled her towards the thick bush bordering the beach. He pushed her gently against the narrow silver trunk of a tall eucalypt tree.

"Tomorrow, I leave. Let's make this special. Our last walk together." He kissed her. For one brief moment, he protected her from the howling winds as the storm drove towards the shore. Then one large, fat droplet landed right bang on Esther's forehead and rolled down her cheek.

Luca kissed it away. "It tastes like sea water. I taste salt everywhere, now."

"Yes. Our bare skin is always covered with salt crystals. It carries in the air and is permanently in my mouth and on my lips."

The rain pummelled the earth and turned the sand to mud. The sea pounded the shore, the sound echoing around the secluded cove. The sky turned black and thunder roared. "We'll have to make a run for it." He pulled her along, laughing to avoid showing his fear.

***

"Well, I never," her mother said as she watched them crash onto the front veranda of the cottage. "Didn't you see the storm brewing?"

"It came in so fast, there was nothing we could do." She smiled innocently at her mother.

"Come inside and dry off." Mary didn't crack a smile. Esther looked at Luca, who currently resembled a wet mop, and laughed. His hair surrounded his face, and his clothes stuck to his skin. Drowned rats, as her mother would say. It made her forget her heart was breaking.

The house was a flurry of activity due to the rain. Her brother and sister forgot their schoolwork as they watched the storm roll over them.

"This is a bad one, hey, Charles?" Tommy asked. Charles had been sent back from the lighthouse to check on them. Their father would remain vigilant through the rollicking weather.

"We've seen worse, Tommy. And the weather hits more severely here on the Cape as we're so exposed. Perhaps down in Adventure Bay they are listening to the pitter-patter of rain on their tin roof while having a cuppa."

Charles was so like their father.

Tommy clapped his hands together. "Mother, can we play a board game in the front room?" His face lit up waiting on her answer. Mary was usually a stickler for school, so everyone held their breath.

"Yes. It'll give me a moment's peace to have a hot drink." Margaret rolled her eyes, but Tommy raced ahead to choose a game from the bookshelf.

"Let's play Candy Land," he yelled.

"Candy Land?" Luca queried. "We play for American sweets?"

"Not exactly," Esther explained. "It's a journey through Peppermint Forest, over Gum Drop Mountain by matching colour cards. Pretty simple. It'll be good for your English."

Luca followed the fracas and settled himself in the front room on the floor with the children. A vicious clap thundered in the sky and the room went dark. The storm raged over them and the trees swayed violently, the weather bearing all its force. Luca placed his hand over Esther's and held it there while Tommy and Margaret flapped about setting up the game. The noise in the room quietened as her body thrummed from his touch. She would not think about tomorrow. Perhaps if she didn't, it would never arrive.

After three successful rounds for Tommy, Luca asked if she played chess.

"I've never played, but Father and Charles play all the time."

"I'll teach you. Where is the board?"

Charles was reading in the corner, and Tommy and Margaret moved on to snap and other card games. Their mother joined them and sat crocheting.

Esther found the board and Luca set it up. She listened as he named each piece, struggling with their English equivalent. Charles yelled out in the background when he got stuck. With exquisite patience, Luca explained the rules whilst their legs touched under the low coffee table.

***

A door slammed shut. Voices mumbled. Esther woke with a start. Was Luca leaving? She had to see him once more. She reached for her gown and hurried towards the kitchen where she heard the squelching of wet shoes.

Father, Mother, and dreadful Hawkins stood huddled together. Her mother remained in her nightclothes. This worried Esther immediately and her stomach twisted. The whites of Father's eyes were streaked with red and he wrung his hand down over his features, dragging the soft skin.

"Have you been at the lighthouse all night, Father?"

He nodded.

Only then did she notice the world was black. It was five a.m. She saw the rain sheeting against the windowpanes and lightning flashing into the kitchen. The rain provided a steady drum sound. A chill crawled under her skin and settled in her bones. She hugged her robe tighter.

"Has the storm worsened?"

Albert answered. "Not worsened, but not abated one bit. It's been ferocious since it started. The seas are the choppiest I've seen in all my time."

Esther glanced at her father, trusting his judgment more. He gave a curt nod.

"Has there been an accident?"

"No," her father said. "No, no boats in trouble that we know of, so despite the weather being tumultuous, we pray that everyone has been kept safe."

This wasn't the news she was waiting for. "What about the supply boat?"

Did her father stall?

"Well, the good news is that the cargo ship had departed, but the storm advanced and it had sufficient time to make safe harbour back to Hobart. So, everyone on board is well."

Esther released her breath.

"Your friend cannot return today. The weather is reportedly to stay for a few days at least," Hawkins said as he dripped water droplets onto her mother's linoleum floor.

Was Esther the only one to hear the vicious tone to his voice? Was she the only one who spied his cold smirk and pinched mouth? Neither of her parents responded to his words.

Her body sagged and she used the chair for support. She composed herself, not prepared to give anything away.

Moving swiftly across the tiny space, she put the copper kettle on to boil and placed the cups on the bench for both tea and coffee. The first moment she could, she'd be delivering a hot coffee to Luca. He was still here for at least one more day. She forced down her bubbling happiness.

"Mother, Father, sit down. I'll make tea and we can all take it back to bed. Father, you need to get some sleep. Albert, I assume you'll be heading back to the lighthouse so Father can rest?"

Esther flinched when she glanced at him. Albert balled his fists by his side; they appeared to shake, likely desperate to break free and deliver a heavy slap to her cheek. She needed to learn to hold her tongue.

"Yes, he will, thank you, Esther." Her father put her back in her place.

No one commented on the bitter caffeine smell that filled the room, overpowering the gentle tea brewing in the pot. Thankfully, Albert made his exit after he'd gulped his tea. Esther poured her parents another cup and made fresh toast and sent them to their room. On tiptoes, dancing around the kitchen, she prepared another tray and raced down the hall. Outdoors, the sun had risen, but was only visible through grey and ominous clouds. A misty fog hung low over the earth.

The hot drinks slopped into the saucers as she walked too fast.

Esther held the brew under Luca's nose. She was teasing, a broad smile across her face. He roused, as she had hoped. His sleepy eyes opened, and seconds later, taking her in, he sat up, losing the covers and exclaiming.

"What. How, what is going on? Oh no. Did I oversleep? Your papa will be so angry." And he rummaged around for his clothes in a flap.

"Luca, stop. You didn't miss the boat. It never came. It had to turn back because of the storm. You aren't leaving today." Letting it all sink in, she clasped his hand.

It was terrible news. The people on the island relied upon the supplies on board the ships. They were the lifeline in an otherwise isolating and tough existence. Esther knew; she longed for her magazine and treats that she ordered, but these freight trips brought much more than that. They meant fresh food, produce, mail, and news from loved ones on the mainland. She felt bad at her joviality, but it meant Luca stayed. Personally, she'd starve if it meant spending one more day with him.

"I'm not leaving today?" he sought clarification.

She shook her head.

"I have to wait until the boat can safely charter the waters, after the storm." He quizzed her on the details.

"Si," she responded. Luca leaned over and pulled her in close. She couldn't breathe he held her so tight, but she would never let go. The harsh weather had worked in their favour. He drew slowly back and she passed his coffee and they sipped in silence. She hadn't developed a taste for it, but she was trying. She took tiny sips; it didn't taste so bad that way.

Chapter Ten

Esther found him pulling out ripe potatoes. "What on earth are you doing?" Luca was crawling on his hands and knees in the vegetable patch. Rain fell like shards of ice and Esther held her umbrella up close. Despite the rain jacket he wore, Luca was still saturated.

"I have four. I need at least two more." His voice was muffled as his head leaned down near the roots of the bush. "All done." He stood triumphant with his potatoes held aloft. "Special treat tonight, for you." He kissed her cheek, touching the edge of her lips. "And your family." Water dripped off his hood and rolled down his nose.

Esther blushed and placed her palm to her cheek.

"Come, let's go. I must prepare."

After drying off, he summoned the entire family. They sat in seats lined up in the kitchen, facing the bench where various ingredients were lined up. They fidgeted and looked at each other uncertainly. The tiny kitchen was stifling, the moisture from outside making the air muggy and the windows fog.

"Tonight, to thank you, I cook an Italian meal. But first, we must drink."

Luca waved a bottle of red wine in front of his captive audience and smiled with a cheeky grin. He saw Esther gasp and turn to look at her mother, who sat stony-faced. Undeterred, Luca took down their finest crystal glasses reserved for special occasions. With great care, he poured five glasses and went to serve two more, smaller tumblers.

"That's quite enough, Luca. There is ample apple juice for Tommy and Margaret. Quite frankly, Esther is only eighteen and lucky she's having any." Mary's face returned to staid.

Ignoring Mary, Luca raised his glass. "Cheers to my host family. My Australian family. I thank you for saving me." He glanced at Esther first. "And for caring for me." He drank. "You have welcomed me like a son. I am grateful. When I return to *Tassie*," he smirked because Mary hated slang, "I will think of you often and hopefully return to the island to visit."

"We've been grateful for your speedy recovery and lively company," her father said.

Luca nodded. "Tonight, we make *gnocchi*."

"What's that?" Tommy was the first to voice what they all must have been thinking.

"It's pasta, silly," Esther interjected and sipped her wine.

"Si, is potato pasta. And Mary, is perfect for making here, on the Cape. All ingredients from your garden. No need for a delivery. Perhaps after I leave, you will make it often and think of me."

"Well, you'd best show me how to make it first."

"Come, stand with me."

Luca loved being in control. He was not used to being waited upon. Now, he was the master of this kitchen. Everyone gasped when he didn't boil the potatoes to make the *gnocchi.* "No." He shook his head. "Boiling makes them soak up the water. Too mushy." He demonstrated how to mix up the mash.

"I know how to mash a potato, Luca," her mother said, indignant.

"Of course, Mary, forgive me. Let's move on."

The children grew bored of kneading and tossing the flour, but drew in close when he cut the dough into bite-size portions. Setting that aside, he got to work on the tomato sauce. His knife whizzed through the basil before it flew into the sizzling pan.

"Quick, gather around, everyone. Watch this." Luca lowered the pieces into the boiling salty water. "They take little time to cook. They…float? Yes, float—when they are cooked. *Delizioso.*" He kissed his fingers and lifted them into the air. Tommy copied him and everyone cracked up in laughter.

Against the Sunday dinner rules, he refilled their wineglasses. *"Salut."* he cheered.

***

It was the best meal he'd had since arriving in Australia. He accepted their platitudes and even his stubble-lined chin turned crimson in the warmth of the kitchen.

"Luca, tell us about your family back home. Of your mother and father," asked John.

It was an innocent question. But the gnocchi stuck like raw dough to the roof of his mouth.

Whilst preparing the meal, he'd ignored the gnawing hollowness in his chest. His precious *nonna* had taught him how to make gnocchi. Many years later, he still remembered every detail of her lesson.

Now, he was back there. Remembering them. A dark cloud descended upon him, but he felt like unburdening his soul. He wanted to tell the truth about his family and what had happened. The kind Anderson family would listen.

Seconds passed. He lowered his head to his chest to avoid the shame, embarrassment and sadness creeping like fingers up his spine. It threatened to suffocate him.

He knew he couldn't. They wouldn't welcome him if they knew the truth, knew why he'd fled. That someone was dead because of him. That his aunt grieved each day of her life. That his family didn't love him enough to run the family business in desecrated post-war Tuscany. That his brother had the job instead and, in Luca's opinion, failed at it miserably. It was all a mess.

This would be too much for the family to comprehend. They'd feel sorry for him, show him sympathy and commiserate. He didn't want that. This family headed by strong and compassionate John Anderson wanted to hear stories of love and Sunday picnics and newborn cuteness of nieces and nephews. Not what he had to say.

Demons did follow you wherever you went; escape seemed impossible. Millions of miles from his beloved homeland, and he couldn't flee his guilt and deep-seated regret.

Instead, Luca made them coffee. He refused to boil the kettle for tea. "You must try, just this once," he said to John and Mary. They acquiesced *just this once.*

"It's stopped." Tommy was the first to notice.

Finally, silence. It was evident after the rain had rattled the tin roof for days.

John smiled, still evidently weary. "Ah, perhaps the weather has broken now. Let's hope tomorrow is filled with sunshine. The Cape is going to be a muddy mess after these relentless days of rain." He looked at each of them individually. "You must all be careful venturing outside. The ground will shift under your feet. Best to always walk steady."

They retired after cleanup was complete. Perhaps it was the amiable feeling that pervaded them after their pleasant evening, but Mary didn't raise an eyebrow when Luca and Esther left the table together and headed to the front room.

Before leaving, Tommy caught Luca and cradled him in a boy-hug, his arm around Luca's hips. John and Charles slapped him on the back. Mary patted him gently on his sleeve.

"So Australian, aren't we? I imagine in Montepulciano you'd be clasping each other and kissing both cheeks and singing out loud good-byes?"

"Yes, that's exactly right, *bella*. However, this is nice, too. Sometimes it is harder to show restraint than express every emotion all at once."

The house was deathly quiet. Outside, the birds that usually chirped all day had hibernated for the evening. A sliver of fluorescent moon was visible through the shifting clouds. The trees didn't sway; the air was still.

Esther sat close to him. It had been agonizing these past few days with all of them cramped in the house due to the weather. They'd practiced their languages, read and reread her magazine, and they'd continued their novel. They were over halfway through *The Lion, the Witch and the Wardrobe* now, and the children were in Narnia and had made friends with the Lion.

"I've missed you these last few days. I've missed our secluded walks."

"Mmm, me too," he murmured as he buried his head into her neck. Today his hair was pulled back into a low bun. Mary had harrumphed when she'd seen it. "But it's so practical, Mary. The tie keeps it out of my face."

Her retort had been fast. "Practical, my boy, would be cutting it short."

***

Finally, she was alone with Luca. Her lips twitched into a broad smile. She no longer experienced a nervousness in his presence; her shyness, too, had disappeared somewhere over the last week. She talked to him about everything—the perfume she longed to receive for Christmas, silly tales she'd read, anecdotes of past times at the Cape. He'd opened up, too. Esther saw a shadow creep across his face occasionally when he thought no one was watching. At those times, he was distant, his mind on faraway places. She knew memories of home caused him pain. She hadn't asked any further about it after that awful day at the cliff edge. Was there more? The guilt over someone's death was enough.

She was also getting used to the sensations that swirled through her body when Luca touched her. His skin on hers caused bolts of electricity to shoot through her, but afterwards, a deep longing, low in her tummy. More and more, she couldn't bear to be apart from him. It drove her wild. That first day, when she'd scrubbed his legs clean, she'd longed to run her fingers through his hair. Now, she did. With his hair tied back tonight, she felt the length of his short ponytail. She moved her hand down to his shoulder. He still wore his jacket, but also a button-up shirt. With shaking fingers, she poked her finger through the gap and felt his hard chest. She traced there, on that spot.

Luca lifted his head and stared at her. With his good hand, he placed it over her fingers, stalling them. His heartbeat thundered under her touch. Could he sense hers?

He leaned in and kissed her. It took her breath away. She wanted more, but didn't know what exactly. Him. She unbuttoned his shirt and placed her two palms flat against his stomach, moving his shirt to the sides. His body was rigid under her caress. With trembling fingers, she moved across his naked torso, tracing his nipples and along the trail of dark curls leading to his waistband. Stopping there, Esther gazed back up at him again, her mouth open, sucking in little breaths of air. Oh God, she wanted him, craved his touch to her skin.

They stared at each other. His eyes black and smoky, desire pooling in them. Questions dashed between them but neither spoke. Esther didn't want words anymore. All she wanted was his body next to hers as they loved each other.

***

Esther's cheeks ached as if she'd slept with a smile on her face. She'd had a dreamless, deep sleep despite creeping into her bed at a rudely late hour. Languorously, she rolled over, keeping her eyes shut. Had last night really happened?

A rolling wave of contentment pulsed through her. Yesterday, she'd been a child, until she'd made love to Luca. Today, she'd grown into a woman. Cuddling the pillow to cushion her head, she dreamed of telling her parents about her love for Luca. For she did love him, didn't she? What else could she be feeling?

Once her parents knew, he wouldn't be forced to leave. Or maybe she could go with him? They could start a life together in Hobart. They could be married. With these ideas running through her mind, she bounced out of bed and dressed. Strange, the house was quiet. Usually it bustled with morning activity and scurrying feet, particularly now that she spied the sun. To be sure, it was a new day.

No one was in the kitchen. Setting the kettle to boil, she started making herself a tea and a coffee for Luca. She poured the last ground beans into a cup. He wouldn't be pleased that this was his last coffee. Humming, she wiped away crumbs from earlier toast. Opening the window, she sucked in the fresh air. Outside, the world had revived after the battering of the weather. Birds sang and soared in the breeze.

Balancing the tray, she headed for the front room. Esther pushed the door open with her toes.

The tray crashed to the floor. The teacups smashed and hot liquid splashed over the hem of her dress.

Her mother stood in the empty room leaning over the settee and rearranging the cushions. The sheets and bedding gone. The window was wide open, unleashing the outdoors and forcing its life force into the room. It was unbearably bright after the greyness. The coffee table was back in place, the armchairs exactly positioned to each side. Instead of Luca's tobacco and woody smell, the stringent odour of bleach hit her nose.

"Goodness gracious, Esther." Her mother bent and collected the china pieces shattered across the floor.

"Where is Luca?"

"The weather has cleared and a boat arrived this morning. They had room to return him to Hobart. Albert arranged everything. But they had to leave at first light to make the departure."

Esther grasped her mother's arm in a claw-like grip. "He's gone?" Esther's legs could no longer hold her. She collapsed to the ground and cried.

Chapter Eleven

September 1952

Esther's joints ached. It took all her effort to carry her body forward, to lift her feet that weighed too heavy. One moment she was starving; the next, nausea overcame her and the prospect of food made her gag. Her nerve endings were alive and sensitive and sore to touch. Days passed and the wretchedness continued.

So, it was true, like in the stories she read. You could die of a broken heart. Her heart had shattered into a million tiny pieces and she didn't know if it would ever be whole again.

At first, she'd been angry, then came a black hollowness. At times, she was sure there was a physical wound like a gaping hole in her chest. As the days continued, so did an overwhelming lassitude. Not merely with her mind, but her body, too. Was Luca feeling the same?

"Esther, stop daydreaming. Feed the goats, please."

Do this, do that. Esther knew her mother was driven spare by her moping. Had the woman never been in love? Anger festered and bubbled towards her mother. For not waking her that morning, for not showing her kindness or sympathy in the days that followed. It was like Luca had never existed.

Deliveries had always been like a rainbow after a storm to Esther. Now, they meant letters from Luca. She reached into the pocket of her skirt and fingered the edges of the letter protected within. It already curled at its edges and had begun to tatter, she'd read it so many times.

They'd written frequently. His words kept her waking up each day. Those same words she recited during her mundane days. Existence for Esther at the lighthouse had become bleached grey and dull. The colour and excitement gone.

She'd begged her parents, but they'd been unrelenting. She'd pleaded with them to let her join him, to live in Hobart, to forge a life together. At first, they'd thought her jesting, despair having made her go crazy, but when she sobbed at her father's feet, clutching at his legs, they'd understood she wasn't joking.

"We belong together."

"Those are foolish dreams straight out of one of your magazines."

Her mother's words were harsh, and her father's were practical.

"What prospects would you have? Luca cannot work because he is injured. Does he even have work into the future? What if they dismiss him, return him to Italy?"

Esther protested, but Father held up his palm and silenced her.

"Even if he remains part of the hydro-scheme, do you intend to live at the camp where the workers reside? Those camps are hardly fitting for a young woman." He hung his head and shook it side to side. "You have not thought this through, child. It's not possible."

At that she'd doubled over and howled.

Her cheeks flushed with embarrassment as she recalled her behaviour. Of course, he was right, they were both right. But she wanted to be with Luca.

In their letters, they discussed the future. In time, surely this would be possible? She believed it. Until then, she had his written words, sloppy and broken in English. But she understood their meaning, the messages of love they conveyed, and the hope. Occasionally, he spilled into Italian. Despite their lessons, she wasn't able to read it. She was sure those words would cut deep into her soul.

Thinking about him made a shooting pain pulse through her chest. She remembered his touch on her bare skin, her fingers raking through his too-long hair, his earthy aroma, and oh, how she longed for the smell of coffee. The scent personified Luca.

A wave of nausea hit her and that nasty metallic taste was in her mouth again. Whilst her stomach swirled it also sat tight. Instinctively, she rubbed her hands over it. She needed to sit down.

***

Charles stood on the front path, dressed in the hand-me-down suit from their father. For weeks she'd been so miserable that she'd forgotten about her brother's departure. Guilt pressed in upon her. Finally, he was setting off on his own adventure—moving to Hobart to work in the Cascade Brewery.

With Hawkins secure as assistant lightkeeper, there was no position for Charles, no avenue for him to earn an income. Left with little choice, he'd sought work off the Cape. Esther had read in the *Women's Weekly* that the recovering city of Hobart was thriving with work and entertainment and opportunities. That's where he had to go.

The irony was not lost on Esther. At only three years older, Charles was permitted to leave the family home for work. As a woman, she had no such liberties. Tradition dictated she remain living with her parents until she married. She controlled a burst of laughter. How did anyone expect her to meet an eligible husband living miles from civilisation? It was a joke, but not a funny one. Except fate had intervened and delivered Luca to her. Couldn't her parents see the sense in the idea? How else would she follow the expected path?

Perhaps she could live with Charles and they could make a home together. But of course, Charles would eventually find his own wife. Esther sighed in defeat. For the time being, she was stuck.

She lined up behind the rest of her family to bid farewell. Her father would deliver Charles to the ferry at Kettering. Esther watched her mother embrace her eldest son. She didn't cry. Everything was so matter of fact with her. It had always bothered Esther, but now her mother's cold nature infuriated her.

Hugging Charles, she couldn't stem her tears. Everyone knew he wouldn't be back. She gulped back a sob. It could have been her…

Hours later, after the round trip, father delivered her another magazine. Whilst he mightn't shed tears or be generous with his emotions, her father was adept at small gestures. Her heart did a pitter-patter of excitement. She longed to be lost in its pages, to forget for a little while the world she existed in.

She flicked it open and her gaze ran across an advertisement for a newly published book. *How to Care for Children, The Homemaker's Encyclopedia.* It had a beautiful green cover with a mother tending her sick child in bed. Esther's breasts began to throb as she looked at the image. She cupped them with her hands to soothe the pulse, letting the magazine drop to her lap. This new book would guide mothers through each stage of raising a child: infant, toddler, preschool. An image of Mrs Miller from the bait and tackle shop in Lunawanna being with child, her fourth last year, filled Esther's vision. After the baby was born, they'd gone to visit and taken a homemade casserole and a gift. Echoes of the conversation came back to her. With a fisherman husband, three children, and a newborn, Ann Miller didn't stand on propriety. She'd discussed personal matters, much to her mother's disgust. Tender breasts. Nausea lasting months, the fatigue.

Esther clutched her stomach. Her skin stretched where once it had been soft. Sensations swirled underneath. Her tummy felt strange, as if one hundred butterflies had been released. Rubbing her hands across it now, it felt extended and fuller.

No. No. No.

She couldn't be, could she?

"Esther, please stop daydreaming and assist me with dinner."

Pulling herself out of her reverie, Esther rose from the armchair and followed her mother out of the front room where she'd been basking in the afternoon dusk.

"Chicken tonight," she heard her mother say. "I've slaughtered it and Tommy is plucking. Can you supervise him, please? Once it's done, you can put it on to roast."

Esther nodded and did as she was told, leaving the kitchen and entering the yard. Spring had arrived on the Cape and the icy winds and low temperatures had receded, replaced with tepid sunshine and bright blue, cloudless skies. Her mother pulled in a few items that had been set to dry on the timber clothes horse standing near the back door.

Tommy handled the dead chicken adeptly. Feathers surrounded his feet and shifted in the wind. A few escaped and fluttered along the ground until they floated over the ridge and down, away to the water. Fresh blood sat in a pool, the innards in a bucket to be discarded. Esther's stomach roiled. The metallic smell of the blood filled her nostrils, mixed with the rank odour of the gizzards. Her hand raced to her mouth. Esther visualised the blood pouring from the dead neck of the chicken. The bile rose up her throat and sweat beads converged on her brow.

"Argh." she cried and sped to the edge of the garden and retched. Her mother rushed over, holding back her hair in a rare moment of tenderness. Instinctively, Esther cradled her stomach. Her mother's eyes went wider than dinner plates, her mouth formed a perfect "O". Her hand dropped Esther's hair. When she'd finished vomiting, Esther stood tall, wiping her mouth and collecting the strands of hair whipping her cheeks. Her mother's eyes scrutinised her stomach. Esther saw what her mother saw. A rounded tummy, barely discernible but on her slim frame, noticeable. Mary's hands flew to her face and she gawped at Esther before she turned and fled. Esther needed to rid her mouth of the taste of sick and sit down.

The world grew dark.

***

November 1952

Penance started immediately.

"Mother, should I fold the washing for you?" Her mother nodded without looking at her when usually she'd provide a curt response. In the days that followed the realisation of her pregnancy, Esther longed to hear her mother's smart tongue and have her say all the things she thought: that Esther had made a terrible mistake, of her disappointment in her eldest daughter, or perhaps that she was a whore. After the initial polite discussion—her father didn't argue, her mother only glared—her mother didn't acknowledge the baby. Sometimes, she caught her mother staring with measured disgust. How hard it must be to look upon her daughter and see her swollen belly, a daily reminder of her sin. That's what her mother had called it: a sin. The comment would have been laughable if it hadn't hurt so much. Her parents weren't even religious.

Esther tried to soften her mother's anger. She talked of names or clothes she might need. Of how she was feeling. Or asked advice about her growing stomach and the ache in her back. Mary answered with practical and sensible advice. But Esther longed for a strong embrace, a sympathetic look, or even a pat to her arm to confirm that everything would be all right.

It was difficult to learn about what was happening to her body. All she'd learned about pregnancy came from the *Women's Weekly*.

Those images captured women dressed in powder-blue suits cradling their arched backs as a dear husband rubbed their sore spots. Not much for her to learn there.

In the end, her father spoke of the practicalities in a matter-of-fact way.

"You will have the baby here on the Cape. When it arrives, we'll say it's an unexpected addition to the family."

Esther stared dumbstruck. "You mean we'll tell people that the baby is yours and Mother's?"

"Yes. We don't see many people anyways, but word will spread. You will, of course, care for the baby. Your mother has enough to do."

"Yes, Father."

She had to accept that she had brought undeniable shame upon the family. If people knew the truth, their family would be shunned and the brunt of local gossip. Her mother would not be able to bear it.

But how could she feel ashamed when her baby had been created out of her love for Luca? She would not feel humiliated.

"Can I feel the baby?" Tommy asked. He placed his hands across her widening stomach. His eyes widened in wonderment at the movement. It was something beautiful they shared. Often as he raced past, he'd pause and listen to the heartbeat before running on.

Margaret was more constrained, aware of the tension in the household and conscious of divided loyalties. "What does it feel like?" she'd whisper when their mother was out of earshot.

"At times, it feels the most wondrous thing. A real person growing within me, but also strange and heavy." Esther had laughed. She loved that her siblings treated her normally and that life with them carried on.

Esther filled her days with chores, hers, those of her siblings, and jobs that didn't need doing. She had to be useful, had to be busy, until she collapsed exhausted into bed. Unbridled guilt drove her to be better, to be the best daughter she could be.

At night she cried into her pillow, but despite exhaustion, sleep refused to come. In between weeping, she thought of Luca. Sometimes, under the moonlight, she'd pull out the letters he'd written and reread them.

My dearest Esther,

I have lost track of the days since I saw you. Too many. They blur into one. All I do is work, sleep, eat. And still, I dream of you. I count the days until we can be together. I understand your parents think it silly, and while I may not have much to offer you now, my love, I work hard so that in another twelve months, I will be free and we can be together. It is hard with my arm still weak. I must fulfil my commitments to this beautiful country that has adopted me, but then I might be offered more work, or I can seek another position. I make plans. Dream of wine and vineyards. I'm not sure if that is possible, but I cannot stop imagining. You will be older then, I will have more money. It is all that keeps me going, the thought that I can hold you once more, cradle you in my arms, inhale your sweet scent.

I know I wasn't sent away as punishment, but it feels that way. It feels like we were torn apart. I tell myself every day it is not true. I tell myself it is not further punishment.

How is Tommy? Your family? Has Mary made gnocchi again? Does Tommy still race about everywhere? It was a cold winter here at camp, but now that it has passed, I imagine the wildflowers growing at the edge of the path towards Lighthouse Bay. Our bay. It must be warmer now, yes? I know it is wrong, but I dream of our last night together, of holding you, caressing your bare skin...

I received a letter from my family today for my recent birthday. Did I tell you it was my birthday on 1 November? We will celebrate together next year. When is your birthday? I shall read their letter now, after I send this to you. Next time, I will tell you all about them and their news.

Non posso sopportare un altro giorno senza di te. Ti amo con tutto il mio cuore. (I cannot imagine spending one more day away from you. I love you with all my heart)

Dearest. Love. He addressed those words to her.

Esther kissed the letter on the spot where Luca had scrawled his name and drawn a pink heart. She held it close to her cheek and inhaled a faint scent of him. She'd never wanted something so desperately before.

Esther ripped out her pad and started furiously writing, with one hand resting on her belly. *Dear Luca.* He needed to know about his baby. Now was the time. Naively, she'd been waiting until they were together to break the news. How stupid she'd been to wait. If he knew she was pregnant, he'd come and get her. She knew it.

She avoided pleasantries about family and dove straight in. After a sentence, she paused, scratched over the words she'd written, screwed up the paper and tossed it in the bin. Started again. Twice more and each effort landed in the bin. She kicked the leg of the desk. Starting again, she took a deep breath, rubbed her tight stomach, and simply told him in words that he'd understand.

They were having a baby.

Chapter Twelve

To dear Luca,

Oh, the baby is kicking. It's the strangest feeling. It's difficult to imagine our baby is growing inside of me, but then she kicks with all of her force, making my skin stretch at odd angles—perhaps her foot or maybe an elbow? I wish you were here to feel it.

I talk to her about you. Her brave father working far away. I tell her you'll teach her Italian and that one day we'll travel to your homeland and introduce her to the rest of her family. How wonderful these dreams are.

I have grown so big that none of my clothes fit anymore. Margaret calls me fat and says I waddle like a penguin. Damn her for being so unkind and for being so thin. But it's true, even my ankles are wide and at the end of the day they are swollen and I must rest them on the settee. At least I am not as tired. The exhaustion of those early weeks was hard. Now I have more energy.

Plus, the indigestion. Sometimes I can taste my lunch all afternoon long.

Mother remains as frosty as a snowman. Will she ever forgive me? It doesn't seem so. I know you could fix it, Luca, if you were here. You could make her smile.

And how are you, my love? Has your hair grown long, does it touch your shoulders yet? How is your family and life at the camp? Your arm? So many questions that I want to ask you. I dream of you speaking Italian to me and teaching me the rest of your beautiful language. I try to practice, but I cannot remember all the words and how to roll my Rs.

By any chance have you seen Charles in your travels? If you do, please give him a big hug from me. We miss him dearly. Life is quieter without him.

When will you visit? Soon—I truly hope so. Each day I long to hear the rumble of a motor car manoeuvring its way along the track. Or sometimes, when I gaze out at the ocean and I spy a boat, I wonder if it's you sailing towards me. Sometimes I swear I can see you standing upon the deck, staring back at me. At night, I wonder if you are watching the same shooting star as me as it falls towards earth.

Oh Luca, I'm not sure I can bear waiting any longer. I don't wish to tell you about our baby via letter...I want us to be together.

I'm scared, Luca. Scared mainly that you won't come. Scared, too, that the birth will hurt. That I will not know what to do with her when she arrives. That you will not be here with me to meet her and help me through it.

Please write again. Receiving a letter from you brightens my day. Tommy sends his love.

I miss you with all of my heart and pray and hope that we can be together again soon.

Ti amo.

Esther.

Today, she wasn't doing her chores, damn the consequences.

In her letters she talked of the beautiful parts of pregnancy. Not about her constantly aching body. Nor how the simple act of walking exhausted her, let alone carrying pails of scraps. One of her most hated jobs was sweeping. How it made her middle throb.

She snuck away and sat beneath the lighthouse, out of sight of prying eyes, and watched the waves roll in the gentle wind. The weather was neutral today. The sun shone golden over the island and held warmth. Esther closed her eyes and lifted her face to capture each ray. She relished the heat and the quiet, but didn't dwell for long. Closed eyes meant she wouldn't spy Albert should he be out and roaming the paths. Occasionally, she'd glance up and spy him watching her, a slavish glint in his eye. He was such a worm. Esther shook those vile thoughts of Hawkins away. On such a pleasant day, she didn't want to crowd her mind with nastiness.

In her pocket she held Luca's last letter. On top of her bump, she balanced crackers and her magazine. Desperate to reacquaint herself with the frivolity of the outside world, she couldn't wait to dive straight into its pages.

But could she concentrate? Luca was coming. For the first time in months, a lightness entered her chest and the darkness that had pervaded her mind lifted.

She left the magazine at her side as she took out his note.

While I work hard and my employer is happy, my arm is still healing and he thinks it best if I find other work. The scheme is, what you say? On a tight deadline and I am slowing them down. Your government will release me without a penalty. I have been talking with my Italian friend, and he has work in a company that build blocks. Sounds strange, doesn't it? Like a child's game. But these blocks build houses. My friend tells me I can do the work with a less-than-perfect arm. But in time it will improve, I am sure.

Of course, I would rather be tending to a delicate grapevine, watering its brittle leaves and smelling the ferment of wine, but I have to work. Be practical. I still dream of an Australian winery; I shall keep that hope alive. But until then, I shall build blocks, but not until after Christmas. This means I should have time to visit. Can I come? Will your parents allow it?

Her mother had read the letter. The seal was open when Margaret handed it to her. Had she read all of them? Regardless, she'd written by return post and said he should come pronto.

That had been three weeks ago. Why hadn't he written since to confirm his arrival? And why hadn't he mentioned the baby? None of it made sense.

She scoured the letter for detail she might have missed. Her fear grew. He wrote regularly. At least once, usually more a week. But Christmas approached and he said he'd visit. Even if their letters had crossed paths, when he learned about becoming a father, wouldn't he have written straight away? Did he prefer to wait until he saw her? He was coming. That's all that mattered. She pictured him arriving as they sang Christmas carols and ate fruit cake and roast pork specially delivered for the celebrations. Then everything would be all right. He would come.

***

February 1953

Esther screamed as the pain gripped her middle. It squeezed her belly like a vise being tightened until she feared she'd rip in two.

"Mother, make it stop," she whimpered. "Please, make it stop."

She knew her mother was present, although she didn't speak. She could hear her soft footfalls as she moved around the room. A ding here, a tinkle there as she shifted things. Occasionally, she placed a cup of water to her dry lips and Esther sipped, but the act was perfunctory, as she would treat a child who needed a drink.

As the contraction receded, Esther rolled onto her side and curled her legs as far up to her chest as her stomach allowed.

Please, let it stop.

Esther breathed in deeply, longing for the brief reprieve between the waves of agony to last. Her brow was wet, her clothes moist and stuck to her. The urge to rip them away from her sticky skin was irresistible. As she tugged at the collar of her nightdress—it had been riding too high up her neck and annoyed her—a soft touch to her hand stilled her.

Blinking her eyes open, she oriented herself in the room. Her eyes had been squeezed shut for what seemed like hours, blocking out the too-bright sun penetrating the room. Her father stood over her. She grasped his hand, tugged it close, held it to her chest. With his free hand, he gently brushed his handkerchief across her forehead. The gesture of kindness almost broke her after the hours of silence and crippling contractions.

"You can do this, sweetheart. I know you can. Be strong."

The twinges returned, building slowly until her breath caught. No, not again, not yet. "Help me, please." Silent tears rolled down her cheeks.

Without speaking, her father bent down and kissed her forehead, slowly, so that Esther felt the outline of his full lips against her skin. The ache rose through her core with unrelenting force. She couldn't stay on her side. Esther manoeuvred over to her back and threw her head against the pillow. Her father was gone.

Exhaustion worse than hours of physical labour absorbed her, made her want to slump in a heap and sleep. But her body wouldn't cooperate; it could not rest, and it seemed to function as a separate entity to her mind.

As she rode the crest of the contraction, her mind escaped the confines of the room and drifted. Her body floated over the raging seas, atop boats drifting in the white caps, and along the rugged cliff tops of the Cape. She soared with the cormorants and the Pacific gulls and swooped when they did. Then her feet were sinking into the beach. The wet sand seeped through her toes and the gentle waves broke over her ankles. The next spasm hit her like the rolling surf and it tumbled her back to reality, back to the bed, where she lay in her own sweat and fought to remain in control. She willed herself back to the beach, the beach she shared with Luca.

Her brief reprieve was over. Pain tore through her once more and she was thrown headlong back into the throes of anguish. She arched her back as an undeniable urge to bear down couldn't be ignored.

"Push, Esther. It's time to push. This baby wants to arrive."

Was that her mother? The voiced sounded different: ethereal, like an angel. A pair of hands gripped her shoulders and secured her against the bed.

"Argh," she screamed through gritted teeth. It was the first relief she'd felt in hours. It reinvigorated her, spurred her on, and gave her courage. She could do this. She shrieked and panted like a dog, struggling to get air into her lungs.

The pain became bearable if she bore down, so she focused on that, her attention back to the present. Skin stretched and separated as though it tore, and then she felt a sudden give, yet fullness, all at once.

"That's it," her mother cooed in a singsong voice. "Oh, come on, sweet precious, come out and meet us."

Esther wouldn't stop now. Something else willed her on. Her mother's tone? No, it was Luca. This was his baby. She placed both hands on her raised knees, squeezing until her round stomach doubled over and didn't let go, until suddenly she couldn't do it anymore. She was done.

A baby cried.

Esther's head lolled backwards and darkness came to meet her.

Chapter Thirteen

Luca didn't come.

Every day she woke with an ache in her chest and it never left.

Was it possible for her heart to shatter any further? It sure felt like it. It already floated awash in her chest.

"Can I please have a cuddle?" Tommy stood with his arms out.

"Of course. He's asleep now, so be gentle." Her arms felt cold and empty after she handed him over. He'd barely been out of her arms in the five weeks since his arrival.

"Esther, he needs a haircut. His hair has grown so quickly." Tommy laughed as he rocked the bundle.

Esther would never forget her mother's face when she roused after the birth. Esther's mind was foggy, but it was difficult to feel anything but relief that the pain had stopped. She looked at her mother, who held the baby, now wiped clean and wrapped in a blanket. Tears ran down Mary's cheeks and her faith had soared. Her mother had forgiven her. John stood next to her and they stared wide-eyed at the babe in her arms.

"It'll be okay, Mary," her father had said.

Esther lifted up her body onto her elbow, frightened. Was something wrong with the child?

Her mother cried louder. "Look at it, John. It's all black-haired and dark-skinned. It looks like him."

She'd been wrong. Mother wasn't forgiving her. She was lamenting the appearance of the baby and how foreign he looked.

"I don't think we'll be able to pass him as our own."

At the time, Esther had let the voices recede and exhaustion gripped her once more.

Back in the present, Tommy sang a lullaby and swayed, as around them squeals of children and the animated chat of adults could be heard. Tommy was an enormous help and Esther had enjoyed watching the bond develop between him and his nephew.

What a wondrous thing for him not to judge this child who had joined their family. Thankfully, Tommy was too young to understand the dynamics. Margaret loved Antonio, too, but she was too busy looking after herself to worry about the baby.

A child raced past with a bright green kite. The noise of its fluttering made Antonio's lids quiver in his sleep.

The first argument had occurred when she'd announced his name. Esther knew it had to be Italian, in honour of Luca and his homeland and culture. But the only Italian name she knew, other than Luca, was his friend who'd died in the shipwreck. Antonio he became.

Her mother stood her ground. "I will not call him Antonio."

Esther had had enough of her mother's vexation.

"It's not your choice."

The noise of the St Patrick's Day picnic on the Cape echoed around them. She and Tommy sat on the worn timber seat at the edge of the garden. The smell of her mother's roses wafted in the air. Square plaid rugs were laid out across the yard. Women from the local communities of Lunawanna and Adventure Bay, some as far as the north of the island, were sitting with legs crossed, basking in the sun. They kept one eye on their children as they raced around or toddled on legs learning to walk. This was one of the rare times they entertained at the lighthouse.

"Oh Esther, he's adorable. Aren't you lucky to have a younger brother. What a surprise." Gertrude came and sat beside her and reached for his fingers that he promptly curled around hers. Esther blanched.

Her mother's approach saved her from small talk. "Here he is." Mary smiled at the bundle but avoided Esther's gaze. Mrs Collins, the doctor's wife, trailed behind her.

"I can't believe you delivered him without any help, Mary. How frightening. George didn't even know you were expecting." The woman tsk-tsked. "You must have been a great help to your mother, Esther."

Esther smiled at Mrs Collins but stared at her mother. This was a new situation, playing out the lie in public. A flush crept up her mother's neck, the only tell-tale sign of her discomfort. Esther waited, not willing to answer. As the moment stretched on, Mary finally spoke.

"Yes, well, Tony was quite a surprise."

"Tony, so Australian." Mrs Collins laughed.

"His name is Antonio," Esther said. "It's a tribute to the Italian migrants who call our country home. It's lovely, don't you think?" Esther widened her smile, daring her mother to contradict her in front of the doctor's wife.

Mary's face froze, grey and solid like steel.

Antonio grumbled and whimpered in Tommy's arms. He handed him back to Esther, despite Mary gesturing for him.

Thank you, Tommy. Esther clutched him to her chest and held tight. She could play games in public to save face, but Antonio was her baby. Hers and Luca's.

"I have been an enormous help to Mother in caring for Antonio. She already has so much on her plate, with assisting Father and schooling Tommy and Margaret and running our household. It's the least I can do."

Esther beamed at Mrs Collins. If the woman detected any sarcasm, she didn't acknowledge it. Mary pulled Mrs Collins away.

"Gertrude, Antonio is due for his bottle, would you like to feed him?" Esther hated pretending to her only friend on the Cape, but what choice did she have?

"Yes, please."

"I'll go and prepare it. Tommy, can you keep Gertrude company?"

Looking as if he'd rather run off and play, Tommy acquiesced and sat. Gertrude paid attention to the baby.

***

The moment she returned, Tommy raced away, grabbing a finger sandwich off a tray Margaret held on his way. The fare wasn't especially Irish, but the best they could do.

"Why doesn't Tommy fish with the men?" Gertrude asked Esther as she sat back down.

"Father says he isn't old enough yet. Perhaps next year. He's desperate to go. He pleaded with Father this morning, but nope, he was adamant his time will come."

"He's the eldest boy now. Would seem better if he went, even to hold the bucket." The girls giggled together. "I didn't see Kevin

O'Connor before they left. Was he wearing his traditional green clothes and top hat?"

Kevin was their local Irishman and had forged the way for the celebrations. There were few Irish traditions on the island, but he made up for it by wearing his striped green clothes that probably spent the best part of the year at the back of his wardrobe. He'd been instrumental in bringing the island residents together to celebrate, but he couldn't convince them to dress up. It horrified the Irishman that the ladies had English high tea on the lawn and the men went fishing. They'd join the ladies and children at dusk for an Irish whiskey, all the while Kevin lamenting his desire for a Guinness.

***

Gertrude fed Antonio, who sucked eagerly at his bottle. Raised voices came from their right. Everyone looked in the direction of the cliffs.

William Smith, the butcher, arrived and paused on the clearing. His face was ghostly white and his breaths ragged. Behind them trailed more men; a group of younger lads from the island whom Esther didn't know well.

"Mrs Collins," William yelled. "The doctor needs his case. John has slipped on the rocks and fallen. He's hit his head."

Time slowed. Was her father the only John amongst the men? She couldn't remember. Mrs Collins hurried towards the cottage. It was a strange sight as her long frilly party dress flowed behind her, slowing her steps. She gripped her hat. Her mother stood still, one hand covering her open mouth, her eyes wide. It was only when Mrs Collins returned carrying the brown satchel that she tore into action. Mary's simple dress didn't impede her like Mrs Collins. She raced towards the edge of the fenced yard and went to descend the slope. Peter, the new owner of the flash petrol station in town, restrained her. Mother's skirt swirled in the pause, swishing around her ankles. Peter spoke to her. Whatever he said worked; she stood still, peering over the edge of the cliff. No one stopped Tommy though. He was over the rise before anyone could catch him.

Seconds later, the lad screamed. His roaring voice echoed and bounced off the ragged cliff and travelled up the rise.

***

The dirt trickled through Esther's fingers and thumped against the lid of the coffin. Her mother sobbed. Rain bucketed down, soaking them as the grave diggers lowered the coffin into the hard earth. Antonio cried too and Esther's ears hurt from his wailing.

Esther held the umbrella over her mother. Grey curly hair stuck to her face. Ramshackle was what she'd call her mother's appearance today, like she'd thrown together any old outfit with no care. It was a most unusual sight. At least something could penetrate Mother's cold demeanour…unfortunately it was Father's death.

"Tommy, Margaret, look after Mother, please. People are moving inside and I need to prepare the afternoon tea." Her siblings stared, stony-faced and vacant, at her but moved robotically to their mother's side.

Inside, Esther boiled kettles, made sandwiches, and joined in small talk. Antonio continued to grizzle, not helped by the fact he was passed through many pairs of hands like a parcel. Esther wanted to scream. Screech her frustration at the meaningless chat that would never bring her father back, at the pleasant smiles and casseroles shoved into her hands and most of all, at her mother. She wanted everyone to leave them in peace.

"Thank you for coming. My father would have appreciated your kindness. A lamb stew. How wonderful," she said as she placed it next to the other five dishes on the kitchen bench.

Finally, she shut the door on the last guest. The cottage was a mess of teacups, plates, and half-eaten biscuits, but she sank into the armchair, needing five minutes to rest her feet. She closed her eyes.

Her mother sat hunched over and mute as she had the entire afternoon—well, in fact, all the days since their father's accident.

The peace splintered too quickly as the back door slammed and heavy footsteps thudded down the hall.

Albert. Of all people. The sight of him still made her stomach roil.

"Esther, Mary, the formalities are over and we need to talk about the future."

Albert stood, his fingers tracing the brim of the cap he held in his hands. His back was ramrod straight and he averted his eyes and looked at the painting hanging over the fireplace. A prickle of apprehension swept through Esther. Mary glanced up.

"I think it's best if the marriage occurs as soon as possible. I can organise the priest and commence the paperwork within the next couple of days."

"Are you getting married, Albert?" Esther tried to keep the derision out of her tone. Really? Who would marry Hawkins?

Her mother nodded, her eyes focused on a worn piece of carpet.

"Mother?" Esther sat up straight. Albert avoided her gaze and hadn't answered the question. "Albert, what on earth are you talking about?" she said.

He took two steps forward. "Esther, I think it is a good idea that we get married."

It took a few moments for the words to register. Her lips parted. "Us?" she whispered.

"It's for the best," said Albert. "With your father gone, I am the head lightkeeper. I'll move into this house. The only way your family can stay on the Cape is if we are husband and wife." Then he smiled, baring his teeth.

Esther glanced sideways at her mother and stood. "I will never marry you."

"It's for the best, Esther. If you marry Albert, we can stay on the Cape."

"No. You're wrong." Her voice hitched. "There must be another way."

Her mother rose from the seat as if she were a woman older than her years. "Esther, you marrying Albert will save all of us. You have to. If you don't, we have nowhere to live, nowhere to go." Her voice quavered. "Albert agrees it is a good idea. You should be grateful, there are many mouths to feed."

Grateful? A tsunami of rage tore through Esther and she balled her fists in an attempt to keep her voice calm. "You've spoken about this. You've developed a plan without even talking with me?"

"Yes. We think it is for the best. If you marry soon, Albert can move into this cottage and the children and I will relocate into his home."

"That house has two bedrooms." It was a ridiculous and useless piece of information that Esther felt was important to point out.

No one responded.

"The babe has to go."

"What did you say?" Her mother acted as if she hadn't heard. The torrent of rage grew in Esther. Her face flushed hot. "I asked you to repeat what you said."

"I will not accept your bastard child," Albert said. "He can live with your mother. I will not raise a dago baby."

Esther clutched her heart as a shooting pain zoomed across her chest. Her legs wobbled and she worried they wouldn't hold her weight. Her mother would speak up. She'd never allow anyone to speak of her grandson in that manner, let alone permit such language in her house. She might have a grudge against Esther for the way the child came into the world, but she loved that baby dearly.

Silence filled the empty crevices of the room.

Glancing at her mother, Esther saw her head bowed, her arms crossed, resolute.

"How dare you?" She sneered at Albert and lurched forward to stand within an inch of him. "How *dare* you?" she repeated.

As if she'd struck a match, Esther watched his demeanour change, saw the vein pulse in his neck and his hands clench.

"When you are my wife, you will do as I say. Only our children will live in this house. Your job will be to raise them and look after me."

Her anger turned to disgust and she fought an urge to vomit. They glared at each other until her mother intervened again.

"It's the only solution, Esther. Please, do it for all of us. For our future. Think of your brother and sister."

Esther moved to her mother and cupped her hands. Her fingers remained cold. Esther wondered whether they'd ever be warm again.

"Mother, I can't do this. You can't make me. This is unfair."

Mary's nostrils flared and she dropped Esther's hands. "What do you know about fair? You've lived a life of dreams and gossip magazines, wasting time on movie stars and celebrities. This is real life, Esther, not time for girlish fantasies."

Esther backed away.

"It was you who killed your father," she went on. "Of disappointment after what you did. He was mortified, but he forgave you. He always had a soft spot for you, his first daughter. His prettiest and the most charming. If you hadn't shamed us all, he might still be alive."

"What? What are you talking about? He slipped on the rocks fishing. It had nothing to do with me."

"His heart was already broken by then. You changed him. You changed everything."

Esther rocked back on her heels as if she'd been struck. This couldn't be happening. Her mother couldn't truly believe those lies.

Tommy entered the room, roused by the raised voices. Albert moved to stand beside her and grasped her forearm.

Through gritted teeth, she said, "I will never marry you."

"Marry? You and Albert?" Tommy muttered in the background.

"Let go of me," Esther attempted to yank her arm free. Albert tightened his hold.

"She said let her go." Tommy said, his face pale. "Esther said she doesn't want to marry you."

Albert dropped her arm and turned and slapped Tommy across the face, the sound of flat palm against skin reverberating around the space.

"Tommy."

He clutched his cheek where a red welt formed. Tears pooled in his eyes. Esther raced to his side and hugged his broadening shoulders.

In the corner, her mother sobbed.

"I will starve and be homeless rather than marry a vile man like you."

As she cradled Tommy to her bosom and bustled them both out of the front room, Albert shouted after them. "You'll live to regret that decision."

Chapter Fourteen

Luca sat at the breakfast table in the boarding house on Wentworth Street, South Hobart, and sipped his coffee. He winced at the flavour. From now on, he vowed to buy his espresso on the way to work.

Can this country not do good coffee and wine? Two simple little things he would like... for once.

"A group of us are heading to the Cascade Hotel tonight for a drink after work. Wanna come?" Trevor, an Australian who worked at the brewery and lived with him, slapped Luca on the shoulder and waited for a reply. Trevor's jacket hung from one shoulder and his boots were on, ready to leave for work. Mrs Devitt would have a fit if she saw him wearing his boots in the house. Their housemistress was kind, but strict.

"Nah. I don't think so," he responded.

"Ah, c'mon, mate. You can't pine for this girl forever. You need to go out, have some fun. Enjoy Hobart. Have you been to the Cascade yet?"

Luca shrugged. He hadn't been to any hotel since his arrival in Tasmania.

"I've been to many cafes, and you Aussies can still not perfect a good coffee," he ribbed his friend.

"You're coming. I'll look for you after work." And Trevor's heavy steps towards the entrance made the house foundations shake.

His Italian workmate, Maximillian, entered the dining room and poured himself a coffee from the sideboard before coming to sit beside Luca. It seemed he could tolerate the brown muck.

Mrs Devitt entered and fussed around Luca, collecting his dirty plates and brushing the crumbs from the white tablecloth.

"Mrs Devitt, has there been any mail for me this morning?"

"Love, if there was, I'd be delivering it to you right now." She placed her worn and chafed hand on his shoulder as she stood behind his chair.

"What about yesterday, or maybe the day before? I left for work early on Wednesday, perhaps something arrived and I wasn't here to receive it?"

"It would be in the hall, like every other day and like all the other mail." She squeezed his shoulder.

Luca hated being the recipient of her pity. He folded the letters and placed them into his breast pocket. Close to his heart, where he could think about them and Esther all day.

By now, he should know not to talk about her. It only aroused jokes from the Aussie blokes about finding a new sheila, or feelings of nostalgia and heartwarming tales from the others. At mention of Esther, Max launched into a story about his first love that he'd left behind in Venice. Usually he clutched his heart and held his red wine aloft at the tragic tale. Whereas the Australians slapped him on the back and told him to move on, find someone else, *There's plenty of fish in the sea."* Mrs Devitt tolerated talking about it, and on occasion it brought a tear to her eye—most often after a few too many whiskeys—but her no-nonsense approach meant she always delivered him straight back to reality. Even if he didn't want to be there.

No, Luca needed to learn the Australian way of keeping his feelings to himself.

Mrs Devitt and Max talked about the fine weather they were experiencing for autumn but how unseasonably cool it was. Their voices faded as he thought of Esther. Her last letter had been weeks before Christmas. So many days had passed. What could have happened? The letters in his pocket were expressions of love and longing. His heart soared at her exquisite words. It was true, he'd admit, he felt special and loved. He thought finally he could make amends and move on with his life. Esther could help him do it.

Surely she wasn't cross about him not travelling to Bruny? He'd apologised many times for not visiting as promised. In the end, he'd had to choose between his new job—the position he needed to stay in Tasmania—or to visit Bruny Island. He'd explained, written the circumstances, and promised to make it up to her. Was she so angry that she refused to write? Luca couldn't believe it. This new job as a block builder secured his future. Their future. Ever since Esther had relayed her parents' views about his prospects, he'd worked hard each day, saved his money, didn't drink like his Aussie mates, and only worked towards the goal of being with her. This would satisfy her parents, yes?

He dropped his cup and it rattled in its saucer. None of it made sense.

Every week he wrote, even when her letters had stopped. Had he been a fool? Long-held and buried emotions rose up in waves and threatened to overwhelm him. His love for Esther had helped him overcome feelings of self-disgust. Deep-seated wounds were hard to heal. He knew he wasn't worthy. How could anyone love him after what he'd done? Had Esther had time to think about who he really was? Did she regret their time together? After all, who could love him?

He'd thought Esther was different. Freed from the restraints of his past, had he imagined it was something it wasn't? Perhaps he'd never find out, but her silence hurt like a blow to his chest.

"We'd best be getting along, hey, Luca. Time for work."

Luca nodded. Today he'd hear from her.

***

That evening, before he'd had a chance to remove his cement-caked shoes, Trevor yanked him out the door to the pub. Luca didn't resist and got swept along. Perhaps it was time to have some fun. It might cure his melancholy.

Now he stood at the bar of the Cascade Hotel and drank the local beer.

"How do you guys drink so much of this stuff?" he asked the group of men as he patted his stomach. "I am full after just, what you call it, one pint?"

The group laughed. "You'll get used to it. Keep practising." They jostled and downed their own drinks.

A brutish man with tattooed shirtsleeves walked past and joined in the laughter. He stood too close to Luca.

"What you laughing about, wog? Happy that you've taken jobs from the locals?" His words slurred and he swayed on his feet. "We don't need your sort here. We were doing fine before your lot chose to come out here and take our jobs, our women, and homes…." The man peered into Luca's face, his breath stinking of stale brew.

Trevor's mates gathered around. One fellow shoved the man hard to the chest so that he toppled and spilled his beer.

With his balance righted, he stood ready to fight. "C'mon, all of youse. I'm ready, you bunch of losers. Let's go." His fists balled in front of his chest.

Trevor placed himself in front of the man. "We're a group of friends out having a quiet drink after work. We don't want any trouble."

Luca didn't need others defending him. He stepped forward but Trevor held him back.

"Well, you should keep your dago friends at home then. They can drink their fancy wine and not our Cascade beers."

The other men closed in and pushed Luca to the rear of the pack. "Move along, mate. We've got better things to talk about."

With the gang up against him, the man retreated, but not before holding up his fist to Luca and giving him one last leer.

"See, my friend, I was right. This is why I don't drink at the pub. The Cascade, it's famous for fights, yes? At home, we eat and drink and be merry."

"It's not Friday night at the local if there isn't a bit of a biff, Luca. It's tradition," said Trevor. Everyone laughed.

"Don't you worry about guys like him. We aren't all like that. Tell us about your job. Trevor says you work over at that place on Macquarie Street building blocks." The man had introduced himself as Eddie, and he'd only drunk one beer to the other men's several. Eddie told Luca he had a wife and small baby at home.

"It's good job. Hard work." Luca flexed his bicep muscle, which bulged. "We make blocks out of cement, sand, and metal. We stir it together with paddle mixers and they set like a pie." He gestured in a stirring motion. "Then the blocks set and we pile them ready to sell. All good houses here in South Hobart are made with the blocks from Charlie Long. You know Lipscombes? Or the Macquarie Supermarket?"

Eddie nodded.

"Our bricks." Luca puffed out his chest. "I might build my own house one day. Plus—" He hugged Max closer. "Other Italians are employed by Mr Long, and I meet new friends."

"Cheers to that." The men clinked their glasses in a toast.

Trevor, who'd moved away to purchase another drink, snuck up behind Luca and startled him, making his still half-full beer spill. Luca didn't mind if he accidentally slopped the remainder of the drink. He really longed for a glass of red wine from *La Famiglia*. He could taste the tannin on his tongue. Instead, he sipped the beer. It was cold, but he held back his grimace. Like his morning coffee at Mrs Devitt's. Another taste to endure.

"Luca. What are you doing this weekend?"

Luca shrugged. He didn't do much in his free time but read the paper and relax around the boarding house. He tried out new coffee shops and wandered the streets of Hobart, sometimes venturing up as far as Battery Point.

"This weekend, there's a cricket match. The brewery is holding a charity event and you're participating."

"Cricket? It's an English game. I'm Italian."

"Well, you're about to learn how to play cricket. It's Aussie too, you know. If you want to live in this sports-mad country, you'd better get an introduction to the sports we love. It's for a good cause and you can join in and do something useful. You'll love it."

Luca wasn't so sure. But his choice was to sit around and nurse his broken heart or engage with life in his adopted hometown.

Chapter Fifteen

Esther sat at Charles's small round kitchen table and gulped a glass of water to calm her rumbling stomach.

Albert's retribution was swift. In less than seven days they were turfed out of their home, the Cape, and the island. It had been a whirlwind that had her head spinning. They all felt discombobulated. Except for Antonio. He balanced on her knee as she scanned the job advertisements in *The Mercury* newspaper. She circled any jobs in red that might suit. By the end of one column, she'd circled them all.

She was in Hobart. She'd dreamed of this for months. Hobart meant Luca. Once settled, she would find him. A tiny spark ignited in her belly.

Margaret sat on Charles's worn sofa and cried. She'd been bawling like a baby for days. It had been Esther who had wrapped their delicate items in tissue paper, packed their personal belongings, and arranged transportation from the ferry at Kettering to Hobart. Charles had met them on arrival. The rambunctious group of five. Since then, he'd fed and housed them.

But only Esther had acted.

Mary and Margaret had collapsed under the weight of judgment and the fall from grace. Esther wanted to break down like them, but what good would that do?

Esther knew Margaret to be self-absorbed, though she'd never realised how much. But then, it had always been about her. At the hiccupping sound of yet another sob, Esther could barely control her exasperation. And worse, Margaret had loudly protested how it was all Esther's fault.

"You could have avoided this, Esther, if you'd married Albert. He wanted you, God knows why," she'd snarled the words. "But you chose not to save us."

The apple doesn't fall far from the tree. Esther couldn't resist the old adage as she gazed at both her mother and sister. They wallowed in the misery life had delivered while she hadn't a spare moment to indulge in the luxury of crying. Or in the only thing she wanted to do: find Luca.

But it seemed she was to be the provider as well.

What of her mother? One would expect the matriarch of the family to take the lead. Her mother was worse than Margaret, except she didn't sob loud enough to make Esther scream. Most days she was sullen and downcast. Esther hoped her depression over the death of her husband would not last and, once their situation was sorted, her spirits might lift.

With nowhere to live, little food, and no money, the situation was desperate.

How long could they live like this? The burden felt too great. Esther could barely muster the energy to think of solutions.

The door to the flat opened, bringing forth fresh air from outdoors.

"Esther? This is my manager at the brewery, Mr Barrett. He's come to see you." Charles entered with another gentleman.

Esther stood and smoothed down the creases in her skirt. "Hello, and welcome, Mr Barrett. How can I help you?"

"Well, I'm hoping I can be of assistance to you, actually. Charles alerted me to your plight and of your father's passing and your tragic eviction from the lighthouse."

Esther flinched. Eviction was a harsh word and painted them in a poor light. No wonder her mother remained mute. No time to be proud. Esther kept a thin-lipped smile in place and listened.

"I am a member of the South Hobart Progress Association and my colleague requires some home help. A housekeeper, to be precise. And when I heard of your situation, I wondered whether you might be of assistance to each other."

Esther sank down into the chair. "A job? That would be wonderful. I do need work, sir. Um, I'm grateful, but I have my son and my family to consider. We cannot continue to burden Charles by living here. I need a position to cater for all of us."

Mr Barrett nodded. "Yes, of course. I understand." He pulled out the chair opposite and sat down. He removed his hat and placed it on the table. It matched his dark suit. Esther noticed his polished leather shoes.

"I can advise that Mr Robert Hogarth has servants' quarters with sufficient room for yourself, your mother, brother, and sister. Is that who will require accommodation?"

Esther nodded.

"Mr Hogarth is amenable to them staying in the accommodation with you. It's sizeable enough to suit you all, I'm told, and that would allow you to perform the duties of housekeeper. He pays rather well, he tells me, and it should be sufficient to keep your family in good health."

Tears sprang to Esther's eyes. A hush fell over the room and even Margaret stopped bawling.

"Can I start immediately?" she asked.

Mr Barrett laughed. "In anticipation of your agreement, I've arranged with Mr Hogarth that you are to attend at his home first thing in the morning. He will provide you with the instructions you require."

Esther sank lower into the chair. Immediate waves of relief rushed through her. Everything would be all right.

"I am so grateful, sir. I cannot repay your kindness. I will work hard for Mr Hogarth. You will not be sorry you recommended me."

"If you work as hard as Charles here, you'll do well. It's a sorry situation you find yourself in. Mr Hogarth does have high ideals and is a powerful man in our society. He's a lawyer with his own successful law firm, but his real ambition is politics. He might be our next mayor."

His words rushed over her like water. She had a job. Esther tried not to get her hopes up, but she couldn't dampen the rising thrill growing in her tummy. They would have a roof over their head and money to buy food. Her mother would have to care for Antonio while she worked, but she'd be close by and could spend time with him during the day. Once settled, Margaret could search for a job, too.

A housekeeper. Work she was familiar with. She could do it. Mr Barrett pulled her from her reverie as he stood.

"Here's a little something for you and the family." He placed a wicker basket filled with food on the table. Esther spied crackers, fruit, and chocolate. They'd eat well tonight.

She held her breath to prevent her tears from falling. She didn't wish to embarrass herself or Mr Barrett. But unable to stand on propriety, which was what her mother would have expected, she threw her arms around the man and clasped him tight.

"Thank you, Mr Barrett, so much."

He returned her hug and then reached for his hat and made for the door. "You're welcome, Esther. At the brewery, we look after our own. Welcome to Hobart." He gave a curt nod and left.

***

Esther paused to catch her breath after rushing from Charles's flat. She held up the address Mr Barrett had scribbled on a piece of paper, and saw that yes, she'd arrived.

Wow. A stone fence surrounded the property. She peered up at the two-storey Georgian sandstone residence. The home of Mr Robert Hogarth—hopefully her new employer. Esther crossed her fingers in superstition. The house was beautiful. Perhaps her life in Hobart could resemble those images in her magazine?

She took in the front garden. An enormous Norfolk Island pine tree provided a thriving and vibrant green lawn with shade and protection from the sun. The grass shimmered with dew. A paved path led her way to the front door. On each side lay a garden bed of pure white roses. Esther leaned down to smell their scent. Her mother would love them. Lady would have loved them, too, and the ever-present twinge at having had to leave her behind made itself even more prominent until she centred herself once more.

At the end of the path, she ascended five small steps to the front door. She'd never been for a job interview before. She wiped her moist palms down the front of her skirt before she glanced downwards and checked everything was in order. It hadn't been a difficult choice in what to wear. Her only decent dress of pale blue had to do.

Nothing to do but get on with it.

A metallic sign on the wall stated *Norfolk*. Sweet, presumably after the tree. Esther knocked. Seconds later, the door swung open.

"Brilliant. You're on time. Thank you. I've been expecting you. Come in."

A solidly built man with dark black hair and a matching motorcycle moustache ushered her inside. Esther couldn't help but stare at the handlebar.

They stood in a warm yet dim front room. It looked like a formal room to Esther, with its comfy sofa chairs, fireplace, and oriental rug. Plush velvet curtains hung from the sash windows.

"Thank you, Miss Anderson. I've been without a housekeeper for a number of weeks and it's been unbearable. I understand you're able to commence immediately?"

"Yes, Mr Hogarth, sir. I can start right now."

"Splendid." He sounded pleased, but his lips under the moustache didn't smile. He stood with one hand behind his back, avoiding eye contact with her. One hand reached up and twiddled the tip of his moustache.

"So, the job is mine, sir?"

"Oh, yes. Mr Barrett speaks highly of your family and I'm a busy man. I don't have time to advertise and find suitable help. You'll do fine."

At this, his gaze roamed over her, from the tips of her toes back up to her face. Esther grew warm under his stare.

"In fact, I'm due at my office now. Here are your keys. You can acquaint yourself with the house. Your quarters are out the back door and to the right. It has its own separate key; it's this one." Mr Hogarth held up an old bronze key. "Please make yourself at home."

"Thank you, Mr Hogarth, for this opportunity. I'm so grateful. You understand that I have my mother and family to accommodate with me?"

"Yes, yes, you're welcome. This arrangement suits us both. You can accommodate whomever you like in the quarters. I understand you've been through, um, some difficult times. I only require one housekeeper, mind, so there's only the one income, regardless of how many are in your family." He held her gaze.

"Yes, sir." Esther looked away first.

"Spend today getting acquainted with the house, then I expect you to get straight onto things. But I'm not unreasonable." He offered a tight smile. "My only expectation today is that you prepare dinner for this evening. There is a book in the kitchen that details what I like to eat. Choose a menu from there, please. Here is some money to purchase what you require for the evening meal."

Mr Hogarth extracted some notes out of a wad of cash and handed them to her.

"Thank you and good day."

Esther stood, dumbfounded. That was so easy. She'd survived her first job interview and landed the position. Their luck was looking up. *Thank you, Charles, Mr Barrett, and Mr Hogarth.* She danced a little step on her tiptoes.

Then she whooshed open those plush curtains and let the sunshine stream in.

***

Esther skipped back to the flat. The world on Elboden Street woke up to the new day. A kaleidoscope of colour exploded before her. Blues, pale yellows, and greens. The trams rattled past, the hum of the electricity lines overhead buzzing after them. Shopkeepers set up their stores for the day's trade, placing placards on the paths advertising pints of milk and fresh bread. Men dressed in their pressed suits chased after buses. Children in school uniforms were escorted by ladies with fine dresses and court shoes and pillar box handbags. Esther watched the locals of South Hobart, as if seeing them and their city for the first time. Now she was part of the thriving post-war city.

Esther stopped. Up ahead, a man with dark, too-long hair dressed in a pale brown collared shirt walked briskly. Under his left armpit was a curled-up newspaper. *It couldn't be, could it?* Esther attempted to match his pace. She was closing in when he paused at the curb and looked to his left to check for traffic before crossing. Esther pulled up short. No, of course not. It wasn't. Would she one day be walking along these streets and pass Luca? She hoped so. Now their future was more certain, maybe she could find him. Hope sprouted in her chest and blossomed like a budding flower.

At the flat there was a flurry of activity. Esther couldn't believe that Margaret was packing her belongings. Her cheeks were rosy-red and not their usual pale pallor. Mary nursed Antonio and fed him his breakfast but barked orders at Tommy. Charles had already departed for an early shift at the brewery.

"All right, Tommy?"

Tommy nodded. "Charles has arranged transport to take us to Mr Hogarth's house. It should be here soon."

"Fantastic. I did enjoy my walk, but with the five of us and our belongings, it would've been a struggle. It's a grand house, Tommy.

I haven't seen our quarters yet, but if they are half as nice as the residence, it will suit us fine." She gave Tommy a reassuring smile, hoping now that the extrovert and fun child might return. She ruffled his hair and he got on with folding his shirts.

***

Esther left her family to settle into their new accommodation. The quarters weren't large but had three rooms and a small nook that Tommy could call his own. Margaret had been indignant at the prospect of sharing with her brother, so Tommy had chosen the small nook at the front. Esther would have chosen that too, rather than share with Margaret.

The cottage abutted the main residence but was completely separate. Esther sighed with relief. She'd been worried that Antonio's crying might have bothered Mr Hogarth. No worry about that now. The house was neat, solid, and had a fireplace to keep them warm in the cold winter months. It was sparsely furnished but was more than she could ever have dreamed.

However, all of that had to wait. She was on tenterhooks about ensuring she was ready for dinner.

It was early afternoon and she wandered down the street to a local butcher and grocer. The recipe book had outlined many meals, but some of them she couldn't master. She'd have to enlist her mother's help for those; however, shepherd's pie she could manage. She required fresh beef mince and potatoes. Not too difficult for her first night. Esther rushed because Mr Hogarth hadn't told her what time to expect him, so she wanted to be ready.

***

Esther cupped her chin in her hand as she leaned on the dining table. The clock ticked. She glanced at it again. Nine p.m. Still no sign of Mr Hogarth. She'd fed and put Antonio to bed over two hours ago. Did she misunderstand the instructions? The pie was most likely ruined and dried out by now. What if it was and he hated it? Sacked her on the spot for her incompetence? Her family had already claimed ownership over the quarters: their stuff strewn everywhere, toys on the carpeted floor and their toothbrushes in the bathroom.

She heard the key in the lock. She stood, her hands gripping the chair in front.

"Miss Anderson. Hello. I'm later than expected. A busy day at the office and then I had forgotten an urgent meeting of the South Hobart Progress Association."

"I have your dinner ready, Mr Hogarth. A shepherd's pie. One of your favourites."

"Thank you. Unfortunately, it's too late now, I'm afraid. Feed it to the cats. Good night."

Esther placed her chin to her chest as he rushed past her. She held in her sobs until he'd left the kitchen and she could no longer hear his steps on the stairs. Then she collapsed into the chair and rested her head against the table.

Chapter Sixteen

"Where is your favourite toy, Antonio baby?" Esther searched the boxes in the corner of her bedroom. He'd slept dreadfully last night and she'd had to get up at least three times. In the end, they'd cuddled together and fallen asleep for the last remaining hours before the rosy first blush of dawn had penetrated the curtains.

Esther needed to find his bunny so they could sleep uninterrupted tonight.

One box overflowed with miscellaneous odds and ends, memories of a past life. She added sorting it to her to-do list. Of course, it was her job; neither Mother nor Margaret would assist.

"What's this?" Esther lifted out a bundle of envelopes tied with a ribbon. She held them in her hand and spied a red patch of cloth. "There it is," and Esther pulled out the toy bunny. Antonio reached for it. "Not yet, buster, that's for sleep time." His chubby fingers caught the end of the one skinny leg. "Okay, a quick cuddle and then not again until rest time." Esther turned over the bundle and sat down next to Antonio with her back against the bed. Her breath caught at the handwriting on the yellowed envelope.

Luca.

A dozen or more letters from Luca and, at the bottom, the letters she'd written, too.

Esther ripped open the first envelope. November 1952. That couldn't be right. That was months ago. His first line mentioned how long it had been since she'd written. Her body slumped. How had she not received these letters? But worse, how had he not received the letters she'd written?

She skipped the content of that letter and ripped open the next. September 1952. Her vision blurred as she read 23 December 1952.

Esther clutched them to her chest and gulped in deep breaths. None of it made sense. But it did, really. It made perfect sense.

She wiped the tears away with the back of her hand, tidied the bundle, and tied the ribbon back in place. They were precious and she wanted to keep them safe. She was desperate and wanted to devour every word Luca had written. They might provide clues about where he was. But not yet, soon. She tickled Antonio and he responded with a giggle and his little legs circled in the air. Bundling him up with his toy, she strode out to find her mother.

Mary sat in the garden. It was an idyllic scene on a clear Saturday morning. The birds chirped and a gentle breeze brought with it the faintest scent of the late autumn blossoming flowers. Her mother sat at the wrought-iron table drinking a cup of tea, a shawl across her knees. Mary had still not returned to her normal self, but a semblance of that person had made a reappearance since they'd moved into *Norfolk*.

"What are these?" Esther placed the envelopes on the table.

Her mother glanced up at the letters. "It was for your own good, Esther."

Esther would forgive her if she offered an apology for the deception. Then they might cry about the circumstances of the life they'd had at the lighthouse and where they'd ended up. But her mother's voice was steely and, most determinedly, not sorry. Her face was drawn with lips pulled into a tight line as if she was tired of talking about the subject.

"But why? I was pregnant. I was desperate to hear from him. I thought he'd given up on me." Esther's voice hitched and she took a deep breath.

"There was no future for the two of you. It was best to make a clean break, to move on with your life. It was too difficult to do that when you kept writing to each other and clinging to hope. We did you a favour."

A shooting pain spiralled through Esther's heart. Is this what family did to each other? Deliberately cause them pain? Lie to each other?

"Yes, as you kept telling me, it was time to grow up, wasn't it, Mother? No time for silly fantasies. Or lost love. To hope for a better future."

Her mother lifted the china cup from its saucer and took a sip of tea. Esther stood up taller. Her mother was right. She had grown up these last few months. Faster and in ways she wouldn't wish on anyone. A lump in her chest pressed down on her but a steely reserve rose like armour.

"I will never forgive you for this."

***

Esther blew a wisp of hair out of her face and wiped her hands on her apron. She'd been baking all morning and the kitchen was stifling. She measured the last cup of sugar, added a dash of food colouring, and stirred the mixture.

"There is a charity cricket match today. I promised that I would donate some baked goods," Mr Hogarth had said that morning. "I'm sorry for the late notice. I'd suggest trays of cupcakes. The children always love those."

He patted Esther on the arm before he trudged out the door in his cricket whites. Esther glanced at her arm afterwards, at the sensation that lingered there. His hand was heavy on her skin. She couldn't decide whether she liked the feeling or not.

She had one more hour to finish and deliver the cakes. She could do it, had no choice, actually. So soon into her new position, she wanted to make everything perfect. If Mr Hogarth required cupcakes, he'd get perfect cupcakes. The next batch was ready to bake. Now to tidy up the kitchen and herself and she'd be right to deliver them on time.

Mary refused to come, but she enlisted the help of Tommy and Margaret to deliver the cupcakes to the South Hobart District Cricket Club. She pushed Antonio in his pram. They heard the yelps of the players as they approached the green field. Numerous white marquees were set up along the edge of the playing ground for the spectators. Laughter drifted out of the tent.

"Hello there." A lady approached Esther. The tables were laid like Alice of Wonderland's tea party, with white china, pink cloth napkins, and dainty cakes and cucumber sandwiches.

"Hello," Esther responded. "My name is Esther Anderson and I'm delivering cupcakes on behalf of Mr Hogarth."

"Oh, you must be his new housekeeper. How delightful. I'm Mrs Manning. Let me take them." She gestured for the tray that Esther balanced and placed them on a table. Tommy and Margaret handed over their trays as well. "These look delicious."

"What's the charity we are supporting today?" Esther asked.

"Come, please, and have a cup of tea and I'll tell you all about it. Perhaps your friends would like a cake, too?"

"Oh, I'm sorry. This is my brother, Tommy, and my sister, Margaret."

"Lovely to meet you. Would you like one of these delicious fairy cakes? Mrs Scott, a local teacher, made these and the children have raved about them." She offered one to Tommy and Margaret, who eagerly accepted.

"I'll have a cup of tea before returning," Esther said to her brother and sister. "Why don't the two of you run off and have a look around. I'll meet you back home."

Tommy and Margaret separated and headed off in different directions. Esther sighed. Once they would have held hands and stuck together. Times had changed.

"Please come and sit and I'll introduce you to a couple of the ladies. We pretend to be watching the game but rather we are talking and enjoying the cool breeze."

Esther followed Mrs Manning, who wore a pale lemon tweed suit with a high stiff collar in what looked like a brocade pattern. Esther knew the style from her *Women's Weekly*. So… people really did wear those clothes. Mrs Manning matched it with sheer stockings and high-heeled shoes. Esther noticed her heels sank into the plush grass.

"Aubrey, Luella, Deborah, this is Robert's new housekeeper, Esther Anderson."

The ladies rose and air-kissed her cheeks. They were not as young as her, nor as old as her mother. Somewhere in between, Esther surmised. Unlike Mrs Manning, these ladies wore cooler cotton dresses. One was a gorgeous red floral pattern that Esther wouldn't be bold enough to wear. The other ladies were more demure, in pastel tight-waisted dresses that fell to their knees with simpler patterns of polka dots and checks.

"And who is this gorgeous bundle?" asked Aubrey, peeking into the pram.

"This is my son, Antonio." Esther held her breath.

"Oh, he's divine."

And so began a flutter of conversation about his age, his sleeping patterns, and life as a mother. The question that Esther dreaded didn't arise, but that was helped by her being a prime candidate, it seemed, for the charity they were all supporting.

"Isn't that simply perfect. You are exactly the sort of mother the Child Welfare Clinic support. The clinics have been around in some form since the early 1900s, but we've had one in South Hobart only since 1944. Set up with the support of the South Hobart Progress Association, of which Robert is the current chair. We are in desperate need of new premises as we are trying to cater to a much larger market now—so many babies being born. And with the help of the brewery, all money raised will purchase a new home for us."

Luella poured her a cup of tea.

"So, if you need any assistance or have any questions, you must come and pay us a visit. We have a nurse on staff who can assist with all of your baby health needs, or simply come for a cuppa and a chat."

"That sounds fabulous. I could have done with that help in the early days when Antonio wasn't sleeping. Luckily, he seems to have settled down since."

"Anytime. We'd love to see you there."

Deborah Bothwell leaned in with a devilish smile. "How is it living with Mr Hogarth?"

Esther's neck grew warm at the insinuation. Mrs Bothwell tittered.

Mrs Manning noticed her discomfort. "Are you new to Hobart, Esther?"

She nodded.

"Well then, what wicked Mrs Bothwell is referring to is that Robert Hogarth is the resident bachelor and the most sought after of gentlemen. He's unmarried, and all the single ladies are greatly attracted to him."

"Don't you agree he's ever so handsome?" piped in Deborah.

"I'm his housekeeper," Esther stammered.

"Of course, you are, but you're only human." Luella giggled.

"But, seriously, Esther, other than being handsome, he is an influential man. On top of being a well-respected lawyer in his own firm, he's the chair of the SHPA who make great advances in our local community. We wouldn't be who we are today—would we, ladies—without the association. They make things happen."

Esther nodded, eager to hear about her new community. From the corner of her eye she saw Tommy racing along the outside field in a pack of boys. She was happy to see him running again and of the prospect he might have made some friends. There was no sign of Margaret.

"It's an unfortunate business about his arm, though. It's never held him back. Even today, he's participating. He's not one to watch on idle."

Esther turned her gaze towards the field. Men were scattered into the far reaches of the space, others were hunched up closer to the wickets. "Where is Mr Hogarth playing?" she asked.

"He's the umpire."

Esther looked now, and from behind, she saw his trademark stance. His right arm held behind his back. Even at this distance she could see it was short. His hand started at his elbow. The fingers splayed outwards. How could she have not noticed this before? It made perfect sense—he never let that arm sit naturally by his side.

"I've noticed Mr Hogarth always holds it behind him. Is he, do you think, ashamed?"

"It's hard to say, Esther. He never talks about it, but apparently it's been like that since he was born. A birth defect, one of those strange things that happens sometimes. My experience is that he doesn't hide it. One must tire of talking about it, don't you think?"

The ladies agreed, nodding their heads.

"Such a gracious man. Living with his own deformity but doing so much for others."

Esther returned to watching the match. The bowler threw his ball to the batter and it struck the wickets in the middle. The men in the field screamed and jumped up and down and Mr Hogarth raised one good finger on his left hand. In amongst the commotion, Antonio grizzled. Esther soothed him but he wouldn't settle.

"Will you have another sandwich, Esther, or some sponge cake?" Deborah asked.

"It's been so lovely to meet you all. But Antonio is due to be fed and I must be off home to prepare dinner."

"Now listen, I mean what I said, please come and visit at the clinic. I'm there most days." Mrs Manning smiled so that it lit up her whole face.

"Thank you, Mrs Manning. I think I'll do that. Enjoy the rest of your afternoon, ladies, and I hope to see you again soon."

Chapter Seventeen

"I don't understand cricket. A player on the other team throws a hard ball and attempts to hit the sticks behind the batter. If they aren't struck and the batter hits the ball, he runs. But how does a team *win*?"

The men laughed. The brewery had its own large marquee on the edge of the field, backing onto a scenic creek that ran along the boundary.

Luca was teasing. He'd gotten the hang of this silly sport hours ago. He liked rattling his new friends; it was the Aussie way of things, he'd learned. It seemed to him that a game of cricket was more like a ruse to spend hours together with friends and enjoy a drink. The crew from the brewery sure knew how to put them away. But they'd accepted him, and he'd had an enjoyable afternoon. The two teams were a ramshackle bunch of players. Luca's team, brewery staff mainly, were larrikins out for a good time. The opposition, he learned many hours later, after he'd hit their bowler for six on two occasions, were the serious personalities of Hobart. Politicians, lawyers, and the like. If he'd known, Luca might have hit the ball a little softer. In the end though, the umpire had called him out when he'd clearly held his bat across the white line before the stumps were hit. That umpire hadn't cracked a smile all day. He was taking the game way too seriously. That wasn't the Australian way. Perhaps the boys should offer him a cold Cascade beer?

The sun sank low over the horizon, and Luca stretched out his limbs and yawned. The hot autumn sun sapped his energy although the men on the field still played with vigour. A yelp came from his right. A boy of about ten years old ran up the incline. "Help. My sister has fallen into the creek. I can't reach her."

The men sped down the bank. Two jumped in without hesitation and struggled against the current. It was a narrow creek, but the murky waters flowed fast.

Luca went rigid. His mind and body transported back to a different time and place. He gripped onto a tree trunk and stood on the bank. On a day not unlike this one, with people sitting around in the warm sun, eating and drinking, another child had fallen into a river. Sweat droplets formed on his brow and he struggled to breathe. He should be helping. It was five years ago, he should be over it by now. Panic seized him and glued his limbs to the spot. How could a man not help a defenceless child?

Luca placed his hands over his ears to block out the sound of the panic echoing in his ears. The mother of the child ran along the bank as the girl was pushed farther downstream. Luca could hear her despair, feel her fear.

He watched, his tongue thick in his throat. A hand grabbed the child and together they swam to shore. Outstretched arms grappled for her and pulled her little body to safety. A blanket was wrapped around her shoulders and her mother's embrace crushed her in its ferocity. Luca lowered his hands. He locked them together to ease the tremble. He looked away from the unfolding scene and desperately wanted memories of both incidents to fade. It was like he was there as his aunt cradled a lifeless body in her arms and wailed. He would hear that sound forever, like a record playing on repeat.

"Gee, that was close, hey, mate? Thank goodness William is a strong swimmer."

Luca nodded, swallowing to get moisture into his mouth. "Is he from the brewery?"

"Yes," Eddie answered.

"They make you boys tough at the brewery, huh?"

"Yep, sure do," Eddie responded with a slap to his back.

Luca wished he was tough like these boys from Cascade. Then maybe he could have saved his little cousin too and she wouldn't be dead and everything would still be okay.

***

Esther lit the copper and plugged in the electric boiler. She'd stripped the beds and had the sheets ready for washing. Her eighth Monday washing the sheets. Where had the time gone? She acted on rote these days, familiar with the routines and tasks required of her. But Mondays were the busiest of all. After the sheets had been rinsed and the whites given an extra soak with Recketts Blue came the hardest part—wringing out the excess water. Her mother mused that Esther's wrists were too delicate, whereas hers were well exercised having done years of her own washing, as she pointed out.

"It's not done like that anymore, Mother, there's new equipment these days."

She showed her mother the wringer that Mr Hogarth owned. Esther's demonstration prompted a loud harrumph from her mother, entirely unimpressed with the unnecessary and overly complicated piece of equipment that made life "too easy these days." Esther was grateful.

In between hanging out the sheets and hoping that the wind would pick up to dry them before ironing day on Tuesday, the coal was delivered. This was a delicate operation. Mr Fairweather had to unload his scuttle of coal to the bunker without any of the dark soot penetrating her clean sheets. The things she worried about these days. It was worth anything to protect those sheets and her poor wash-maid hands from having to repeat the wash cycle.

With the washing out and the coal basket full, Esther advised her mother that she was heading out to the grocer and butcher.

"Antonio is asleep, Mother. A snack is prepared for when he wakes."

One of her favourite parts of her day was buying the fresh produce for dinner. She could walk in the sunshine and explore Hobart. And secretly scout for Luca.

Each night she collapsed into bed and commiserated with herself that she hadn't found him. Between caring for Antonio and Mr Hogarth, her days were full. But where would she look, even if she had the time? Tomorrow, she would. But tomorrow had yet to arrive.

***

Arriving home on Friday afternoon, Mr Hogarth surprised her with a bunch of native flowers.

Esther was in the kitchen. He held out the flowers, smiling under his moustache. She hesitated, hand still held out, uncertain, but she accepted them. Lost for words, she placed her face in amongst the bunch and inhaled deeply. Their scent immediately transported her back to Bruny Island. Tears pooled in the corner of her eyes. Mr

Hogarth paused, took one step towards her, seemed to debate whether to offer comfort, but quickly stepped back, hands by his side.

"It's my pleasure to give you beautiful flowers. I'm grateful that you like them. It's been lovely having you about the house. It's never been so clean or my dinners so delicious. Thank you."

Esther offered a tight smile. He seemed to assume she was touched by the gift. And it was not that she *wasn't*... She was only more embarrassed than anything, really. Why was her boss giving her flowers?

Esther turned away to find a vase. She stood at the sink, looking out the window that faced the garden, and arranged the flowers. Esther inhaled again. She saw movement to the side close one of the trees in the garden and heard Mr Hogarth's raised voice. He stood close to the gardener, Mr Jeffrey Goodwin, leaning in and pointing his index finger, stabbing it into the old man's chest.

Had something dreadful happened? Why was Mr Hogarth so angry? Esther winced as Mr Goodwin took a step backwards before Mr Hogarth slapped him across the left cheek. The gardener dropped the shovel he'd been holding and it clattered to the path. Esther gasped and quickly looked away.

Mr Hogarth headed back inside and obtained a drink from the cold room. He saw Esther observing him. She remained still, holding the now-full vase. His features did an about-turn and a saccharine smile stretched across his mouth.

"Esther, please join me for a drink before dinner."

Esther's hands trembled as she placed the vase on the table. She wanted to say no, but how could she? He offered her a lemonade and took her outside to the front garden under the shade of the Norfolk pine.

He held out her chair before seating himself. He'd become more comfortable in her presence, and now, he sat with his disabled arm in view. She didn't dare ask about it.

"How is your family settling in, Esther? They are quiet, I never hear them. It's almost as if they don't live here."

Esther took that as a compliment and smiled. "They are settling in well, sir. My mother keeps to herself and cares for Antonio. My brother, Tommy, has settled into the local school. He's made a few friends and likes his teacher a lot."

"Who is his teacher?"

"Mr Smith."

"Oh yes, he's fabulous. We went to high school together. A lovely chap."

"Yes," Esther agreed. "And you'll remember, sir, that we've not attended school, so he's enjoying our mother not teaching him anymore."

"Not attend school, hey. That's rather odd."

"We lived on the Cape, sir. At the lighthouse. School was too far to travel so we learned at home."

"And your sister?"

"Margaret has settled in well, also. She's attending a secretarial course and hopes to acquire a position soon. When she isn't studying, she is out enjoying the sights of Hobart. She's a regular at the cinema."

"Good, good. That's very well then." He sipped his beer.

He didn't say anything else but finished his drink and rose.

"I have some papers to read before dinner. Rather than dine alone, I'd like you to eat with me in the evenings from now on. Thank you, Esther."

Esther sipped the icy cool lemonade to calm her rattling nerves. Eat dinner with him? She loved spending the evening with her family. Damn, this really didn't suit her at all. But he was the boss after all, and she needed the job. She guessed she'd have to do as she was told.

***

Fat tears rolled down Esther's cheeks. Such upheaval in their lives over the recent months, and now she cried at the drop of a hat, as Mary would say. Putting the paper down to avoid the letters bleeding, she swatted at her cheeks. Luca had never stopped writing; the pile of letters attested to that. How could she have doubted him?

Circumstance could be a nasty thing. Circumstance now saw her in Hobart, miles away from the Cape. But, ironically, closer to Luca. He wouldn't be able to find her, even if he wanted to. Was he still writing?

But most importantly, Luca still loved her. Well, he had at Christmas time. It was May of 1953, five months since those last letters. Had he met someone else? Desperation had crept into his words the longer he wrote with no response. He'd become confused; she couldn't blame him. She'd felt the same when his letters dwindled to a stop without any explanation.

But they hadn't.

Esther noticed he never mentioned Antonio, proof her mother had stopped her letters long before she'd broken the news.

Is it your parents? Are they forbidding you to write? To care for me? I wait every day for the mail delivery to hear from you, to read what you've been up to, of when we might plan to meet again. Why do you not write?

Her defences crumbled. Next to her, Antonio played. He was growing fast. He would soon be one year old. And he hadn't met his father. Hadn't woken up in a house with the aroma of coffee. Didn't know that when his father laughed, his eyes crinkled up so he couldn't see and he tilted his head back and opened his mouth wide. Or that he loved his homeland of Italy and his family that still lived there. If they'd been together, Antonio might be proficient at Italian and English. She'd taught him a few words that she could remember, but she couldn't recall the exact intonation.

She watched their baby, and her heart disintegrated. Antonio was a happy and mischievous child who explored everything, placed objects in his hands and chewed at them furiously, ate the dirt from the garden, and gurgled all day long while dribble sat on his chin. He delighted over animals and birdsong. So many things that Luca had missed out on.

Everything made her sad: Luca's hidden letters, her father's death, her family that had fallen apart overnight.

But here she sat in a comfortable, warm room with her son who had enough food to eat. Her employment with Mr Hogarth had saved her family. They were lucky and she was grateful to Mr Hogarth for this job. He was a kind man.

Over dinner, Robert—he insisted she call him by his first name—was softly spoken. They'd eaten together three times now. She'd be lying if she said she enjoyed it. She'd never dined alone with a man, and he was her boss. He was proficient at conversation and she'd learned about his high-pressure job as a lawyer and his community work. His chest puffed out as he spoke about the advances the association had made since its inauguration. They'd built bitumen with proper guttering, improved health care and services. The entire South Hobart community had benefitted.

Esther did her best to avoid staring as he tried to eat with one hand. One evening she'd cooked mutton and sliced it into what she thought were lean pieces. She hadn't realised he couldn't cut his meat into smaller portions. She did it for him, like she would for her infant son, and passed his plate back to him. He offered a curt nod.

Esther's eyes pooled with tears again. She cried for Robert Hogarth and his deformed arm and the man that he was. Her gaze drifted across the room to her mother. To her damaged mother who'd lost the will to live. But she cried for Luca most of all. Where was he right now?

Esther scooped up Antonio and dropped him into her mother's lap. "Mother, can you watch him for a little while? I'm going out for a walk."

Her mother nodded, her eyes glassy and her look faraway.

She had an urgent need to search for Luca. How had she not prioritised this before? He worked here, somewhere, building blocks. How hard could it be? She'd find that business and then she'd find Luca.

Chapter Eighteen

Her one pair of already tattered and threadbare ballet flats were ruined. Her calves ached as if she'd traipsed along the cliffs at the lighthouse for many miles.

Out of *Norfolk,* she'd headed for Macquarie Street, passed All Saints Church, towards the hub of South Hobart. If anyone wanted for something, rumour said it was to be found on Macquarie Street. Could it deliver her Luca?

Esther saw a grocer, baker, chemist, and a hotel. But she wasn't window shopping, so she barely glanced in their direction.

She spied a newsagent. A chubby baby stared back at her from the cover of the latest edition of the *Women's Weekly*. Esther placed her hand to her chest and took in every detail. Her copies were most likely still being delivered to the lighthouse. And until now, she hadn't thought of them.

She felt for loose change in her pocket. A couple of loose shillings fell into her palm, not enough for the magazine. Her shoulders slumped.

Her fingers itched towards her purse. There were pence in there and a note. Some of it was change for Mr Hogarth after she'd purchased the sausages for tonight's dinner. It would go back into the kitty for other expenses. The other pence were for a pair of new school socks for Tommy. He'd worn out his one pair and things were getting desperate.

Damn it. She wanted that magazine. To smell its freshly inked pages, feel the card cover and gaze at the images inside. Only those pages could transport her somewhere else. She released a deep sigh. Not today. She'd become well accustomed to going without, and this was one more thing she couldn't have. She dragged herself reluctantly away. There was always next week.

Esther kept walking but her feet dragged now. Where was Luca? Did he shop along this strip? Lost in her own sorrows, she didn't see Mrs Manning until she approached.

"Esther. How lovely to see you again."

Esther felt pressure on her arm and looked down to see a fine silk glove resting there.

"Are you all right? You appear quite lost in your thoughts."

Esther offered a smile, though it felt strained. "Mrs Manning. Hello. How are you? I'm well. There's simply so much to take in along this street."

Mrs Manning removed her hand and they resumed walking. "Are you searching for anything in particular?"

"Well, actually, yes. It might sound a bit strange, but are there any block-building businesses near here, by any chance?"

Mrs Manning laughed. "That's an odd question."

Esther could feel the heat crawling up her neck to her cheeks. In a moment they'd be on fire.

"Well, aren't you mysterious?" Mrs Manning gave her a sly smile.

Oh no, could Mrs Manning be a notorious gossip? Esther couldn't stand it if the woman spread some ridiculous rumour about her and it got back to Mr Hogarth. She thought quickly. "Um, no, I'm not purchasing any blocks. You see, an old friend from the Cape moved to Hobart and mentioned they were working in a block-building business. That's all. I was wondering if I could visit if they were nearby."

"I'm sorry. Unfortunately, I can't help you. I'm not familiar with any such businesses. But I can ask my husband, Joseph—he knows all there is to know about this area. Would you like that?"

Yes. Esther wanted to jump up and down with glee, but she stood firm on her feet. "That would be wonderful. I'd be so grateful."

"Agreed then. I shall ask him this evening. Should I let Robert know?"

Esther's mind went blank. Robert? "Oh no."

Mrs Manning's head shot up.

Esther softened her tone. "I wouldn't wish to bother him. I'm due to attend your clinic anyway with Antonio, so you can let me know then."

"That sounds lovely. I'll find out and I will see you shortly at the clinic." Mrs Manning kissed her on both cheeks and started to walk away. She paused mid-step and turned back. "Esther, would you mind taking this and perhaps giving it to someone who'd like to read it? I've finished with it." She handed over the most recent edition of the *Women's Weekly* Esther had been drooling over only minutes before.

Oh, happy days. She knew she liked this woman.

This was a good omen. She was one step closer to Luca, she could feel it. As she turned for home, the bright afternoon sun dazzled and she sparkled along with it.

A twirl of blue caught her eye as she approached the gate at Elboden Street. Esther didn't call the gorgeous Georgian house home. Her heart hadn't yet made any attachments there. Somehow, it still seemed as if they were passing through. And, of course, it wasn't her house to love.

Margaret danced down the street from the opposite direction. Rays of sun struck her blonde ringlets and they appeared translucent. A smile as broad as the Cheshire cat spread across her beautiful face and she moved faster upon spotting Esther.

The scowl that had been perched upon her sister's features these past few weeks had been pushed aside. It lifted Esther's spirits. Momentarily. What could make Margaret so happy?

"Esther." Margaret shrieked. "We are to have work experience towards the end of term. Some of the proprietors of the businesses attended at school today to meet us. We'll be allocated by our teacher, Miss Northcote, in a few weeks. But this one gentleman, he was so handsome and tall. He appeared like a giant towering above me. And he took a real shine to me. The other girls noticed. We shared a cup of tea and a scone. At the end he kissed me on both cheeks and said he'd see me soon." At this, she swirled on the spot, her full skirt swishing around her.

Esther controlled the roll of her eyes at Margaret. Of course, the girl who struggled to be pleasant to them, jostled on the spot. Over a boy.

If only it was because she'd secured a job as a secretary and there'd be another income to add to the household. *That* would cause Esther to jump on the spot.

She couldn't judge though, could she? She'd wasted an afternoon walking the streets of Hobart on the ridiculous whim of locating Luca.

Her sister deserved some happiness, didn't she? At least someone should be happy.

"Well. What do you think? Will he be in touch?" Margaret clutched her purse and looked at her with swooning eyes. Only a few short months ago, Esther herself had behaved like this about Luca. Innocent and hopeful. That felt like a lifetime ago.

She mustered up a slight smile. "I'm sure he will be. Where does he work?"

Margaret shrugged and turned into the gate. "I can't remember. He does drive a fancy motorcar, though. His car was the shiniest and newest, and I'm sure it would be the fastest and most expensive as well."

Okay, Esther had been patient, but now Margaret was being frivolous. They were lucky to have food on the table each day—and this girl was impressed by an automobile. Had she not learned anything since their father died?

Esther tried to bury the anger that surged through her. Her shoulders tightened. She paused under the Norfolk pine and breathed in its scent. She had grown to love that smell.

Just think of Antonio. He is what is important.

Margaret didn't notice Esther had stopped. She raced away into the house, no doubt to dream more about her mysterious fellow and their first date.

Esther imagined the time she'd be reunited with Luca. Her wish would come true. It *would*, because Mrs Manning would ask her husband where the block-building business was, and within a few short days, she might be dancing down that path too, like her sister. She sucked in a deep breath and smoothed down any wayward strands of hair, then walked the path towards the house.

As she turned the corner of the yard, she spied Robert reading in the sun. He sat in the wrought-iron chair her mother sometimes occupied and concentrated on the book he held. It was rare for him to be sitting quietly. He always rushed from home to work to another meeting and back.

Hugo the black cat, one of two attached to the cottage, wandered outside. He strode over to his owner and curled himself around

Robert's crossed legs. Esther imagined the cat's contented purr as he rubbed against him.

A frown creased across Robert's brow and his foot jerked. Esther watched in slow motion as he kicked the cat square in its belly. The force lifted the cat and tossed it through the air like unwanted garbage thrown into a bin.

Esther stifled her gasp with a hand over her mouth. Her urge was to go after the poor animal, but it had run into the bushes.

He resumed reading his book. *What about Hugo?* With her eyes trained on Robert, Esther took a small step backwards. A branch cracked and she crouched down low, the foliage covering her. Robert gazed up, his finger lingering on the page he was about to turn. He gave a cursory look around before resuming. Esther stood now and raced back around to the front entrance and the safe confines of the house.

***

"Thank you for dining with me, Esther. I appreciate your company. You have no need for frivolous conversation." They sat at the dining room table, eating the dinner she'd prepared.

Esther could hear the drop of toys out the back and longed to be with Antonio.

"These sausages are delicious. Did you get them from Mr. Pullman?"

Small talk. She hated these conversations. "Yes, he said they were his best. A new recipe apparently—pork with herbs and spices."

Robert listened, but Esther sensed his distraction. She longed to ask why anyone, particularly its owner, would kick a defenceless cat. But she kept silent. The scene replayed in her mind over and over, and it made the sausages roil in her stomach.

"I almost forgot. I bought you something." Robert rose from the table and moved over to collect a small package from the sideboard. He placed it before her and waited expectantly.

"You shouldn't buy me gifts." And Esther meant it. Why buy someone gifts if you cannot be kind to your own pet?

"Open it, please."

It was wrapped in bright pink paper with a bow. Pushing her plate aside, she carefully unwrapped it to reveal a white box. She glanced at Robert and he nodded for her to continue. She opened it. Perfume. She lifted it out and held it up.

The words were out before she could stop them. "Why did you buy me this?"

Robert sat up taller in his chair and shuffled his feet. She didn't often see him ruffled.

"Why? Don't you like it?"

"No. I love it. It's kind of you. I don't really have anywhere to wear it, though."

"Well, we'll have to fix that, certainly. Yes, we will. Thank you once again for dinner."

He rose and she was left alone with the perfume. She traced her fingers down the elegant, miniature bottle. Unable to resist, she twisted the lid and inhaled. Floral. It reminded her of wattle. A frisson of unease curled through her gut. Placing the bottle carefully back into its wrapping, Esther got on with the job of cleaning up.

Chapter Nineteen

Margaret was right. Perhaps she'd wished upon a shooting star and made her dreams come true. Arthur Stuart began to call. His courting began with an evening to the pictures and then a barbeque with friends until he was at the house frequently. Margaret rose out of her doldrums and life became beautiful again.

"Esther, what do you think of these tighter curls in my hair? Arthur is taking me to a dance and I need to dress up. The most important people in town will be there."

"Is Mr Hogarth attending?" Esther asked.

Margaret laughed and stopped preening herself for a moment. "No. Don't be silly. This is a dance for young people; he's old."

"But he's an important person in South Hobart."

Margaret groaned. "Don't you know anything, Esther? You aren't invited to a dance, you go along. Society dictates who attends. So, I'm going with Arthur and his friends and they are all important businesspeople. They've done well after the war."

"Prospered, you mean?"

Margaret didn't answer, and instead checked her makeup in the mirror. Esther glanced at her sister's hands—smooth, pale, and unblemished. She held up her own hands. Red and raw with peeling skin. Esther picked at the scaly flakes on her knuckles. What a treat it would be to slather some of Margaret's hand cream onto her dry skin. But it would be a waste. On her next laundry wash, all the softness would be gone.

To complement Margaret's already beautiful hands, tonight she wore a sparkly bracelet—a gift from Arthur, one of many she'd received. It really did seem as if her sister had found her Prince Charming.

A knock to the door and her sister harried. She smoothed her palms down her dress once more and tucked a strand of hair behind her ear, then immediately pulled it loose again. She puckered her rouged lips and smiled, happy with the image that shone back at her.

Arthur entered. He was a tall fellow and suave. A white-toothed smile dazzled in Esther's direction. Arthur was hard to dislike, even if he was way too clean and sharp. Add to that his charm, and he was too "shiny" for Esther.

"How is the antiques business, Arthur?" she asked him after the exchange of pleasantries.

"It's fantastic, thank you, Esther. You should come along to the shop and see if there is anything that takes your fancy."

She glanced at Margaret. Surely Arthur understood she was unlikely to purchase any of his expensive antiques.

During his visit last week, Arthur had talked about the history of the business of which he was enormously proud. His father had been a capable carpenter and he'd purchased premises where he acquired and repaired antiques. Quite modest in the early days, Arthur said. Given his father's natural skill and ability, he'd become sought after and customers came from all over Hobart. Eventually, he'd expanded into auctions and bought, repaired, and sold furniture, turning it into a successful business. Esther had never seen Arthur with dirty fingernails or dust on his jacket, or tired from a hard day's labour, so she figured he must be the boss. Too good for real work? A perfect match for her sister then.

Instead of responding to his invitation, she asked him to describe the newest piece he'd acquired. His eyes sparkled as he described it in great detail. She did admire his passion, though—despite his excessive polishness.

They left in a puff of perfume aroma, the perfume Margaret had borrowed from Esther. The soft purr of Arthur's car drifted away into the distance, and now the cottage was quiet. Antonio was long asleep and her mother was never good company. Tommy snored in his room.

Esther reached for Luca's letters and fingered the tattered corners once more. She didn't want to read them again; they only made her heart ache. It had been three days since she'd run into Mrs Manning on Macquarie Street. She couldn't wait any longer for news. She'd go to the clinic tomorrow.

***

"He feels hot to me, Esther," said Mrs Manning. "Has he had a fever?"

Esther shook her head and placed the back of her hand to Antonio's forehead. It spiked warm. "Yes, he is warm. He was fine yesterday. Happy and playing as usual. But he has been grizzly this morning."

She bounced Antonio on her knee, which usually made him crack up in fits of giggles. Instead he placed his entire fist into his mouth and chomped. "I didn't notice he had a temperature. I should have."

"Don't be silly. It might have just come on. He's sure munching on those fingers. Perhaps he has some teeth coming through? That causes the poor things to be unsettled, those nasty teeth piercing through their tender gums. It can't be pleasant." She went to remove his scarf and outer jumper. "Given the poor mite is warmish though, we should take off some of his layers."

Esther gave a tight smile and nodded. "Of course. It was so windy this morning I thought I was back on the Cape. But, yes, maybe it's his teeth. He was such a champ when his bottom two came through. One day it was all gummy smiles and the next, he had a tooth."

Mrs Manning had staff to manage these clinic appointments, but she attended to Esther herself.

"Are you a nurse?" Esther asked as she took Antonio's temperature. Before answering, Mrs Manning checked the thermometer and wrote the results into a leather-bound notebook.

"No, not at all. I've acquired basic skills volunteering here. We have medical staff who attend regularly. After moving into one of our bigger premises next year, we hope to implement a training program for young women to gain the skills to care for the children. If they wish, they may continue their studies to become qualified nurses or even doctors. Wouldn't that be fabulous?"

The woman beamed. What drove Mrs Manning to be so philanthropic? During her examination of Antonio, staff often approached her and asked questions, both medical and administrative. She was clearly the go-to person. Esther experienced an overwhelming feeling of envy. She hated being inflicted with that ridiculous emotion, and she'd been experiencing it often lately. For the briefest of moments, she imagined that she could become like

Mrs Manning and assist at the clinic. Of course, she already had a job that took up all her time. She couldn't afford to spend even one hour helping others, even if she wanted to.

Esther emitted a lengthy sigh.

Mrs Manning petted her on the arm. "Don't worry, Antonio is otherwise well and healthy. He's obviously eating well. He does have a temperature and is a little grizzly today, but I suspect it's his teeth. You'll have to keep an eye on him over the next couple of days. I'm confident tomorrow he'll wake and be his usual cheery self." She lifted Antonio and nuzzled his tummy. "But that depends, doesn't it, little man, if that pesky tooth arrives." She was wonderful with children.

"Thank you, Mrs Manning. My visit was timely, wasn't it?"

She handed Esther back her son. "Call me Eliza, please, Esther."

Esther placed him in the baby carriage and rocked it with her foot. "Thank you, Eliza. I'm grateful. You were going to ask your husband about the block-building business?"

"Oh yes, thank you for reminding me. I did ask Joseph. He said there is a place." She rattled off a street name that Esther tried to memorise. "It's run by Mr Long and he employs a number of Italians. It's doing quite well, he tells me."

Bingo. Esther wanted to scream with joy. "Thank you, Eliza." Her feet did a little tap dance under her long skirt.

Eliza regarded her. "I think there is more to this than you're telling me. Let's enjoy a cup of tea together and chat some more."

***

Esther didn't want to deceive Eliza; the woman treated her as a friend. So, Esther told her of the fellow who had been stranded in a terrible storm upon the Cape and had been injured and his friend had died. Esther laughed as she recalled him recovering and teaching her family how to make gnocchi. It felt good to speak fondly of Luca, but she deliberately held the real story back. It was not for Eliza to know that she'd fallen in love with him.

Eliza acted like it was a wonderful tale of adventure, and she voiced her hope that Esther could locate her friend.

The two women could have chatted much longer, but Eliza was called away to see a baby with worrying symptoms. Eliza kissed her on both cheeks and asked her to call back whenever she was free so they could sit for a cuppa. Esther knew she would.

Rugging them both back up into their warm jumpers, a sprig of hope sprouted in her chest. Finally, she could find Luca.

Plus, the visit to Eliza had provided a good dose of reality for her. Not everyone had shiny lives that bounced off the pages of the *Women's Weekly*. Esther had learned that despite a deep longing for a family of their own, Eliza and Joseph had never been blessed with children. There was no medical reason that she'd been unable to conceive. Eliza said she'd fallen into deep despair with the realisation that she'd never be a mother. Joseph had coped by throwing himself into his work and had become a successful parliamentarian. Eliza was proud of him and deeply in love, Esther could tell. When she spoke of him, her eyes twinkled and her voice softened. But what was she to do? A woman who didn't need to work and had no role at home? The answer was the Child Welfare Clinic and the gap in services her husband had identified. It wasn't only for their politicians to fix the needs of society. It was her job, she'd decided. As a result, she had devoted her time to the health care of others.

We all have our rods to bear, as her mother would say.

Esther walked home in a more determined mood. She had nothing to complain about. But she couldn't deny there was a cavern in her chest that she feared might not repair. To be whole again she needed to find Luca. Her fantasy of a different life had long disappeared, but it was still unbearable to think about what might have been, what could have been. Soon, if she didn't find him, she'd have to get on and accept her fate. That was what she dreaded.

Chapter Twenty

"Excuse me?" Esther moved inside the entrance to the large warehouse and shook her umbrella of excess water. She approached a man busy sorting packages. Around her, men scooted on forklifts, moving boxes and pallets. Rain pelted the tin roof.

"Yes, love?" He paused after stacking a box.

Esther wiped away a water droplet rolling down her temple. "I'm sorry to bother you. Is there a block business next door? I was given this address but there's only an empty decrepit building. Perhaps they've moved?"

"Block building—like bricks, you mean?"

Did she? "I'm not sure, blocks to build things, so maybe bricks, yes…"

The fellow scratched his forehead. "Gee, there hasn't been anything next door for ages. You need some bricks? I have a mate who can help ya."

"No, I need this specific business. You see, a friend works there. Is this the street? And number fifty-four?"

"Yep, that'd be right. But there's no business of any sort next door. You sure you got your details right?"

No, Esther wanted to scream. But they should be, her source was reliable. Did she have it wrong? She'd memorised it but perhaps she'd made a mistake?

"Well, thank you anyway. I'll keep looking."

"Righteo, love." He waved and kept on with his task.

Okay, a setback. If only the bloody rain would disappear, then she could walk around this industrial estate in the sunshine and search for Luca. But the sky was grey, her toes numb, and the hem of her wet dress stuck to her.

Thank goodness she hadn't brought Antonio. He'd be miserable. The next workplace appeared to be a painter; she spied a lady behind a desk inside a small office space.

The door whacked shut behind her after another unsuccessful attempt. She asked three more people and tried to rein in her despair.

This was her chance. Today she was supposed to see Luca. See his bright smile and stubble-lined chin. It was like the rain was dousing her lit fire, and hope disappeared with it. She spied a corner shop…her last chance perhaps.

An hour later, Esther threw her broken umbrella into a bin and dragged her feet home. She let the rain saturate her as she took one step at a time. First, she'd have a hot cup of tea and dry off. Then, she'd devise her next plan. The next plan to find Luca.

**

A month later and Margaret was married.

The impetuous girl didn't even finish her secretarial course. Esther attempted to reason with her, but Margaret wouldn't listen. She covered her ears and argued, "He's rich, Esther. R-I-C-H. I will not need to work. He'll take care of me."

Mary didn't help. She said nothing was more important than securing Margaret's future. "If you hadn't ruined your life, Esther, by having a baby out of wedlock, this could be you."

Esther stared, gobsmacked.

Where had the morals and values of her family gone? Or was it, perhaps, that Esther had changed?

After all she'd done for this family, *this* was what they thought of her? Her heart turned to stone each time they jabbed at her with their insults. Her mother and Margaret were a great team. Only Tommy seemed to maintain the values her father had held dear.

It didn't matter what they said. She swallowed back her retorts at their ungrateful behaviour.

But Esther was smart enough to know when she was beaten. She backed down and watched Margaret get swept away with wedding preparations. Arthur's wealthy family paid for everything and that gave them the right to make the decisions. Margaret was heavily guided by her mother-in-law-to-be and was being groomed into the position of a prominent society member so fast Esther couldn't keep up.

At the ceremony, one pew was allocated to them. Tommy was not a page boy, nor was Esther a bridesmaid. Out of nowhere,

Margaret had an array of new friends—Arthur's sisters and acquaintances. At least she had permitted Charles to give her away. Esther couldn't stem the flow of tears as she watched handsome Charles escort his younger sister down the aisle.

At the reception, they were allocated a table at the rear of the large hall hired for the occasion and hadn't spoken to Margaret all evening. Charles spent the majority of his time dancing with a beautiful blonde woman in a dazzling magenta frock. Esther was happy for him. Perhaps he could find the perfect girl, too? Hopefully not a friend of this crowd, though.

Esther felt invisible and lonely.

Back at the cottage, Margaret's presence wasn't missed. Especially when all her belongings remained. Determined to leave any semblance of her former life behind, she didn't take any of her things. "Arthur is buying me everything brand new."

Esther should have been ecstatic. Margaret's remnants fitted her perfectly. And as she hadn't lifted a finger in a day's work, they were in impeccable condition. Another few dresses to add to her collection. But somehow the prospect didn't fill her with any joy. Ironically, she'd left Esther the dregs of perfume.

Margaret didn't visit. Esther observed her sister as she drove past in their expensive motorcar. Esther saw her waving out the window at the crowd as if she were the Queen. The jewellery on her fingers and neckline dazzled in the sunlight. Esther touched her own bare arms and rubbed the toes of her worn shoes against each other, embarrassed. It seemed as if her sister was lost to a better world and had little recollection of the family she'd left behind or of their struggles that were no longer her own.

***

"Esther. What is this?"

In the kitchen, she sat scrubbing the silverware. Her hand was dipped into the bowl of scalding-hot water ready to polish the next piece, a sizable rectangle baking tray. She yanked her hand out.

A lump formed in her throat and she turned, drying her hands. Robert's face wore a scowl and his brows were knotted. She went to take the small slip of cream paper he held in his hand.

"It's an invitation to dinner," she observed. It was a neat square of cream card with gilded edging. The words that swam in the middle were curved and loopy.

More deep crevices appeared across his forehead.

"Are you acquainted with Joseph Manning?"

"No. I met his wife, Eliza, at the charity cricket event when I dropped off the cupcakes. She operates the Child Welfare Clinic and I have been there to visit. Why? Is something wrong?"

"Joseph Manning is the Premier. I am a loyal supporter and member of his government and party. They have invited us to dine with them. How do you explain that?"

Esther paused. "I don't know. Eliza didn't mention an invitation. I'm sorry, I wasn't aware. Of course, you should be invited, but not me. It's because we've become friends. Well, I mean, close—no, we've talked..." Esther's words petered out; she wasn't sure if she should be apologising and for what.

Robert pinched his fingers together under his chin. "Mm, I see." He kept Esther hanging as he digested the information.

"This is simply wonderful." He leaned forward and embraced Esther, his arm brushing across her shoulders. "Yes, this is fabulous news. Well done, Esther."

She let her shoulders drop.

"This is a coup. Perhaps other members of parliament will be in attendance?" Robert gazed at the invitation with wonder. "Can you please respond that we would be delighted to attend?" He lowered the card. "Do you have an appropriate dress to wear?"

"Um, I have some nice dresses. Do you think they will be suitable?"

"No. You must purchase a new one. It's a formal dinner. Buy a new suit for me, too. I will give you my tailor's details. Ask him to arrange it urgently. The dinner is next week."

Robert hurried over to the sideboard where he kept the housekeeping kitty.

"Take this and buy a dress. Blue, I think. Blue will suit your complexion perfectly and it's not by any means an offensive colour. Midnight blue, in fact, even better." Esther stood back, partly amused yet unsure of how to respond. Discomfort grew in her tummy as he pulled out a roll of notes.

"Oh no, Robert. I cannot accept so much money to buy a dress. You should attend the dinner without me. I'm your housekeeper." Esther took a few small steps backwards, away from his outstretched hand.

"You will attend this dinner with me. You are invited and presumably, we are invited because you have gotten to know Joseph's wife. You must go. *I* must go. This is important, Esther. And you must be attired appropriately. Buy a new dress."

She looked away but allowed the notes to be pushed into her palm.

"You will not have enough to order a new suit from Mr Lewis. However, he will place it on my account." He held up his hand with a motion. "Now, go, go."

Dismissed, she turned away, head down. She put the money into her skirt pocket and picked up the silver tray, placed it into the now lukewarm water, and scrubbed.

"Oh, and Esther? Well done, I'm so pleased."

One wouldn't know it, given his features hadn't altered out of their scowl. Nonetheless, Esther worried less that she'd made a mistake. Now the concern was to find the right outfit and present herself suitably for attending the Premier's home. Inexplicably, tears welled in her eyes and she fought to conceal them.

***

The dinner was all Robert could think about. He asked Esther each evening about the preparations.

His intensity heightened her anxiety, and with the pressure of choosing the perfect new dress, Esther become a naïve young woman again. Something she hadn't been since leaving Bruny Island. Added to that, for over six months, she'd become accustomed to thread-worn clothing, holes darned tight, and pale and muted colours after many washes. New clothes were a novelty she didn't have the privilege of enjoying. Now, she had the chance. It felt wrong.

She dithered about what to do. For once, she wasn't up with the latest fashions in the *Women's Weekly* and couldn't seek advice within its pages. She couldn't ask Eliza because it was her dinner.

With great reluctance, she asked Margaret. It was her forte, after all, and Margaret happily stepped in and ordered Esther around as though she was the older and more sophisticated sibling. Esther had to admit, she hated that selfish, egocentric Margaret had one up on her.

They met at a local boutique. By the looks of the fancy window dressing, it was expensive. Margaret's taste, no doubt.

Margaret arrived in her motorcar and parked immediately out front, pulling the car to an abrupt halt. She was overdressed for a simple shopping trip, wearing a long dress in mint green. The colour reminded Esther of a bull's-eye lolly that sat in a glass jar on the counter at a confectionary store. The lollies that dazzled little children. The dress was pinched terribly tight at her waist, making her appear impossibly thin, and on her head she wore a soft, floppy, broad-brimmed cream hat. It sat low over her face, covering her eyes. Esther tried to ignore the fact that she could have been one of the celebrities from her favourite magazine.

"Hello, darling," Margaret said, and air-kissed her on both cheeks.

Who is this woman? Esther stood back, taking in the transformation of her sister. She no longer wore hand-me-down clothes or smelled of talcum powder and cheap soap. Before her stood a confident woman who carried herself with an air of arrogance. It was the way her lips were set tight and she didn't look around as she walked, as if people walking past should be taking notice of her and not the other way around. Not a strand of hair was out of place when she whipped her hat off to enter the store. She wore court shoes and carried a leather handbag. Diamonds sparkled at her ears.

Esther smoothed back her own hair. After the walk from the house, her armpits were damp and she hoped she didn't smell.

Margaret gave her hat to the owner, who greeted them upon entry, and they immediately started talking about dresses.

A range of ridiculously overdone dresses were paraded in front of them. Esther tugged on her sister's arm.

"Margaret. I can't afford these. Mr Hogarth has given me a lot of money, but not that much. Plus, they're too fancy. I'm not attending a ball, simply a dinner."

"Yes, at the Premier's house."

"Yes, and at a budget."

"How much do you have then?"

Esther showed her and Margaret pulled a face, obviously not used to skimping. With a motion to the assistant, half of the collection was removed and a select few remained.

"Mr Hogarth insists it be blue and that he will be paying for the dress." That left only three. Margaret rejected one as too dowdy, and the two remaining were low cut. One had beading threaded throughout the bodice and the other had flounces in the skirt. Esther couldn't say she loved either of them. In the end, the beaded one sat better and the decision was made.

Outside the store, her sister strode away to her car. "I'd offer you a lift, Esther, but I'm rushing off to afternoon tea with Arthur's mother." With a wave, she got into the car.

"Thank you for your help," Esther sang out, but the door had already slammed shut and the engine purred to life.

***

That evening, Robert insisted she model the dress. Esther watched his eyes rest on her exposed chest in the low-cut bodice, then slower over her hips to her ankles. She pulled her gaze away when his eyes lifted back up. She dragged in a lungful of air when he moved close and bent down low to examine the needlework.

"Superb. Let's eat."

"Yes, Robert. I'll change and serve dinner." She walked away towards her quarters.

"No. Stay in the dress."

"What? No, I'll risk spoiling it before we attend at the Mannings. I'll change."

He blocked her path with his arm. "Stay in the dress." Only when she'd acquiesced did he lower his arm.

Esther wanted to cry for the woman she'd become. She used to be fiery and self-determined. She remembered the way she spoke to ghastly Albert Hawkins when he treated her the same way. The old Esther had never tolerated such behaviour. Now, despite her own wishes, she would serve up their evening meal of mutton stew with mashed potato and sit at the table in her new gown. A frock she would never have chosen if given the choice.

Instead, this pathetic and submissive Esther, desperate to keep her job and an income to support her mother, Tommy, and most of all, Antonio, did as she was told. The meat refused to dissolve in her mouth and took too long to chew. It was tender, having simmered in gravy for hours, but it tasted bland and rubbery.

Oh, Luca, where are you?

Chapter Twenty-One

"Everyone at home is on their summer holidays, hey?" Alessandro patted Luca on the back. "We shiver with these nasty winds off the Tasman and my family is lying in the sun and enjoying a most deserved break. It is the only time of the year that they holiday. An Italian tradition, no?"

Luca worked with Alessandro. His friend was older, married with children, and had lived in Australia longer than Luca. Alessandro had his immediate family with him, his wife and three daughters, the youngest of whom had been born here. Alessandro was an example of a man who had made the most of his opportunities. Luca thought he might run the brick-making company one day. If not, he would succeed in another entrepreneurial venture.

Like Luca, his parents remained in Italy. Alessandro spoke of his longing for his family. Luca listened and longed for his family, too. But he longed for a *happy* family, the one he remembered before his niece's death and before his departure on bad terms. He longed for the family that had lived prosperously before the war, of a family who accepted his ideas. A father who wanted him to be part of the family business. At least here, Luca couldn't disappoint his family anymore.

Alessandro stopped talking.

"Si, where is their holiday home?"

"Sorrento. It's lovely, but many tourists."

"Si." Luca nodded. "Do you think you will travel home in the future? Or will they visit here?"

Alessandro shook his head. "No. They will not come here. Too expensive and too far. Plus, I don't think they want to come to this strange dry place with odd animals." He chuckled. "Taking five people home is not possible for us right now. If I am not working, no money. Perhaps in the future."

"We may not ever see home again."

"That is true, my friend. But we are making new homes." Alessandro gestured towards his seventeen-year-old daughter. For months, he'd been trying to interest Luca in her. Many dinner invitations had been extended and accepted. He loved talking fast and fluent Italian and eating the dishes of his homeland.

He looked at Angeline.

Like most Italians, she was dark: black hair and dark features. Tall for her age. No doubting she was an *Italiano*. Angeline noticed his attention and lowered her head. Her younger sisters had run off to play. She didn't play like her siblings, but she was still a child. He couldn't compare eighteen-year-old Esther to this young girl. Esther had spirit, determination, and seemed so much more mature than this demure girl sitting across from him. That could go in his favour if he wished to have a subservient wife who cooked and cleaned and waited for his return from work each day. However, he didn't want that sort of life. Luca wanted Esther. But months had passed and he'd had no word. Despair was setting in.

Angeline was pretty. Perhaps he needed to move on? Should he give the girl a chance? She was Italian; they had much in common. They could start new lives together.

"Would you like some panna cotta?" she asked him in her singsong sweet voice.

It was the voice that did it, fragile and timid. Esther's voice had honey tones to it but perfect English pronunciation. Like the Queen she read about in her girlie magazine. And when she talked, he wanted to listen, wanted to hear the enthusiastic rhythm to her words and the purpose in everything she said.

Luca offered a warm smile, like a kind uncle would to an adored niece. "Your mother's panna cotta is the best in Hobart. I would love some."

Angeline served him a generous portion.

"You are so kind, Luca." Alessandro's wife approached from behind his chair. "I guess you will also have some amaretto biscotti with your coffee?"

"You are spoiling me, Elizabetha. Your coffee is the best, too." This elicited a grin and a light swat to his shoulder in thanks.

He turned to his friend. "My heart belongs to someone else, Alessandro. It isn't fair. Stop this. A good Aussie girl has captured me and I can't relinquish her. Not yet, anyway."

His friend lowered his head. "I understand. But this girl is not here. Eventually you will realise that you must leave her behind and hold those good memories close to your heart."

"You might be right. But until that time comes, I cannot. I don't want to."

***

"Esther." Robert held the tips of her fingers in his, caressing them with gentle strokes. Esther controlled a wild urge to jump back away from him. The touch wasn't repulsive exactly, but shocking and uncomfortable.

"Tonight was a wonderful success. My own private audience with the premier. He's an intelligent man. So across the issues of our state, innovative and forward-thinking. I got the impression he was interested in some of my ideas." Robert gazed at her like an excited child. "If I can gain a seat at the next election, I might have a place on his cabinet. Did you get that sense, Esther?"

She pulled her hand out of his grasp. Rarely did he speak with such tenderness. Waves of nerves flitted through her tummy. She needed to create some space between them. Esther stepped away but her back hit the timber buffet and she winced.

Robert didn't notice. He moved closer. Placing his left hand to her waist, he appeared to compose himself. Esther watched his chest rise and fall with his breaths. He hadn't even removed his dinner jacket. The suit had cost a fortune, was made of the finest cloth, and had delicate pinstripes through the fabric. He presented as a fine figure. For the briefest moment, she imagined him as the premier standing to make his acceptance speech.

Robert leaned in towards her. Esther experienced a flicker of fear uncurl in her tummy. Was he trying to kiss her? Surely not.

"Esther?"

"Mother?"

It was then Esther heard the wailing.

"Antonio is sick. He's been unsettled for a while, since you left, and now he's distressed. He has a temperature. I've been using wet flannels but he's not settling. You must come."

Esther bumped into Robert in her rush to leave the room.

Antonio wrestled around in his cot, rolling from one side to the other. Esther touched his chubby face. His head was so hot her hand burned.

"We need to take him to the hospital. Mother? How long has he been burning up?"

"He's been grizzling for more than an hour, but the temperature has been steadily building." Mary moved closer and felt his forehead. "He's much warmer now, even than ten minutes ago. I thought the wet flannels were working, but they don't seem to be."

"I'll drive you to the hospital."

"Oh, Robert, would you? Thank you."

"Yes, no need to worry, I'm sure it's a virus or some such thing. I'll fetch the keys."

Antonio's grizzles continued and Esther picked him up to comfort him. It was like cradling a hot water bottle. No matter how much she jiggled, he didn't quieten.

"Mother, can you grab his nappy bag for me?"

Her mother assisted silently. Her usually solemn face had deeper lines surrounding her mouth and dark puffy bags under her eyes.

Esther experienced a shot of guilt; her mother appeared to have aged without Esther even noticing. But then Antonio wailed once more and her attention was diverted. She flung the bag over her shoulder and rushed out to meet Robert.

***

Esther woke with a start. She gently moved her neck and winced as she eased out the crick. Her eyes shot open. She'd been leaning on Robert's shoulder. Awake now, she sat up straight.

Robert sat in the plastic hospital chair, eyes straight ahead.

"How long have I been asleep?" she asked.

Robert checked the time on his gold wristwatch. "About forty-five minutes. You needed it. The nurses haven't come back; I would have woken you if there was news."

"I'm sorry, um, about leaning on you. I hope it wasn't uncomfortable."

"Not uncomfortable in the least."

"I can't believe Antonio has measles. Where do you think he picked that up?"

The news had shocked Esther. But the doctor had reassured her that it was not unusual and hopefully it was a mild case. Most importantly, he was sleeping now and they had managed to lower his temperature. Poor mite. How awful he must have felt. He'd had other obvious symptoms too: runny nose, dry cough, and sore red eyes. He'd been like that for a few days and Esther had believed it to be a common cold.

"Yes, that's how the symptoms start," the doctor told her. "In a few days, perhaps even as early as tomorrow, he'll most likely come out in a nasty rash. It's one of the last symptoms to appear. But it was the spots on the inside of his cheek that gave it away."

Antonio would remain in hospital until they were confident he wasn't contagious anymore.

Esther rose and stretched out her stiff limbs. She leaned down close to his crib. Relief swept through her to find him sleeping soundly, his little chest rising and falling with each breath. She tucked the blanket in around him tighter and closed her eyes, inhaling his scent. A sob formed deep within her chest. She fought to control it; she didn't want to cry now. He was safe and all would be well.

From his seat, Robert spoke. "Esther." It sounded like a command for her to turn and listen. She did instinctively. "You need someone to look after you and Antonio. He is unwell. I can provide for him. I can give him the best medical treatment he requires. When he is older, I can send him to the best school in Hobart. If you or your mother or Tommy fell ill, I could look after all of you."

Esther noticed his able hand move up and down his thigh, then move to rake through his short hair.

"You are a capable housewife. The cottage has never been so clean, my clothes so neatly ironed, or such delicious meals prepared. You manage the budget well and are sound with your choices. You carry yourself with an air of dignity."

Discomfort unfurled in Esther's toes and shot up her body, bringing with it a sense of dread. She gripped her arms across her stomach. What was he going to say? She calmed herself with intakes of shallow breaths as a heavy pounding started in her chest.

"But tonight you showed me a whole other side to you. At the dinner with the Premier and his wife, I mean. I've been mistaken in not getting to know you better. You are a woman who can hold a conversation on intelligent matters and be courteous and kind to others. You would be the perfect wife."

Had Antonio made a noise? She longed to hear him wake up to distract her from this situation.

But the room was silent. Esther could hear her own breathing. She snuck a peek at Robert.

He stared in her direction, his gaze glassy-eyed and distant. "I will run for politics. That has always been my intention. But with you by my side we can achieve great things. The public will love you. The illegitimate child is an issue, but we can make up a story about a dead husband." His words rushed on, as if he was in a hurry to finish. "You need me, and I need you. You need me to take care of you and your family and secure your future. Otherwise, you have no one and nothing. If I marry someone else, I'll have no need for a housekeeper and you will have no job."

Esther sucked in air through her teeth.

"This is the ideal situation. You cannot afford health care, schooling, even somewhere to live. I can give you all of those things if you agree to marry me."

Esther's entire world rushed before her. An ache, like a crack of thunder overhead during a violent storm, careered through her chest.

What he'd said was true. Even with her income, they had so little. It was barely enough to feed and clothe them. It might have been sufficient for one person, but for four? Their clothes were threadbare and they had no furnishings other than those provided in their quarters. But with a sudden veracity, as if the world was suffocating her, Esther realised that if Antonio needed medication, she wouldn't have enough money. How could she provide these necessities?

Had she been kidding herself these past few months? With dawning solemnity, it appeared as if she had. What sort of life was she providing for her child? For Tommy, who deserved so much better? They couldn't rely on Margaret to help them. She'd all but disowned them, couldn't spare a few minutes to have a cup of tea with their mother, let alone a few coins to provide a warm jumper for winter.

How could Esther have been so stupid?

Was Robert the answer? Could he save them all?

Images of Luca clouded her mind: on the sofa rolling in pain, holding his splint aloft, walking on their secluded beach together, eating nougat on the plaid picnic rug, his touch, sitting in the front room as they read *The Lion, the Witch and the Wardrobe* and those dark eyes penetrating her innermost thoughts.

Luca, where are you?

But Luca wasn't here to help her when Antonio was sick. In fact, she had no idea where he was and no idea of how to find him. What would happen next time? What if Tommy fell ill? What if she lost her job because Robert got married? Where would they go? *God damn it, Luca. Where are you*, she wanted to scream.

The worries of the future swirled in amongst the images of him. But what simmered to the surface, consumed her, and sat like a hard clump of rock in her chest, was her desperate need to do whatever it took to care for Antonio. Their son.

Esther moved across to the window of the small hospital cubicle. She turned, clutched the back of the chair she'd vacated. She couldn't form the words, they seemed stuck to her tongue, to the roof of her mouth that was inexplicably dry.

She knew what she had to say—what she *needed* to say—but forming those words caused a great gulfing pain.

"So, we have an agreement, yes?" Robert spoke out loud to the room at large, not to her.

She paused. The words still didn't come. Then he turned sideways in his chair, his short and deformed arm on display. He looked at her.

She nodded.

Chapter Twenty-Two

Esther became Mrs Robert Hogarth before she could blink. The man was on a mission to make her his wife as swiftly as possible. Esther understood it had to do with the impending council election and his selection as candidate for the local area. Everything had to be perfect.

Esther undressed with care. After releasing her feet from the ivory wedding shoes, she rolled down her stockings, forming them into a tight snake-like shape as she slipped them off. The plush carpet under her soles felt luxurious as she massaged them against the pile. She knew she was delaying the inevitable.

Robert had dismissed her quickly as they'd entered his bedroom. He expected her to return out of her wedding gown but perhaps wearing not much else. Esther thanked her mother in this instance when she'd insisted upon the silk robe. She fingered the smooth fabric now. It would save her modesty.

For the moment, she laid her gown across a velvet chair; she could pack it away properly tomorrow. Her body felt light and free after the restrictions of the dress and its weight. Despite its simplicity, it had a full skirt of ivory, a lace bodice, and long, sheer sleeves.

The wedding itself was a carefully orchestrated affair with important people in attendance. Esther had the impression it was more a business meeting to Robert than a joining of souls. But she couldn't comment, could she? She didn't love Robert; she had married him because he assured her and her family a secure future. It really was a business transaction that was mutually satisfying to both parties. However, she'd have liked a bit more personality injected into the serious service and formal dinner that followed. The Premier attended and Robert beamed whenever he was near. Esther was delighted to have Eliza by her side.

It wasn't quite a society wedding, but Margaret had graced them with her presence. Esther watched her sister smiling and mixing with the right people. Margaret had even spoken to Robert, a man she'd never had a proper conversation with when they'd lived under the same roof. Esther shook her head in wonderment.

Antonio had not been allowed at the reception and she'd missed him. She longed to hold his chubby frame in her arms and inhale his sweet scent. Tomorrow.

"Esther?"

"Coming," she called.

She raced to remove the rest of her clothing and the pins in her hair. It tumbled free. Her hair was shorter these days and barely brushed her shoulders. So much easier to handle. She raked her fingers through the fine strands and smoothed it down on her scalp. She plumped up her cheeks by pinching them and blew out a breath. The silk gown sat nicely and she turned this way and that to check in the mirror. Now or never. At least she knew what to expect. But she brushed those thoughts away fast and focused on the man on the other side of the wall, because thinking of Luca only delivered heartache.

This was her new life and she would embrace it.

With a confidence she didn't feel, Esther opened the dressing-room door and entered Robert's bedroom.

It was dim and her eyes adjusted. Robert lay in the bed with the bedclothes covering his body and pulled up to his chin. His arms were bare.

"Take off your robe."

Esther paused, a million thoughts splintering and ricocheting around her head.

"Take off your robe and stand there, let me see you."

She was about to say no, but she caught the words before they sprang off her tongue. She wasn't on the Cape anymore, and she wasn't dealing with Albert Hawkins. In one way, she wished she was.

Reaching to the belt holding the robe in place, her hands moved in slow motion.

Esther didn't see him reach to the bedside table and turn on another lamp. Suddenly, right where she stood was bright with light. She gasped out loud. She didn't know how to feel. This was her husband. Her wedding night should be a happy event and the beginning of a wonderful life.

But those were the frivolous dreams of a young, innocent girl. Not the woman she'd become.

Standing naked before a man was not the hardest thing she'd had to do in her life. Burying her beloved father, never seeing Luca again: those topped the list. She could do this.

Esther removed her robe and it fell to the ground. She stood tall with her shoulders back. She would not be embarrassed.

Robert ogled her. Holding her breath, she waited for him to critique her—for that was how it felt. What would he do if he was dissatisfied? Divorce her, send her away? Never sleep with her?

Humiliation thrummed through her, but she refused to feel ashamed. Luca had loved her curves, her breasts, and long limbs. She was beautiful—to *someone*, anyway.

Luca.

"Come and lie down."

That was it?

Esther strode over to the bed with a conviction that she could endure anything. Hadn't she already? Her life had crumbled before her and she still existed, had survived. She copied his position and lay with her head on the pillow, eyes staring at the ornate ceiling.

Robert lifted the sheet off her and rolled it delicately towards the base of the bed. Usually, she'd help him as he struggled with one hand, but not today. He was setting the course. He'd been naked under there, but Esther didn't want to see. She spied a hairy white chest and the flop of his manhood as he moved towards her.

Robert rolled to his side and slid his hand up and down her body, pausing on her breasts, roughshod. Then he was on top of her, feeling around as if he was unsure of the geography and was charting his way. Within seconds, he spread her legs and was inside her. Thrusting. Esther fought the urge to squeeze her legs tight and fend him off. Instead, she screwed up her eyes up until stars shone inside her lids.

Was this what it was like between two people who didn't love each other?

In an instant, his movements became faster and his breathing quicker. With one final shove, she balled her hand around the bedsheet, and he groaned and slumped against her, his body heavy as it lay on top her. His skin was moist and his moustache tickled her collarbone. Even his breath was hot.

Esther felt the bed sink beside her, and he moved away and back onto his side, their skin no longer touching. The moistness gathered between her legs and trickled down her thighs. Then the throbbing started and she winced as she closed her legs.

"I have an early start in the morning. You can make yourself comfortable in the spare room. I'll call for you when we are to be together."

Have sex, you mean? she wanted to scream at him. Those tender words he'd spoken, the touches, was all of that a lie? Disgust welled up within her and she needed to escape. Without a word, she rose up, gathered her robe around her, and fled the room.

***

Six months later
February 1954

Cold and cordial was how Esther described her married life. Pleasant if she was being kind. That is, until Robert lost the council election. After that, their relationship turned nasty.

As soon as the wedding ring adorned her finger, Esther became involved in the campaign trail. She straggled behind Robert as he strode the path to hopeful victory. She became the trophy wife, rarely called upon to offer her opinion or invited to discuss issues of significance, but required to stand close by, smile and nod at the appropriate times, and agree with the policies as stated.

It began with little incidents. Robert gained an entourage to advise and guide him, some recruited from his law firm, others provided by the political party. As she became a keen observer, Esther noticed two sides to Robert. He presented as approachable, friendly, and interested to his constituents. However, the moment the person turned away and had finished their chat about the need to improve health care, provide better schooling, or tackle the rising cost of living, he'd denigrate them and what they'd said.

"Wasting my time, that one, and as dumb as an uncut loaf of bread." Robert would shake his head and jest as his staff grinned along with him.

His staff acted cautiously around him lest they be the next target. They'd learned after one advisor had incurred Robert's wrath. "Mark, do you seriously think I will have time to attend the opening of this new building in the centre of town and make it across to the quarry to talk about the redevelopment there, and then attend a dinner with the management of the Cascade Brewery? It's ridiculous, man. Fix it." Robert had yelled at him in front of the group. Mark, a young university student gaining his feet in the political arena, had scurried away with his head down.

Robert's temper frayed more frequently as voting day grew closer. He strained to hold it together and smile amiably at the cherubic babies being held by their mothers and the elderly who wished to shake his hand.

On a quiet reprieve at home one evening, Antonio was bawling during their dinner and the noise carried through the cottage.

"Can you not shut up that bastard child."

Esther gasped. Deliberately dropped her cutlery so that it clattered against her china plate and rose from the table. She did not return to dine with him. The next day he'd acted as if he hadn't called her son by that dreadful name.

On election night everything came to a head. As per tradition, everyone supporting Robert gathered at the local RSL to watch his landslide victory as the votes were counted. The Premier was due to make an appearance, too.

The evening did not commence well. Tommy rushed forward upon his arrival. Whilst her status might have improved by marrying Robert, little had trickled down to her family, and Esther still struggled to provide for them. Appearances mattered to Robert, so Tommy was now enrolled in a more prestigious public school, but this generosity didn't seem to extend to a wardrobe of clothes or other necessities. Tommy had two good outfits and often wore one as the other was cleaned. With Esther occupied with Robert's campaign, she hadn't been as attentive at home. So, tonight, Tommy wore tattered pants with a loose hem down and a ratty T-shirt. Unfortunately, his hair was unbrushed, too.

"Best of luck tonight, Mr Hogarth. I'm confident it will go well," Tommy had declared and held out his hand to shake.

Robert pushed him aside. "Get out of the way, child," he said, as if he didn't even recognise him. Tommy's face fell.

Esther jumped in to rescue the situation.

"Tommy, where shall you and Mother sit? Over here, right in front of the television will be perfect." Esther placed her arm over his shoulder and guided him away. As she passed a waiter, she ordered a chocolate milkshake. That put a smile on his face.

The evening quickly worsened. It became apparent early that Robert was behind in the votes. He drank expensive Scotch. As the hours dragged on, people drifted away and he sat alone. He shouted belligerent remarks as the member of the opposition party was announced as the new local council member. The Premier did not turn up. Robert threw his crystal tumbler and it smashed against the wall, narrowly missing a young woman whom Esther had seen helping with the delivery of pamphlets.

Security guards had to guide Robert out of the club in the wee hours. Esther's head ached with fatigue; she dreamed of bed.

The moment the world was shut out behind him, Robert raged. He approached the buffet in the kitchen and swiped at it, causing everything to smash to the ground.

Esther moved herself into the shadows and stood against the wall.

He moved on to the dishes in the sink.

"What are these doing here? I have a wife, don't I, to tidy up? To do what I ask of her, to keep a clean house. Esther?" he bellowed loud enough to wake the entire house.

She stepped silently beside him. He slapped her across the cheek. If not for the wall, the force would have bowled her backwards. On instinct, her hand flew to stem the sting and cradle her face. A welt formed where his ring scraped along her skin.

"You made me lose this election. It had to be you. Explain to me how else this happened? The public must not have liked you. Low stock and all, I should have realised. It's probably that bastard dark child of yours. Or your pathetic family. It's all your fault."

"Robert, don't speak like that. You know that isn't true." She kept her voice even, not wanting to agitate him more.

"So, you're saying it was *my* fault, are you? I had the best policies, did the most work, talked to more people than my opposition. Had the notoriously well-liked and supported Premier on my side, and still I didn't win."

"You can try again, Robert."

He grasped her wrist tight and dragged her along with him as he moved towards the stairs. Given his crazy campaign schedule, he'd rarely called for her since their wedding. Much to her enormous relief. Now, her heart hammered out of her chest. She tried to pull back. In response, he yanked harder.

Esther thought of grabbing one of the tall candelabras that stood on the balustrade at the base of the stairs. Could she hit him over the head with it and stop this madness? Too late, they'd passed and were taking the steps. With her long dress, Esther misjudged the rise and tumbled twice. Nothing caused him to stop.

In his room, he threw her towards the bed and ordered her to get undressed. He started to undo his belt and nudged her in the shin when she didn't move.

Oh God, please let this be over quickly.

Impatient, he pushed up her dress. He ripped her underwear and manhandled her over onto her stomach. When he entered her from behind, she screamed.

Chapter Twenty-Three

After that, everything changed. Robert had always been mean, but was an expert at hiding it. She remembered him kicking the cat in the garden and the heated conversation with the gardener, his control from day one and his brusque manner.

Now she was being punished for his failure. Her house kitty was reduced. Occasionally, he refused to eat with her, and other times forced her to sit through a silent meal. He criticised her work: the house was never clean enough, there was too much dust on the ledges, the sheets were not ironed, his breakfast late, and the cats unruly. He targeted not only her but her family. Tommy cowered in Robert's presence. Esther did everything possible to keep them out of his path.

One fine warm afternoon, Esther took a breather. The back garden beckoned to her and she sat and watched Antonio crawl around on the grass. He marvelled at the ants and bugs he discovered on the ground. She'd poured a hot cup of tea and was savouring a sweet arrowroot biscuit.

Malcolm Crosby from Robert's office bounded around the side path and paused in front of her, panting, his hands resting on his knees.

"Afternoon, Mrs Hogarth." The title still made Esther bristle. "An urgent message has arrived for Mr Hogarth. He's not at the office and I have another important errand to run for him. Can you pass it on?"

Malcolm's tongue darted across his dry lips. The seventeen-year-old was frightened. Esther understood, but as paid staff at Robert's law firm, couldn't they sort it out? Another task to add to her list.

Once, she would have made enquiries about the envelope, its urgency, asked after the lad's welfare, that of his family and so forth. Now, Esther simply nodded and took the letter. No point griping about it.

"Thanks, Mrs Hogarth."

Esther paused, her guard crumbling. She placed her hand on the young man's arm. "It's okay, Malcolm, I'll ensure Mr Hogarth gets this. Where is he?"

"At the brewery, ma'am."

The boy rushed away. Esther took a gulp of her now tepid tea and collected the pile of letters from the table. Perhaps it was for the best. She'd intended to wallow in Luca's letters again, but it only caused her terrible melancholy. Yes, she decided. All for the best. No time to dwell on the past today.

She collected Antonio and took him inside to her mother. The brewery wasn't too far from Elboden Street, but a long walk down Cascade Road. She'd take the bicycle. As she imagined the wind blowing in her hair and the breeze against her cheeks, a spring entered her step. She'd grasp any chance to get out of the house and away from her usual routine.

The Cascade Brewery sat tall and regal at the base of Mount Wellington. It was breathtaking and easy to spot as she approached. Its caramel-coloured bricks contrasted with the deep green of the hills surrounding it. The unmistakable aroma of brewed hops filled the air. Esther screwed up her face as the astringent smell tickled her nose.

Men bustled, rushing towards carts whilst rolling barrels and talking loudly. She had no idea where to find Robert.

A workman hurried past.

"Excuse me. I'm looking for Robert Hogarth. Apparently, he's here today. I have an urgent message."

"He's in a meeting about the Queen's visit, lass. You'll find him on the second level in a meeting room."

She thanked the man, who carried a bag of something moulded to his shoulders, and entered the building.

The Queen. Esther had forgotten that the Queen of England was visiting Hobart in a few short days. If she'd been up to date with her *Women's Weekly,* she would have known all the minute details of the tour, but she wasn't—hadn't read one since the discarded copy from Eliza. But the city had been abuzz for weeks about the impending visit. Robert had mentioned it many times. If he'd been elected, he'd have met her personally, another reason for his ill-temper.

A man in a suit passed her inside the entrance. "I'm so sorry to trouble you, but this is an urgent message for Mr Hogarth."

"No worries. I know where he is, I can take it." The young man smiled and took off. A twist of nerves formed in Esther's stomach. She should deliver it herself to ensure it made Robert's hands. Imagine if he never received it. Esther panicked. She watched the man ascend the stairs to her right and head towards a room. She climbed a few short steps and saw him hand over the envelope. Robert glanced up. Instinctively, she raised a hand to wave, but he ignored her and turned away. Oh well, job done, he had received his message.

Outside, doors opened and slammed and men in suits exited vehicles. She had to move out of the way of the line of traffic. With her head bowed, she walked towards her bicycle.

Conversations flurried around her. She heard an accent that sounded like Luca's. She paused her step. Barely breathing, she lifted her head. A dark-haired man exited a car, holding the door for someone. Hearing those rolling Rs made Esther's heart beat faster. This fellow was rounder and heavier than Luca. He laughed at something and his belly shook. The man moved away from the car and another figure emerged from the passenger side. His back was to Esther but he was tall and lean, with dark wavy hair touching his shoulders. Esther mis-stepped and tripped over her own feet on the uneven ground.

In an awkward fumbling gesture, she balanced herself and prevented a fall. Righted, she looked back up…and gasped.

Luca.

It was him. Luca watched the fellow move away from the car as the three men continued to shout across the distance.

"Esther." A voice called her name. Luca?

Luca turned his head.

Their eyes connected. His eyes widened, and his mouth opened.

"Esther." Her name again and it wasn't Luca calling. She didn't care who it was, she kept her eyes on him.

Robert arrived to stand beside her. She blanched and refused to look at him; she could not take her eyes off Luca. Her whole body tingled and her heart felt like it was going to burst out of her chest.

She'd found him.

Robert blocked her view. He must have seen her expression for he turned and gazed across the way. His forehead creased. He looked from Esther to Luca and back again. She moved her head to see around Robert and their eyes connected again. She locked on those dark black pools. Oh, how she'd missed them. Her face must be filled with awe. And she didn't care.

Robert squared in front of her. His arm went around her middle, pulling her close. He kissed her full on the mouth. "Thank you, darling, for bringing me this urgent message." He spoke loud enough for Luca to hear. He swung her forcibly around so that her back was to Luca. Robert's lips found hers again.

"You, dago," Robert shouted, still holding her tight and talking over the top of her head. "Mr Long is required for at least two hours in this Progress Association meeting. He doesn't need you hanging around like a bad foreign smell. Come back later."

Esther wriggled under Robert's grip. He sensed her urgency and pulled tighter, only to loosen his grip moments later. Esther turned swiftly, her hair swinging into her face. *No. Don't go.* Her fingers stretched out, desperate to reach him, to prevent him leaving. But it was too late. Luca retreated and hopped into the passenger seat of the car. The door slammed and he was gone. Through tinted windows all she could see was the outline of a head until the car reared away down the street. Esther started to trail after it, but Robert held tight to her wrist.

"Let go of me," she spat at him.

He held on to her until the car disappeared. Satisfied, he pushed her away and she fell to the ground, landing on her knees. Esther stayed there, head lowered, staring at the pebbled walk until Robert strode away.

***

Luca asked Roberto, the driver, to stop the car as soon as they turned the next corner. He had the door open before the vehicle rolled to a stop at the kerb. Luca tumbled out, mumbling his thanks. The hot February wind picked up and buffeted him as he walked along Cascade Road. He stuck his hands in the pockets of his jeans. He didn't know where he was headed, but he needed to walk. In the distance, the mountain range loomed large and ominous above him. He breathed out long, heavy sighs.

Esther.

But instead of being ecstatic, bile burned in his belly. This should be one of the happiest days of his life.

He allowed himself a brief, tight smile. She was still beautiful. Her straight blonde bob sat shorter than usual and she was dressed differently. Demure. All brown and grey and sensible shoes. A long-forgotten memory of a shimmering blue dress came to mind. He couldn't deny that she'd aged. She'd stood rigid, her neck solid, her stance tall but her face was set hard and her movements jerky. Like a robot performing its duty. Where had her softness gone?

Luca remembered that luminescent smile that made him light up. The crinkles that formed at the corners of her eyes when she smiled so broadly, her entire face joined in. Her laughing, lilting voice that carried him along like a song. Eyes that had once sparkled and were now dim.

What had happened to her?

Did it have something to do with that horrid man? Luca shuddered. One glimpse and Luca knew exactly his sort. Powerful. It was all about how mean he could be to others to make himself feel better. Luca noticed his deformed arm. Guaranteed that man had spent his entire life trying to make up for his physical shortcomings. Had he seen him before?

Esther was in Hobart and hadn't told him. Or found him.

Why?

Did she still love him?

Why would she? Her lack of contact answered his questions.

Luca balled his fists in his pockets, thinking of that man with Esther. Was he a good person? Where was his love or affection? Instead, he'd gripped her arm too tight. Maybe she needed help? No, they were *together*. Married? He couldn't believe it. Why would someone who had so many dreams, was so vivacious and wanted to conquer the world outside of her tiny island life, marry a man like *that*? Luca had so many questions, but honestly, he wasn't sure he wanted the answers.

When they'd seen each other, Luca had detected a pause in her step. Her shoulders slumped too, he was sure of it. Then she'd taken the tiniest of steps towards him before her path was blocked. Yes, he remembered now.

Head down, he walked with a steady pace through the afternoon crowds, accidentally bumping a few people. He uttered apologies and kept going. When his feet ached, he stopped at a cosy corner shop near Battery Point. *Boy.* He'd walked a long way. He needed sustenance for his return walk to the boarding house. Roberto would return to collect their boss, Mr Long. Thank goodness, because right now, Luca didn't want to be anywhere near the man with the ridiculous motorcycle moustache. Any self-respecting Italian would have better facial hair than that.

Luca sat at a round table in the corner and drank his espresso. He braced himself for the usual bitterness burning his throat, but it actually tasted okay.

"Excuse me, sir. I must tell you, this coffee is good. Almost the best I've had here in Hobart."

"Thank you, kind sir." The jolly man slapped Luca on the back.

Behind the counter, a young woman wiped down the benches. Her bright red hair, made up in tight ringlets, was matched by freckles that scattered across her nose. Is this what they called a white English rose? Striking. Why couldn't he fall for an Australian girl like her? Live a solid, hardworking life—perhaps in this café? He could make Italian food and good coffee and talk with the customers. It's not like he was going to achieve his dream of a vineyard anytime soon. Maybe he should serve coffee instead? At least one of his two passions could be fulfilled.

Luca hung his head. It didn't matter if he wished it, this was not the life for him. He longed for Esther. Seeing her made everything worse. Had all he'd believed been wrong? His chest tightened, like someone had pushed down upon it, waiting to crush him. What was he going to do?

"Thank you for the coffee." Luca offered the man a thumbs-up and left the I. No point dwelling on it. Luca knew what he would do. Just like last time. He would go to sleep tonight, a scattered sleep filled with troubled dreams, and then he would wake in the morning. Mrs Devitt would serve him breakfast with unpalatable coffee and he'd dress for work and spend the day building blocks. After a day of hard work, he would return home and repeat the pattern. Whilst grateful for this routine, it provided little comfort.

The world outside had dimmed. Clouds hung precariously low, trapping in the cooler night air. The streets began to empty as people headed home for the evening. A brisk walk would get his blood circulating, so he increased his pace.

At a screech of tyres, Luca looked up. Ahead, a car swerved dangerously on the road before there was a loud thump and he watched something fling through the air. Because it was getting dark, he couldn't see what it was. The car squealed to a halt farther on. Luca ran, but was still some distance away.

Someone alighted from the car right as he reached the tyre marks on the road. The man wore a light, camel-coloured jacket with black pants. The right arm swung loose and free. Luca paused his run mid-step and pulled up sharp. No, it couldn't be.

The timing was about right. Maybe two hours had elapsed.

Hunched down into his coat and skulking rather nervously, the man searched around him. A cat sprung out to his left and he jumped, colliding with a dust bin that rattled.

Luca came to a complete stop. Waiting. He had a direct view of that shiny, thin moustache and all desire to assist deserted him.

Esther's husband approached the mound on the footpath. A tentative kick with the tip of his shoe revealed nothing and the man leaned down close. He recoiled up and back as if attached to a spring and then took two steps backward. After a pause, he placed one foot in front of the other and fled. Without looking back, he raced to his vehicle. The engine roared and the car sped away.

Luca made careful steps forward, avoiding some wet patches on the road. The lump rolled over as he advanced closer. It was a man—a fellow with a long, untamed grey beard. Lying prone on his back, he tried to sit up but couldn't.

"It's okay. I will help you. You've been hit by a car." Luca spoke to the man who gazed at him, unseeing. "I call for help. Be back in a minute."

Luca smelled the stench of beer. It mixed with a pungent aroma of body odour and made Luca wince. He was most likely a drunk or homeless, but regardless, how could anyone not stop and help someone they'd injured? Luca raced to the nearest house to raise the alarm.

Chapter Twenty-Four

Two hours. Esther would return to the brewery in time for Luca to collect his friend.

"Look where you're going," a driver yelled as they nearly collided. She paused the pedals, gulped in large breaths and forced herself to calm down.

Back at the house, she'd performed her tasks methodically, only thinking of Luca. Distracted, she lost her grip on the mixing bowl and it smashed and scattered across the kitchen floor. Damn it, she didn't care. She'd seen Luca. If she hadn't spied him with her own eyes, she wouldn't believe it.

She prepared the leftover casserole and cut fresh bread. Laid everything out, ready. She did a quick sweep of the kitchen and tidied the dirty dishes, took out the rubbish, refilled the fruit bowl, and ensured everything was in its place. Perfect.

Esther had no idea if Robert would return straight after the meeting or later. Usually he worked into the evening. There should be plenty of time for her to ride back to the brewery—in the dark—and return, and Robert wouldn't be any the wiser.

After checking on Antonio and snatching an extra-long, deep cuddle, she gathered her coat and shoes and rushed out to the shed to retrieve the bicycle. The path was dim in the dying hours of the evening, but she knew her way.

The back door of the cottage clicked shut and her heart started its own dance. Finally, she was going to see Luca. She'd be able to explain everything. Arrange to meet him again. He'd understand, she knew it. Whilst she wanted to sing out loud with joy, she'd become adept at controlling her emotions. Recent months had delivered her too much disappointment. Now she prepared for anything. There'd be plenty of time to celebrate when she found Luca.

Head down as she walked, Esther thought only of Luca. Would they embrace? What would he say? Two paces and she was blocked on the path.

"Oh," she exclaimed as her foot twisted at the unexpected force.

"Esther? Where do you think you're going?"

The light in the world went out. Demonstrating the power he held over her, it was like Robert flicked a switch and her pluck dissipated.

She had to think quick. It was dark, the shops were shut. Where would she be going?

"A walk, Robert. You're not usually home this early. It's a beautiful time of the afternoon—"

"A walk?" His words snarled as they curled off his tongue. "A walk," he repeated.

The pause before he spoke again had Esther breaking out in a sweat. She could feel the drips trickling down the inside of her dress. Could he tell she was lying? Robert knew nothing of Luca, so his suspicions should not be raised. But it wasn't about that, Esther understood. She was not permitted to do as she pleased.

"Well, that's wonderful when I'm not here. But I'm home now. Let's have a drink in the parlour before dinner."

Emboldened by something in his demeanour, Esther gazed at him directly. She saw defiance in his eyes, as if they dared her to misbehave. Yes, that was exactly what he wanted. For her to refuse, make a fuss. That way he could punish her without guilt. A recalcitrant wife who won't do as she's told.

But something was off. He sloped to one side, his malformed arm weighing down his right side. He cleared his throat and his leg jiggled. An air of uncertainty hung around him. If Esther didn't know better, she'd have said he was rattled.

None of that mattered. Her opportunity to catch Luca was disappearing like sand seeping through her fingers. God damn Robert. She wanted to cuss the most unspeakable of profanities. But, of course, she bit her tongue. She'd waited this long and she could wait longer. Luca was here in Hobart and she would find him. Of that she was certain.

***

Esther had never seen the streets filled to capacity before. Everyone had come out to catch a glimpse of the Queen of England.

Hobart had felt like such a metropolis when her family arrived all those months ago, and the feeling of claustrophobia and congestion had made her chest constrict. Today, she stood amongst the jostling crowd comfortably. How quickly you get used to people pushing you in the back and craning for prime position. Of the noise and commotion.

Esther hadn't been able to help herself. She'd been glued to the new television set at Eliza's house following the new Queen's visit to Australia. She'd already visited Melbourne and boy, what a welcome she'd received. Hobart had high expectations to live up to. So far, the city was meeting the challenge.

Esther was fascinated by the Queen, yet her heart yearned for the young twenty-seven-year-old woman. She'd not long lost her father, and here she was travelling to a faraway nation—a trip her father had been rumoured to have made if he'd still been alive.

Now, like everyone else, Esther had come out to see her. She stood well back from the crowd, Antonio on her hip, oblivious to the fuss. The Queen's itinerary was vast during her brief stay, but Esther headed to the wharf where the Queen's ship was to dock after travelling along the Derwent River. She'd be one of the first to spot the royal visitor.

Murmurs amongst those around her assured her the arrival was imminent. Moments later, the crowd erupted in rapturous applause. Antonio clapped his hands, too. People pushed from behind and Esther swayed forward, bumping into others. The *Royal Britannia* loomed large above them as it berthed and the crowd held their breath.

Esther checked around for her mother. Remarkably, she'd agreed to come. Esther had never seen her demonstrate any interest in the monarch, simply raising an eyebrow when she'd show her a photograph of the glamorous princess at a ball in England. Her *Women's Weekly* had covered many features on the royal family over the years and particularly since Elizabeth had been crowned.

Esther stood on tiptoe.

She spied her as she descended the gangplank. Esther sucked in her breath. Real-life royalty here in Tassie. The blazing hot February sun didn't prevent Her Majesty being attired in long sleeves and white gloves and an elegant pillar-box hat. She transcended beauty. Her skirt and matching jacket were blue. Pale blue? Powder blue? A string of pearls sat at her neckline and she held a handbag. In accordance with tradition, the duke trailed behind. Esther felt sorry for him, but in her romantic fantasies, she imagined a wild love affair between the two.

The horde cheered as she met the dignitaries. Cannons exploded in welcome. Antonio startled and cuddled in closer.

Esther wondered where Robert was and turned around, as if she'd spot him amongst the thousands of people present. He'd stormed around the house these last few days. If he'd been elected, he would have had special duties during this visit. Now, he was most likely relegated to the common folk like her, needing to crane their necks to gain a vantage. His party colleagues would be sitting in the makeshift stands comfortably, resting their weary feet and no doubt shaded from the searing sun. Nothing she could do about that. It wasn't possible to turn back time, and even if she had that power, what would she do?

All these what ifs…

Wiping her brow with her damp hand, she glanced at the crowd, looking for someone different now. Would he be here? Would Luca know who the Queen was? Each day since she'd seen him, Esther dreamed of Luca. Of what he did now, of where he lived, of coffee. They'd lost so much time. What had he been doing since she last saw him? So many questions… Esther turned every which way, but the crowd was twenty abreast.

Esther spied her mother, standing still and poker-faced a few paces away. She couldn't even muster up a smile for royalty.

In a matter of minutes, the Queen stepped into an open-topped limousine and was escorted away towards the streets of Hobart. People behind Esther started to run, keeping pace with the blur of black car as it sped past. She strode with them, ebullient. The mood of the day lifting her. She allowed thoughts of her mother to drift away; she could find her own way home.

But with Antonio at her hip, Esther couldn't keep up the fast walk for long. The limousine sped away into Hobart town. The farther it drove, the crowd thinned, slowly becoming quieter now that the show had dispersed. Some men and women milled around, broad smiles on their faces and clutching each other, aware something special had occurred this day. Esther spun in a circle on the spot with Antonio. He giggled his boyish laugh that made her smile.

As she spun, a flash of darkness crossed her vision and she paused. Antonio's chubby fingers clawed at her face, urging her to keep playing the game.

Luca.

Across the road, behind barriers like a cage keeping them apart, and out of the path of the cavalcade, stood Luca.

He hadn't seen her.

He stood, his teeth showing in a broad smile, looking to where the Queen had recently passed. People around him danced, confetti covering the path.

People pushed past her too, as if her life wasn't flashing before her.

She had to get to him.

Esther forced forward, the barrier trapping her. It swayed, nearly losing its footing. Antonio pulled at her earlobe now. Esther swatted it away and searched the fence converging on all sides around her. She needed to find a gap, a crossing; she had to traverse that road. Tracing her fingers along the railing, she frantically looked to her left and right. The barrier went for miles. *Where was the goddamn gap?* She wanted to scream until she gazed up again. She could not let him disappear.

Now, his eyes zeroed in on her. Probably the only person not dancing on the spot. He'd discovered her in this melee, amongst the crowds out in Hobart today.

A miracle.

His own barrier buckled under his weight as he leaned against it, his hands outstretched reaching for her.

"Luca." It sounded like a whisper above the racket on the street.

"Esther."

She reached across the gap. It was too far. Impossible.

She watched him search for an exit. He moved left, then right, swerving around children with their parents. Instinctively, Esther moved too. She kept up with him, pace for pace, left for right.

"Let's meet at the next crossroads."

Esther nodded, and kept walking, mirroring his steps on the other side of the footpath. Her attention did not sway from him.

This time, she would not lose him.

A man bumped her from behind, pushing her forwards, and she stumbled. Hands grappled at her elbows to prevent the fall. Her full skirt swished around her, catching in her legs as she walked too fast. She switched Antonio to her front for balance.

"Sorry, love." With a hearty grin and a wave, the man propelled onwards, eager like everyone to follow the momentum and the excitement the Queen had generated.

Steady now, Esther paused and clutched the rail, catching her breath. She cradled Antonio's head and held him close. She cooed in his ear, more for her comfort than his. He seemed okay.

It had taken only a matter of seconds. But it seemed as if the world had shifted. Where was Luca? Now it seemed as if more people had descended upon the street and with no queen to watch, they gathered in groups and cheered, some standing outside pubs enjoying a pint. The sun glared into her face and momentarily, she couldn't see across the space. Esther searched for his black hair. Her throat dried up. Breathing in deeply, she tried to dampen her rising fear.

"Esther."

A hand tugged at her arm, pulling her roughly backwards.

Mother.

"It's time to go."

Esther tried to move around her. Where was Luca?

"Esther."

His voice this time.

Rougher than she intended, she pushed her mother aside. Mary was solid and didn't even stagger. Esther heard him again; her mother did, too. She turned towards his voice, and a path cleared as the sun suddenly hid behind a building, giving her a clear view of the street. Luca stood tall on the other side, his arms waving.

Thank God she hadn't lost him.

"There's no way across." He shook his head. "Meet me at two p.m. at St George's Church at Battery Point."

Her mother stepped into her line of vision and he was lost, again.

"Get out of the way, Mother," Esther snapped.

Her mother shook her head and refused to meet her eye.

"Urgh." This time Esther shoved her hard and she shuffled sideways.

Luca reappeared, his features screwed up and frustrated. With his hands raised, he yelled again.

Two p.m. at St George's Church, Battery Point. Yes. She could do that. She had no idea where it was, but she'd find it.

Esther nodded and grinned, a cheek-aching smile. With one free hand, she waved at him, her arm circling wide.

It was then his eyes dropped from her face to the bundle in her arms. His grin plummeted. Esther stepped forward, again frustrated by the makeshift barrier. She shook her head, the energy buzzing around her only moments before seeping ever so slowly away.

What was he thinking? No. He'd still come to meet her, wouldn't he? Who did he think this baby was? A sick feeling filled her belly that Luca really didn't know they had a child. Did he think this was Robert's baby? It would be okay, she would explain everything this afternoon.

She communicated these thoughts to him, made them travel across the space that felt cavernous between them. The crowd gobbled Luca up.

This time she let her mother drag her home.

Chapter Twenty-Five

Luca spotted Esther sitting on a park bench facing the church. Her delicate head was upturned, hair down and dancing around her shoulders as she stared at the neo-classical tower, its calming presence standing tall and majestic over Battery Point.

And yet it didn't calm him today. He wanted to run to her, embrace her and lift her off her feet so that she clung to him. Instead, he hesitated. His stomach fluttered with nerves. The child sitting in her lap waved its arms, flapping like a bird.

Luca had dreamed of this moment. Every day of the eighteen months they'd been apart. But at no time did he expect it to be like this. He'd fantasised about a reunion that had them enveloping each other, tears of joy and happily-ever-afters. How could he have ever imagined anything else?

Nerves turned to dread. A warning that his dream may not play out today. A spasm gripped his chest, a shooting arrow of pain at the thought of having to say good-bye instead of it being a new beginning.

Damn it, Luca. You've always been too soft. A criticism embedded in his brain after years of having it shoved down his throat. With the arrogance and enthusiasm of youth, he'd ignored it—until he'd stuffed up and ruined his life and that of others. And then, too, when he couldn't live up to expectations.

Luca knew what he was doing: he sabotaged himself and he loathed it. Man up, as his Aussie friends would say. So he did, forcing his feet to move forward and not stop.

Esther turned in the seat and watched him approach. He couldn't deny the spark that lit up her eyes or the smile on her rosebud lips. His spirits soared.

"Hello, Esther."

"Luca."

He sat so no part of their bodies touched. Esther inched closer. The cotton of her brown skirt skimmed his leg and gave him an electric shock.

Her hand lifted, slowly, paused in mid-air and retreated, back to her lap.

Luca didn't know what to do, what to say, how to act. He sat paralysed and mute. Nothing like his usual persona.

The baby didn't have any such intimidation. Luca ignored him until he lifted his hand and touched his face. Those plump little fingers pulled the hairs of his short beard. Luca moved away. Incomprehensible babble erupted from the child, annoyed at being deprived of fun. Luca leaned back in and the child yanked again. The murmuring stopped.

Deprived of touch for so long, excepting a slap upon his back from workmates, a hand to his arm from Mrs Devitt, he hadn't experienced skin on skin, well, since he'd been with Esther.

A sob formed and he couldn't swallow it back down in time. It erupted like a cow mooing or some sort of ignorant burp.

Esther laughed.

"Excuse me." Luca smiled too. That ridiculous noise dispelled some tension between them. The child giggled. Luca reached out his finger and he grasped it.

Luca squared his gaze at him for the first time. The child had black hair. Dark eyes and brows. He looked at Esther then the child and back again. *No.*

Jumping up quickly, he almost lost his balance. He paced back and forth in front of Esther and the baby. At each return, he stared at the child again. Thoughts pierced his brain and he couldn't grasp them.

On one pass, Esther placed her hand on his arm.

"Luca…" She nudged him to return to sitting on the bench.

"This is Antonio. He is twelve months old. He was born in February 1953 on Bruny Island. Five weeks later, my father slipped on some rocks while we were celebrating St Patrick's Day. He hit his head and died. Since then…" Esther paused, looked down at her feet and away, up at the tall church tower again.

Luca sat still, his breath stuck in his throat.

"After Father died, we had no means of support and Albert Hawkins wanted me to marry him so that we could remain as a family on the Cape. My mother thought it was a good idea."

Luca raised his eyebrows but detected the tone of sarcasm to her voice.

"I refused and we were all turfed out. The baby, Tommy, and Margaret. We had seven days to leave. We had no choice but to come to Hobart. Charles helped us and I found a job and somewhere for us to live."

Esther had a faraway look in her eyes, like she was suffering that pain all over again. Luca touched her. She turned her head sharply towards him and immediately placed her hand on his. Her body sagged. So did his. Her touch felt so good. He positioned his other hand over the top so they were tangled together. A thrill raced up his spine. He couldn't drag his eyes away from her. Tears rolled down her cheeks and he wiped them away with gentle strokes.

He wanted to know every detail of what had happened to Esther since they'd parted, but he needed to know. Needed to know about this child first.

But he couldn't form the words. "Esther?" His eyes darted between her and the baby.

"I'm sorry, Luca, I wrote, told you that I was pregnant, but my mother was keeping the letters. I didn't realise, I thought you knew… But, yes, Antonio is your son."

A son? Luca had a one-year-old son.

"Luca?" Esther stared at him.

He didn't know what to think. He had a son? Luca kept his head down, reading the pattern in the pavers.

Esther kissed Antonio's head—his baby's head—and the child responded with a giggle.

"How could this have happened?"

Anguish crossed Esther's features and her lips pinched.

"Luca, I was desperate to hear from you. I told you about Antonio and you never responded…but I know now that it was my parents. They kept all our letters. I wanted you with me. And then my father died and my life fell apart."

"Your life fell apart? I was sent away that morning. You realise that, don't you? They wouldn't let me say good-bye—that stupid, mean Albert refused to have the boat wait. For me to rush to your side and kiss you once more. Your father let him behave that way. Then your letters stopped and I had no idea if you were alive or dead or what had happened."

He cupped his head in his hands, his body curling over itself.

Antonio jiggled in Esther's arms and it was difficult to hold him. She placed him down onto his little feet and he stood at the bench, hardly rising to its height.

Luca looked at him. The small child standing with his tiny hands gripping the bench, his knuckles pale. And then he smiled, revealing a few pearl-white teeth. The grin caused his cheeks to pillow. They were the chubbiest cheeks Luca had ever seen.

Luca split in two. A pulse started at his temples and throbbed.

Only one other question remained unanswered.

"Are you married to that man, that man from outside the brewery?"

Esther nodded.

Bile rose up Luca's throat, burning. He did the only thing he could, what he was good at. He turned and fled.

***

"What's going on here then, my loves?" Mrs Devitt entered the dining space, her ample body taking up all the available room.

Luca, Trevor, and Maximillian gave her a curt nod but didn't respond.

"Has someone died?"

"Well," Trevor said. "Mrs Devitt, you remember Luca's young lady, the one he's been pining for every day he's lived here at your fine boardinghouse?"

She nodded.

"He's found her. Can you believe it? They run into each other in the crowds at the Queen's parade, no less. Fancy the chances of that? Anyway, they lost each other and then agreed to meet up later."

Mrs Devitt plonked herself down at the table. "That's fabulous news, isn't it?"

Luca hung his head.

Maximillian said, "No. She's married and has a son…"

"Oh." Mrs Devitt covered her open mouth with one hand.

"And that son is Luca's."

"Oh my," she said and rose from the table. She went to the sideboard, unlocked one of the doors, and took out a bottle along with four glasses. "Well, I'll be," was all she could say and placed that bottle down on the table. She poured shots of the Jack Daniels straight up, no ice, and handed one to each of them. The men downed them. Everyone was silent as the burn hit the back of their throats. Luca coughed.

"So, you didn't know anything about your son, Luca?"

"Not a word, Mrs Devitt. Esther said she'd written but her mother kept the letters. How could a woman do that? Keep something like that from me? I always liked her mother, but now, maybe not so much."

"Yeah, that's a low blow, I agree. But not Esther's fault, right? This is the woman you love, and she tried to tell you."

"Loved."

"Honey, I've watched you these past months. This girl has consumed you. Most unusual, isn't it, boys, to pine over lost love like that. Most Aussie boys, they'd be back out there, finding a replacement—but not you. Now, that tells me something."

"What?" Luca said in his most belligerent voice.

"That you care for her."

"Mrs Devitt, I did. I do, but I feel let down. He's a one-year-old and I never knew about him."

"Yes, it's unfair, yes, you should have known, but I'm sure there's more to this story. What else did she say?"

Luca told them about her father's death and their eviction from the island.

"Je-sus, Luca," said Maximillian. "That poor girl, she's been through a lot. And then giving birth alone, with unsupportive parents and without you. That sounds terrible."

Luca considered his words.

"It's true, Luca. Can you imagine what she's been through? It sounds as if she was waiting for you. She didn't lie, she told you about the baby. It sounds as if she had no choice about how things played out." All present murmured assent.

Luca regarded each of the three people sitting at the table, drowning their sorrows with him. They'd become his Australian friends. He trusted them and their judgment. Mrs Devitt poured another drink.

"What about her husband?" Trevor asked.

Luca shook his head. "She didn't talk about him, but I've seen the man. Run into him around town. He's nasty."

"Does she love him?"

"I don't know, Mrs Devitt." Luca held his head in his hands, relishing in the warmth the alcohol provided him. "I swore her eyes sparkled when she saw me today."

The boys collectively slapped him on the back.

Mrs Devitt scraped her chair back and replaced the whiskey in its hidey-hole and locked the door. "You need to talk to her. You don't know anything. Stupid boy." She grasped his shoulders in an embrace that a mother would give her son. "Go to her, tell her you love her, and ask her what you need to know. You have a son, Luca. He needs you."

Trevor and Maximillian nodded their agreement.

"Dinner at seven p.m., boys," Mrs Devitt said her piece and slammed the door behind her.

Problem was, how would he find Esther when he'd run away like a fool?

***

Esther was wracked with guilt. Sitting in the back garden, Antonio explored the flowers and plants whilst she read and reread Luca's letters.

Esther rubbed the back of her neck and rolled her shoulders. Seeing Luca again had been both exhilarating and overwhelming. But she'd badly misread the situation. Her excitement at simply finding him had buoyed her. She'd been naïve, expecting him to feel the same when so much had happened since they'd last seen each other.

Esther had given birth to their son, who was now twelve months old, moved from Bruny Island to Hobart, and married Robert Hogarth. What an enormous shock it must have been. No wonder he'd fled. If she'd been faced with that news, what would she have done? She hoped that she'd have listened to him if the situation were reversed. Instead, he'd run off and left her flailing.

They needed to talk. She had to see him again. Even if he remained angry at her, she had to explain, make him try to understand. Even if he never wanted to see her or Antonio again, she had to try.

What an idiot she'd been. In their brief conversation, she hadn't elicited any idea of how to contact him. Where did he live? *So stupid.* Had she lost him again?

Rewrapping the letters, she clasped them to her chest, hoping they were not to be her only memories of her first love.

Chapter Twenty-Six

Esther moved through her chores by rote that week. Once again, Luca consumed her every thought.

As she wiped down the benches, she wondered what he might be doing. Without realising, her hand stilled and her gaze glued to the garden outdoors, not even noticing the blossoming daffodils or roses. She had so many unanswered questions. Did he still build blocks? Where did he live and with whom? And really, the only one that mattered—did he still love her? Had he missed her? But did she have any right to ask? So much she yearned to know, so much her chest ached.

Since the island, she'd adjusted, gotten on with life, she'd had to. But now, circumstances were different. She'd found him. And she knew with startling clarity that she had no right to wonder if he loved her—she'd married Robert. Disgust pooled in her tummy that Luca might think she loved her husband.

With no idea of what else to do, or where to find him, Esther returned to St George's Church the following Sunday. Same place, same time. She waited until the sun dipped low and the crisp night air cooled her skin.

The next Sunday she performed the same ritual. Dispirited but determined, she went the third Sunday and the fourth.

On the fifth, Esther plonked Antonio into her mother's lap. "I'm going out."

"Where do you go each week?"

"Out." Her mother's sharp turn of head must have made her neck crick.

"I can't look after him this afternoon. I'm busy." Mary rose and handed Antonio back then went to leave the room.

"Doing what?"

Her steely stare made the hairs on the back of Esther's neck rise. "Things."

Esther's body went stiff. "Might I remind you, Mother, that I do all of the work and provide for you and Tommy to live here comfortably. You've not done a day's work since we arrived in Hobart."

"Might I remind you—" her mother stood her ground, "—that you are Robert's wife. He is a good provider and an honest and reliable man."

Did her mother know where she was headed? She couldn't.

Esther felt as though she was back on Bruny Island as a seventeen-year-old girl being dictated to by her old-fashioned mother.

"I'm a grown woman, a mother. A wife. I care for Robert well. Not that it's any of your business. Now, I'm asking you to care for Antonio while I go out for the afternoon. Perhaps you might like to think about how you would fare living with Margaret?" She glared at her mother until she looked away, then called out, "Tommy."

Her brother strode in

Esther gripped his shirt and tugged him from the room. Lowering her voice, she handed him Antonio, who gurgled loudly and held out his hands for his uncle. "I'm going out to find Luca, Tommy. It's important to me. I saw him in the crowds recently at the Queen's parade. I want to talk to him, make sure he's okay. I haven't seen him for so long." Her voice cracked.

Tommy's eyes went wide. The poor love looked stricken and not sure what to say.

Instead, Esther stroked his cheek and thanked him.

She stomped along Elboden Street. It was no surprise her mother had turned into a major disappointment. She'd been a hard-nosed woman before her father had died, but ever since, she'd been nothing but a sour so-and-so. If it hadn't been for Esther, they'd all be destitute.

The bright sunshine hit her face and a breeze tickled her ankles. Thank goodness for the outdoors and the distance from *Norfolk*. Her stiff shoulders loosened and her steps slowed.

As always, she passed the newsagency. As usual, the magazines had prime position in the window. The newest edition of the *Australia Women's Weekly* had the most beautiful shot of the queen on its cover. Damn it, she was going to get a copy today.

Esther inhaled the fresh page scent. It was like a drug, an addiction that she'd been deprived of for too long. God, it was only a magazine, but what it could do to her spirits.

She hadn't forgotten her mission, though—find Luca.

Sooner than expected, she reached the church. Her anger turned to foolishness as she neared the once-again empty bench where they'd sat all those weeks ago. She'd given up hope of him miraculously appearing, so why did she still come and torture herself?

Visiting the church was futile and stupid, but now remained her only connection to Luca.

Esther sat and watched the people mill past her. Today she'd rest and read a few precious pages of her magazine before real life came crashing back to her.

***

"Twinkle, twinkle little star…" Esther sang to Antonio to lull him to sleep. Tommy stood at her shoulder, performing the hand movements to the words.

The door slammed back on its hinges with a thwack and the noise reverberated around the four walls of her bedroom. Antonio startled in his cot; his heavy lids snapped open and his face crumpled into tears.

"Where are you going?" Robert asked as he entered the room. His eyes crawled up and then down her body, taking in her walking shoes and handbag over her shoulder.

A pause. One moment too long.

Robert strode over and gripped her forearm, the skin pinching.

"Ow." She yanked her arm away, but Robert held tight. The blood stopped flowing through her veins and her arm paled. Antonio's cries escalated.

"I'm going to visit Mrs Manning." That was the best she could come up with. Plausible at least.

"Why?"

"She invited me for afternoon tea." Her insides cramped. She was implicating other people in her deceit and could too easily be discovered.

It was, of course, Sunday afternoon, and whilst Luca was unlikely to ever return, she had learned to quite enjoy sitting in the sun, and today she would reread her copy of the *Women's Weekly*.

But she hadn't expected this. Robert must need something from her. Those were the only occasions he cared where she was.

"I need Tommy to run an urgent errand," said Robert. "And he needs to do it now. It's more important than your afternoon tea. The boy doesn't have time to babysit." He dropped her arm.

When Robert was running for a place in the council, he'd never let her give up an invitation with the Mannings. Now, she figured they meant nothing to him; they were no longer of any use.

Esther wondered why he insisted on burning his bridges with those who had helped him gain pre-selection. Wouldn't he want to try again next election? But the more Esther thought about it, she realised that Robert couldn't stand the humiliation of defeat. The arrogance that ran through his veins meant he hadn't contemplated losing, and when he did, well, his shame was too great. He couldn't risk the same fate again. So, he'd given up his political aspirations and, in the process, grown more and more bitter about his lost dream.

Esther uncurled her limp body, a fierce determination coming over her. Why did he talk to them like that? Why be so mean and not simply ask for Tommy's assistance?

She opened her mouth to speak but saw the steely glint in his eyes that had turned slate grey, before he raised his hand and slapped her cheek.

It stung. To prevent the tears falling that pooled in the corner of her eyes, she ground her teeth together so hard her jaw clenched.

Tommy gasped and stepped forward to break contact between her and Robert. With surprising agility, Robert flung his hand towards Tommy. By the time it connected with his jaw it was a balled fist. The punch of knuckle against chin jolted her as if the hit had connected with her.

Esther twisted to comfort her brother. But Robert grabbed her shoulder, pinning her to the wall. He peered at her, his lips snarling and his ridiculous moustache twitching. Esther stared back, trying to communicate her disgust as it rode in waves through her.

You will not defeat me.

Robert's chest heaved. Esther thought that would be the end of it. He'd made a point, showed them the man that he was. Instead, he pushed her harder against the wall. How did he have so much strength with only one hand?

Her middle back connected with the bookcase. A crack of pain seized her torso. She breathed through it until it receded, and she lifted her head to receive a backhand on the other cheek. A whimper gurgled from her throat.

Tommy ran at him, buckling him around the torso. The two toppled sideways. Robert was a foot taller and his arms thicker than little Tommy's shins. He turfed the boy sideways like discarded rubbish. As Tommy lay in the corner, a loud crunch made Esther wince as Robert's boot stomped on his bare foot.

But Tommy wasn't his target. He bunched her long hair in one fist and pulled until she looked at him, their faces perilously close; she could smell his cheap soap and the stench of alcohol. Veins pulsed in his neck, his face red and glazed, as if he were possessed.

He was going to kill her.

Antonio screamed and she realised that she *couldn't* let Robert kill her. Her baby needed her.

She raised her hands, hitting his chest, scraping his arms, pulling at his collar. Nails scratched his face, drawing blood and forming ragged lines over his chin.

An animal roar erupted out of his chest. He released her with a shove, sending her reeling backwards and into a nearby chair. Antonio kept wailing.

Robert turned towards him and Esther watched his eyes bulge. *No.* She didn't know if the scream actually left her mouth or merely reverberated in her mind, but that word became the ultimate truth.

Adrenaline kicked in.

She pushed between Robert and the cot, blocking his route. His rock-hard body pressed against her, his hand reached for her neck, his one thumb pushing down on the hollow of her throat. Her screams were blocked and sucked back in with the gulps of air she struggled to take.

Blackness entered the corners of her eyes. Her head felt light, as if it lolled on her neck. For the first time, she wanted it to end. Now. To stop. No more. Let her be free.

But Antonio's little fingers touched her back and she fell into the present once more.

Her vision cleared enough for her to see Tommy slowly rising to his feet, one hand on the wall, keeping his woozy balance.

The pressure on her throat suddenly released and Esther coughed as the air travelled through to her lungs.

Robert sank to his feet, his knees buckling.

Glass shards fell noiselessly onto the carpet, glinting in the afternoon sun streaming through the window.

Esther shook her head to clear the fog. She looked at Tommy. He held the base of a lamp that had sat on the chest of drawers. It had a brilliant night-time scene of the stars that she loved, bought especially for Antonio.

Now she liked it even more.

But instead of dwelling, she ripped Antonio out of the cot and gestured to Tommy. They had to move fast. They had to get out before Robert recovered his senses and sought revenge.

***

Tommy leaned his head on her shoulder and cried. The young lad had not shed tears since their father died. Poor Tommy, what a life she'd given him. Guilt wracked her once more.

"Tommy, I'm so sorry. I will fix this, I promise."

They sat on a bench in their local park and tried to calm themselves. Esther leaned her head on his and balanced Antonio in her lap. Thank goodness she'd been able to settle him and he seemed happy enough now, away from the house, away from the ruckus.

It wasn't only guilt she felt about Tommy. What about her baby? The most precious thing in the world to her. What if Robert had hurt him? Could she have stopped him? His physical strength outmatched hers easily. And she had a sense, deep down inside, that Robert would get to him because he knew how much that would hurt her. He also knew that she'd do anything, *anything*, to keep Antonio safe.

Tommy sucked in his hiccupping sobs. "It's not your fault, Esther. He is mean. He wasn't at first, but he's getting worse. Why does he act like that?"

"I think he's an unhappy man, Tommy. He has wanted great things in his life but hasn't been able to achieve them."

"Everyone in the community loves him. He's a local hero, but at home he's horrible. We've never done anything to him." Tommy's adolescent face crumpled again.

Esther cuddled him and Antonio together and squeezed tight. "I am so, so sorry, Tommy. I need to think about this and what we can do. Okay?" She felt him nod his head under her chin. "Until then, you need to stay out of his way, promise? Don't do anything that might cause him to become angry. Stay clear. Can you do that?"

Tommy, with his bright blue eyes so like their father's, nodded again.

"Will you be all right?"

He responded affirmatively and with a tight smile.

"Okay. Can you take Antonio to the playground to cheer him up? He loves that swing at the moment. I'm going to clear my head and take a walk."

Chapter Twenty-Seven

Sunday, Luca was alone. He paced the hallway of the boarding house, sat down, but his legs twitched. He got up, paced again and searched for something to do, something to keep him busy. His idle mind thought of Esther: of past regrets, the what ifs and if onlys. Fatigue consumed him. The backs of his eyes ached and he wanted to shut them and forget.

Perhaps he should have gone fishing with his friends. But since the shipwreck, boats frightened him. On land, he was safe. Sometimes, when he felt this way, he would stand at the edge of the world at Battery Point and watch the waves crash against the shore and roll back outwards again. It was comforting. But he'd rather watch the water than be in it.

Perhaps he should do that today? He could wander the streets of Hobart and search for a good coffee. Something he'd done many other Sundays.

Luca headed towards the Point. There was so much history in the area; it was pretty and busy on this sunny afternoon. The tower of St George's, the largest structure in the skyline, dominated the blue sky. As if his feet were communicating with his brain, they walked in the direction of the church.

He didn't want to think about that awful afternoon only those few short weeks ago. Or that he hadn't seen Esther since. His chest tightened as he remembered.

The church came into view. It appeared stoic, strong and everlasting, and as always when he saw it, waves of calm washed over him. He'd been raised as a good Catholic boy, but religion did not form part of his modern life. Once he and his siblings were adolescents, they'd skipped out of church at the first opportunity, much to his mother's disappointment.

Today, those sandstone walls were calling to him.

Imagining that his muddled mind might find relief inside the church, he headed towards the slight incline to enter. He passed the park bench where he'd sat with Esther and then fled, like a little schoolboy.

A woman occupied the seat. He noticed the long brown skirt first. The woman had shoulder-length blonde hair. Similar to Esther. Luca did a double take.

It *was* Esther.

He stalled. His mind screamed at him to run away but his heart told him to hurry towards her before she could disappear again. His mouth went dry and, with certainty, he knew that today he wouldn't flee. How could he turn away from the woman he loved? He approached and sat down next to her.

"Luca." Esther turned and cupped her open mouth. He noticed her hands were dry and red and her nails were short.

"Esther."

Esther bent at the middle and wept quiet tears into her hands, covering her face.

Luca teared up too and touched her hand, silently asking her to look at him. His fingers stroked her skin until she gazed up.

"Oh, *mio Dio*."

Luca jumped up and broke into Italian. His hands rose above his head and then dropped to his sides before he flung them outwards, his arms gesticulating in each direction.

"Luca, English."

English? He knocked his palm against his forehead. "Ah, sorry." His face became solemn. "Who did this?"

Esther touched her face, tentative fingers caressing her cheek, moving down to her throat. She traced them to the hollow crevice and winced.

He sat again and found her hand and held it in his.

"Does it look terribly bad?"

"*Si,* yes. You have a red handprint on your cheek. You were hit hard, and here," he pointed to her throat, "is like a necklace of bruises."

They stared at each other.

"Who hurt you, Esther?"

She hung her head low and looked around them. "Robert."

"Robert." His forehead creased in concentration. "I know him?"

Shaking her head, Esther replied. "No. He's my husband."

"Your husband?" he shouted the words.

"Shush, Luca, people are staring."

Instead, he spoke through clenched teeth. "Your husband, that man, he did this to you? But why?"

"He isn't a nice man. He hurts Tommy, too."

He couldn't comprehend it. A man hit a woman, and his wife? But of course. They were talking about the man who had hit a pedestrian with his car and driven away. With a force that frightened him, Luca wanted to find this man and make him bleed.

"No. No, this is wrong. Bad. You must leave now." With a frantic flick of his head, he shot out of the seat and sat back down. "Where is Antonio? Is he hurt?"

Esther rested her palm to his forearm and rushed to reassure him. "No. He's with Tommy. In good hands."

"Okay, that is good. Let's get him and you can leave."

She shook her head.

"What? Why you shake your head no? You are hurt, he did this. You cannot stay there." It made perfect sense to him. In his agitated state, his English became more broken.

"Where will I go, Luca? Where can I live with Tommy and my mother, plus the baby? Who will take us in when I have no money, no job?"

"I work, have money. Is okay."

Esther smiled at him and he thought she'd agreed. He made plans in his mind.

"I want to leave, Luca. I hate him. But I cannot." Luca sat up straighter. "I agree I need to get out. But you have to understand, to have no money, nowhere to live, no support, it's frightening. I've been destitute, and I won't be again. I have responsibilities—to Antonio, and poor Tommy, and to myself."

Her tears dried up and her eyes turned grey and hard. He hadn't seen this determination before. This strong posture, her ferocious but coherent words. Luca could see she meant it. But to stay with a monster? That he did not understand. Risk her life and his son's life? That didn't make sense.

"I'll talk to my sister." Esther turned her head away and looked to the sky.

"Your sister?"

"Yes, Margaret is married and lives elsewhere now. She might help me."

Luca thought about this plan. There was only one thing he wanted her to do—come with him now. He could protect her, keep her safe. Couldn't he? Instead he said, "Okay. Your sister will help. Can you go now? I come."

Esther didn't move. Luca tugged her hand.

"Why are you here, Luca, why did you come back? I've been sitting on this bench every Sunday afternoon for weeks."

His voice reduced to a murmur. "You've come each week?"

She nodded.

"Ah, I didn't think of that. I was sure you wouldn't want to see me again after what I did."

Their knees touched. "You didn't do anything. You were shocked. I'm so sorry that you had to learn about Antonio that way."

"I understand. It was bad timing for us. We can talk about it, now that we've found each other. I want to hear every detail. But we need to make sure you are safe first. Most important."

Tears welled in Esther's eyes again.

"Don't cry, my love. We will work it out." He moved to embrace her.

She held up a flat palm. "I really want you to hug me right now, but not here. Robert has many friends…"

"I found good coffee not far from here. Can I buy you a cup?"

"I would love that."

Keeping his hands firmly by his side, he led the way.

***

Dusk fell upon the streets of Hobart and provided an orange glow. Despite an aching cheek and a tender neck, Esther walked with light steps. Seeing Luca, even if she'd had to say a brief farewell— because it *would* be brief—made everything in her life seem balanced again. A reluctant smile graced her lips.

But as her steps drew closer to *Norfolk,* the joy seeped from her. Usually after an incident with him, life returned to normal…well, as normal as was possible in his household. He'd made his point and didn't again refer to whatever the transgression had been. Today's incident had been worse than any before. Prickles crept up her spine at the uncertainty, at what she might face. She hadn't retaliated before. Never had she hurt him back. A lampshade to the head would not be taken lightly.

Her body braced for more abuse and her heart hardened once more as she strode up the path.

Random strays of the receding daylight lit the front room enough for her to see, but the room was dim. The door clicked shut behind her and she tiptoed. Ludicrous. Did she think she could sneak back into the house and everything would be all right?

The sizzle of a cigarette caught her eye.

Robert sat in a single armchair across the living space and smoked. He'd never smoked before. Other than his slow intake of breath as he dragged on the cigarette and its crackle, the room was silent. A spiral of smoke trailed above his head into the air. Esther imagined it pooling at the ceiling and hanging there, literally like a bad smell.

Esther heard a gurgle. Robert's knee bounced. She took two quick steps in his direction and saw Antonio sat in his lap.

Her hand lurched to her chest and she struggled to breathe.

"Welcome home, Esther. We've been waiting for you."

Was Antonio hurt? Stunned, she didn't respond.

"Antonio and I have been getting to know one another better."

"Where is Tommy?"

Robert touched the tip of his moustache with two pinched fingers and twirled the hair.

"Always so concerned about him, aren't you? Perhaps that's where this marriage went wrong. You spent too much time worrying about others and not your husband."

"Robert, where is he?"

He smirked and waved his hand in the air. "Back there somewhere. Where you always seem to gather."

"May I have Antonio, please? It's time for his bath and to prepare for his dinner."

"Oh, but he and I are having a wonderful time together." For emphasis, he jiggled his knee and Antonio released a giggle.

Her defenceless child was perched on a monster's knee and was oblivious to it.

She needed to get him away, and Esther knew she'd have to say all the right things to appease Robert to make that happen.

"You're right, Robert. I've been distracted at times with the baby and my family. I will do better in the future, I promise."

He was nodding. A good sign. Her adrenaline slowed a little. A change of topic would work well.

"Are you hungry, Robert? I can prepare your favourite, sausages and mash. I bought some delicious-looking sausages from Mr. Pullman yesterday. They will be tasty and fresh."

"Yes, that sounds delightful. Prepare them now and I will keep Antonio entertained. Then you will eat with me."

No. no. She had to get Antonio to safety. Her mind wracked over different ideas.

"He will get fractious soon as he'll grow tired and hungry. My mother can take him and you can relax until dinner."

Robert remained quiet.

She took a step forward and faltered, reaching out. He lifted Antonio upwards, one arm secured around his waist and aided by his knee.

"You love this wog baby, don't you, Esther?"

"Yes." And Esther cursed herself for her pathetic whimper.

"If you tell anyone about what happens in this house, I will hurt him. Do you understand?" His fingers tightened around Antonio's middle.

She nodded.

"If you entertain ideas of leaving, let me assure you that Antonio will remain here. You are my wife, he is my son, and he will live with me. If you leave or attempt to *escape*," the word snarled off his lips, "the baby will not go with you. If you do sneak away and take him, I will find you. No one in this community will believe a word you say. They will think you're crazy. That you are an unfit mother, and no one will award a crazy mother custody of their son when there is a fit and upstanding community citizen, let alone his father, to care for him. You will never see your child again. Do you understand?"

"Yes, Robert. I understand. I understand that you will do whatever it takes to hurt me. Whether that be by your fist or with words or by hurting those I love."

Esther moved closer. What else could he possibly do? He'd made his threats, but would he try to hurt her again?

"Give him to me, and then I'll start your dinner."

With his threat delivered, Robert handed over the baby. Esther took him and rushed away from her husband's side.

She held Antonio tight, squeezed him too hard. He didn't like it. Moving fast now, she didn't have time to waste. Inside their quarters, she relaxed when she saw Tommy.

"I'm sorry, Esther, he insisted on taking him. I couldn't do anything. He said he'd hurt both of us if I didn't comply."

"It's okay, Tommy. I understand." She placed a reassuring hand to his shoulder.

Her mother sat across from them in front of the unlit fireplace. Without asking, she placed Antonio onto her lap.

"What have you done now?" she said.

"I guess that's what I should be asking you, Mother." Esther paused for effect and shook her head. "Regardless, do what is right for now and care for Antonio. Tommy will help you. He needs his bath. I have to prepare Robert's dinner." Hatred rushed through her and she quickly dispelled it. That sort of hatred was reserved for men like her husband who hurt and threatened women and children. Her mother was better than that, but Esther wasn't sure by how much.

Esther strode away to perform for Robert. Pretend to care for him, and lovingly cook his meal. She was up to the challenge, but boy, how she loathed it and him.

Chapter Twenty-Eight

Esther stood in Margaret's entry out of the slashing rain. Wiping off the droplets and shaking out her umbrella, she took a moment to compose herself. Margaret always made her nervous…well, this new adult version of her sister, anyway. Esther didn't recognise—and dare she say like—this woman she'd become. Plus, she was not at all convinced that she'd be of any help.

Inhaling a deep breath, she lifted the knocker and let it fall. The door opened and she was instructed by the housekeeper to wait in the parlour.

Esther took the opportunity to look around her.

It was opulent. The walls were white with matching single armchairs facing into a square pattern. The cushions matched the garish curtains in a brown gable pattern. The coffee table in the centre was deep mahogany and had thick legs that curled at their bases. The other furniture, of which there wasn't much, complemented this style. Esther thought it made the room seem dark and overdone. Margaret had obviously wanted a modern room. Could be worse, Esther thought. Bright colours were the fad at the moment, and houses across Hobart were filled with pastel greens and yellows.

"I wasn't expecting you, Esther. You can't drop in and expect me to be available," her sister said by way of greeting as she entered.

"I'm sorry, Margaret. Are you busy?"

"Well, yes. I'm planning a dinner party for next week. Arthur is having a number of important people over and everything must be perfect. It's exhausting planning the menu…"

Margaret reminded her of Scarlett O'Hara from *Gone with the Wind.* Extravagantly overdressed with her hair curled and jewels on her fingers, sassy with a quick wit and words like barbs. Esther had always admired the smart young Scarlett O'Hara and the adversity she'd had to overcome, often at others' expense, but with her heart always in the right place. Would Margaret have to experience her own downfall? Esther sincerely hoped not, but her sister sure needed a good shake-up.

"I need your help, Margaret."

"Help? With what? If you're planning a dinner party, I'm sure you've got people you can call on. It's hard enough work organising my own... Or if it's another dress, well, surely you can choose something for yourself now? I'd only have time to give you a few tips."

Margaret was still the sixteen-year-old girl who had fled from Bruny Island. A deep gulf developed in Esther, a hole ripping open her stomach that she was related to this woman, a deep disappointment that Margaret was her sister.

Putting these thoughts aside, Esther reached over and clasped her hands. "No, it's nothing like that, Margaret. I need to leave Robert and I want you to help me."

Margaret ripped her hands away from Esther. "Don't be ridiculous. You can't leave Robert. Why would you? He's a prominent man in Hobart, not as prominent as he'd hoped, I understand, but still worthy. And of course, we do not divorce. The scandal, Esther. You'll ruin me."

"He hurts me, Margaret. And Tommy."

For a brief moment, Margaret seemed appalled and Esther thought she understood. "Esther, you're always so dramatic. Marriage isn't like those magazines you read. It isn't a fairy tale. My marriage isn't perfect, but it provides me all this." She swept her arms wide. "You've never been tolerant or forgiving."

Esther made an "O" shape with her mouth, but no words came out.

"You know it's true."

What a fool she'd been. She'd hoped history and sibling love would triumph in her time of need, but no, Margaret was not someone she knew anymore. Esther had to accept that they were nothing alike.

"He hits me. Look at this bruise." She turned her cheek for a clearer view.

Margaret leaped out of her seat and placed two hands over her ears. "I don't want to hear it. You're being absurd." She paced. "You need to go home right this instant and make him happy. Cook his favourite meal, make sure the house is clean, take an interest in his affairs. He's the man of the house, out working all day, and needs these comforts when he gets home. You need to work harder."

Esther took it all in, incredulous, but not unexpected. She backed down and became her subservient self, the one who cared for Robert and did as she was told. The person she was determined not to become—or not to remain, at least. The one she despised but seemed to be the person she needed to be to survive this life.

"Yes, of course. You're right. I'll try harder to be a better wife. I'm being silly. Robert is a wonderful husband…" Some lies didn't easily roll off the tongue.

Margaret nodded and smiled, like she'd saved the day.

"One thing, though, Margaret. It's been difficult to keep up with the care of Mother and Tommy. You're well provided for by Arthur and have this beautiful home with plenty of room. Could you take them in? Particularly Tommy—he deserves better."

"I must go. I still have this menu to plan and I'm intending to go gown shopping. I need the perfect dress for this event. And you have plenty to do as well. Mother can assist you with these things and you need her help with Antonio. Honestly, they are best with you. I'm not sure what you're thinking. You're not yourself today." Margaret leaned down and kissed her on the cheek and left the room in a flurry of blue skirt.

Well, at least she hadn't been cruel enough to say she didn't want them. But that's what she'd implied, wasn't it? It meant the same thing, even if she didn't utter the words.

Esther pulled the door shut after showing herself out. Not the result she'd desired, but nonetheless, it had been a useful exercise, because now Esther understood unequivocally that Margaret would never help. She was on her own. Esther had known it, but she was desperate.

And she *was* desperate. Since the incident that weekend, Robert had kept her within reach—aware of her every movement and leaving her a list of chores each day that would render punishment if she didn't finish them. In fear of what he might do, she didn't pause for a moment until every job had been completed.

As a result of the gruelling schedule, she'd missed seeing Luca. And because Robert was always present, she wasn't able to deliver a message. He'd be concerned. Something else she worried about. If she didn't speak to Luca, what would he do? He knew the truth. He might believe she was injured, or worse, dead.

The burden of those difficult early days in Hobart came back to haunt her. All these years later, and she felt as if she hadn't improved her circumstances at all. How had she gotten it all wrong?

No point dwelling on the past. *Think, Esther, think.* She needed a plan and it had to be a good one.

***

An opportunity arose ten long, agonising days later.

Robert had to attend to an urgent legal matter at his office. Esther couldn't believe her luck. She glanced at the wall clock. Only ten a.m. Problem was she had no idea how long his task might take. Thinking quickly, she collected her purse and the nappy bag. There was no way she'd be leaving Antonio here, even in her mother's care. She rushed to the servants' quarters where Mary sat in the armchair whilst Antonio played with coloured blocks on the rug in front of her.

Esther checked he was dry and clean and scooped him up into her arms. "I'm going to the grocer and butcher, Mother. If Robert returns, can you send Tommy to me with an urgent message? He'll expect me home."

She hoped her mother didn't notice the tremor in her voice. She had always had a gut instinct that unsettled Esther. But Mary merely glared at her. A novel sat in her lap, unopened. She picked it up and commenced to read.

Once out the door, Esther walked faster than was safe with Antonio in her arms. The pram would have been useful, but she'd been too harried to think of it. It would slow her down anyway.

Esther recited the address Luca had given her. He'd wanted to write it down, but she'd refused, not being brave enough to commit anything to paper. Any evidence that Robert might find to incriminate her was too dangerous. On her walk home that afternoon, weeks ago, she'd repeated his address until it was embedded in her brain.

His boarding house was in South Hobart, on Wentworth Street. Luca had given her directions. Those details now escaped her. Did he say it was near Macquarie Street school? Or was it opposite the grocer? A billboard of a Cascade beer at the bus stop she raced past jogged her memory. *Near the brewery.* A couple of his fellow housemates worked there.

Cycling to the brewery that day had been easy, but it was a much farther walk. Sweat droplets rolled down the dip in her chest, pooling at the waistband of her skirt. Esther covered her eyes as the mid-morning sun beat down upon her. Bugger, she'd forgotten her hat. Luckily, Antonio's cap was in the bag and she rummaged for it.

There was no mistaking he was Luca's son. No wonder Robert had never taken to him. One look and it would serve as a reminder the child wasn't his, and moreover, belonged to an Italian migrant. Esther imagined it must have cut deeply. Robert had no appreciation of foreign cultures.

Wentworth Street. She'd made it. Esther sighed with relief. Hugging Antonio closer, she kept walking, her anticipation growing with each terrace house she passed. Searching every street number, Esther scanned for 120 and the white stucco two-storey building that Luca had described to her. Number 5. Esther slumped. She was at the opposite end of the street.

The sky started to darken with thick clouds gathering on the horizon. Goosebumps erupted on Esther's arms as a slight wind whipped through the street. Fallen leaves swirled in the gutters.

As she reached 120, Antonio grew fractious and grumbled in her arms. He'd been so good.

"Antonio, Mummy needs to visit this house and then we can go home and have a nice snack. Okay?" She jiggled him in her arms and with one hand searched the bag for a toy or teething stick, anything.

With him on the verge of crying, Esther pounded her fist on the green panelled door. After only a moment, it swung open.

"Oh, hello," she said and wiped her brow. She must look a fright.

For some reason she expected Luca to answer. Ridiculous, she now realised. It wasn't his house. He boarded here.

"Hello, love." The lady before her wore a white frilly apron that hugged her curvaceous figure. The white contrasted against her wild, red curly hair. Fair to say that she would not grace the cover of the *Women's Weekly* anytime soon. But she did wear a broad and welcoming grin. "How can I help you?"

Antonio wailed.

"I'm looking for Luca Moretti. Is he here?"

"Luca." Her face creased and deep pockets formed at the sides of her mouth.

Did she have the wrong house? Esther checked the number on the door. 120. Wrong street? As Antonio's cry increased in volume, her legs went weak and she stumbled forwards.

The lady stopped her fall. Then she reached for Antonio who went into her arms without fuss and twiddled her long hair around his fingers. A raucous laugh erupted from the woman. "Aren't you a wee little one," she cooed and moved up and down on the spot.

Esther recovered herself. "I'm sorry about that."

The woman turned back towards her. "You'd better come in." She opened the door wider.

Esther entered into a bright and breezy hallway that seemed to run the depth of the house. Rooms came off in both directions. She entered the first room to the left. It was nothing like her sister's catalogue parlour room, but warm with pastel yellows and whites mixed with indoor plants and lived-in furniture.

"Luca is at work, love. It's the middle of the day. I was finishing off the laundry. Devil of a job it is when you have six rooms to care for. But enough of that. Can I tell him who came by?"

"He's not here?" She'd walked all this way and he wasn't home?

"I'm Mrs Devitt, boardinghouse missus," the lady introduced herself as she sat in the opposite chair and indicated Esther do the same. Happy now, she kept jostling Antonio on her lap. "What's wrong?"

"I'm Esther."

"Esther," Mrs Devitt mused. Then realisation hit and Mrs Devitt leaned forward, her eyes twinkling. "You're his girl, aren't you?" Her voice rose a pitch higher. "Oh my goodness." She clapped her hands together. It made Antonio jump. "He will be so pleased to hear you dropped in. He's told us all about you."

"He has? I need to see him."

Mrs Devitt checked the time. "Well, he won't be returning until dinner. I know, I'll make us a cup of tea and then I can direct you to where he works. It ain't far, and I'm sure his boss won't mind if you drop in quickly."

Esther nodded agreement. Yes, she could visit him on her way back to the cottage. She didn't have time for the tea though.

"Mrs Devitt, that would be lovely. Thank you, but I'm in a rush, I'm not sure I can stay for morning tea." Antonio chose that moment to erupt again. His eyes scrunched up and closed and his lips quivered.

"I don't think you have a choice, dear. If I remember rightly, that smells like a dirty bottom to me." Mrs Devitt inhaled and placed Antonio onto the carpeted floor. "You'll need to clean him up. While you do that, I'll put the kettle on. You can lay your things out on my bed. It's the last room down the hall."

She left, and Esther felt like she couldn't refuse the kindness.

But she did need to hurry. If Robert returned and she wasn't home, God knows what he might do. The thought brought the taste of bile to her mouth.

Back in the sitting room, Esther perched at the front of the comfortable sofa chair, a clean Antonio on the floor, her bag on her shoulder. She was primed and ready to go at the first opportunity. However, that opportunity didn't seem to present itself.

Mrs Devitt returned with a tray laden with matching floral teapot and cups with scones and clotted cream and jam in their own dainty dishes.

"Here we go. I hardly ever have female company. This is such a treat. Luca will be beside himself when you visit him at work. He's been pining over you, my girl. Thought he'd lost you."

Esther sagged back into the seat. A quick getaway appeared impossible. Usually, she'd love talking to this vivacious woman and eating the delicious spread. So kind and civilised. Unlike everything about her life right now.

She couldn't scamper away after Mrs Devitt had made such an effort. Despite her predicament, she couldn't be rude. Dread pooled in her tummy though. What awaited her back at home would not be pleasant.

Antonio squealed as Mrs Devitt handed him an arrowroot biscuit that immediately became mushed in his mouth and crumbled down his hands.

"Yes, that's better, he's happy. He's clean and has a snack now. And he is Luca's son, I take it? The resemblance is uncanny."

Esther nodded. She'd kept that information so tightly coiled inside, it felt strange to talk about it out loud.

Twenty minutes passed before she could politely remove herself, and even then, she had to make promises to return.

"I would love to come back and visit you. Thank you for the tea and snack and the directions to Luca." Again, she refused the offer to write them down.

"It was so lovely to meet you." Mrs Devitt kissed her on both cheeks.

What would life have been like if her mother was like Mrs Devitt, Esther wondered. As she walked away, images of Sunday lunches and picnics with family floated in her mind. Lost in thought, she didn't see Tommy rattling down the street.

"Esther," he shouted.

Her body came alive at the call of her name and suddenly the day felt much hotter. Tommy chasing her could only mean one thing.

"Tommy, are you all right?"

He caught up with her and had to catch his breath before speaking. "Yes, but Robert is on his way back. Mr Crosby from the firm had to call around to collect something from the study. He said Robert had been in court all morning, but it was due to adjourn for lunch at one."

Esther glanced down at her bare wrist. She didn't wear her watch. Tommy wasn't wearing his either. "What time is it?"

"I left home before noon. It must be at least twelve thirty by now."

"Okay. We have time. We must rush, Tommy. Here, you take Antonio and I'll be able to walk faster. Let's go."

Chapter Twenty-Nine

"Soooo," Mrs Devitt dragged out the vowel, "how was your day?" she asked Luca before he'd even closed the front door.

A strange, luminous beam emanated off his landlady, an aura he hadn't detected before.

Luca shrugged and removed his work boots and placed them in the entry.

"Oh, come on, tell me everything." Her hands on her waist, she waited, expectant.

Luca checked behind him. Was she talking to him?

"Like every other day—I made… maybe, twenty-five blocks, did some deliveries. It was okay."

Her hands dropped to her sides. "You had a visitor at work today, no?"

"Visitor? A few customers came in to make orders. There was one large order for a new house over on—"

"No," she said. "Your young lady. She came to the house and I directed her to you at work. She said she needed to see you. It seemed important."

She'd caught his attention now. "What do you mean? Esther?"

"Yes, Esther."

"She was here, at the house?"

Mrs Devitt nodded. "Yes, I made her a cup of tea and the little bubba had a biscuit. He made a right royal mess, if I may say so."

Luca plonked into the nearest chair. "She came."

"You definitely didn't see her today? Maybe you were with the customer and missed her?" It was Mrs Devitt's turn to shrug.

"No, I was out the front, I would have seen her arrive. There'd only one entrance in and out."

"That's strange. She was insistent about seeing you and I gave her the directions, spelled it out so she would find her way easily."

"Damn."

"Luca," she warned.

"How was she?"

"When she first arrived, she was a little frazzled. The baby was crying. He settled after he had a clean bottom and a snack. The moment she finished her tea, she wanted to be away. To see you. Personally, I could have chatted to her all day, Luca. She's a delight. And your son, how precious. Looks exactly like you."

Luca stared. Esther had missed their last two dates, but she'd come today. Something was wrong.

"And you're sure she was coming straight to see me at work?"

"Uh-huh, yes, definitely. No doubt about it. She was in the most desperate rush. Do you think she got lost?"

Luca rose and paced the front room. "Mrs Devitt, was she upset? Nervous? Tell me everything she said. Was she hurt?"

"What. No. No, she wasn't hurt. Like I said, she seemed anxious to see you, but that's normal, isn't it? Should she have been worried?"

"I'm not sure. I think for her to come here, something is wrong. We'd arranged to meet last week and she didn't turn up. We promised each other..." He marched the length of the room and threw his hands in the air. "She didn't leave a message?"

"No. She left here with the intention of visiting you. There wasn't any need for a message."

"Okay. I need to find her. If she intended to visit me and didn't, well, I can't bear to think that something dreadful prevented her. I will find her."

He pulled his boots back on, still caked with dirt from the workroom floor.

"Luca, where are you going?" Mrs Devitt stood in his path, her face etched with concern.

"Her house, of course. Where else? It will be dark soon, I must hurry. I will find a way to see her."

As he placed his hand on the doorknob, she rushed over. "What about your dinner? Eat first."

"No, I go now. I'll be careful."

***

Norfolk stood ominous, eerie, as if it were taunting her, luring her into its clutches. All appeared quiet. The cats scattered as they entered the front garden. As she stared at the imposing structure, she was sure she saw a curtain flutter.

Was Robert home?

Tommy bent over, hands on his knees, gulping in air. Esther matched him, her chest rising and falling in unison.

"Tommy. Tommy," she repeated when he didn't look up. "You need to take Antonio and go around the back. Keep him safe. Lock the door and don't open it unless it's me. Do you understand? Can you do that?"

He nodded and held his arms out for Antonio.

She watched her brother and son walk around the back of the cottage. She was buying time, bracing herself. She'd done a lot of that lately, and quite frankly, she was sick of it. Pandering to Robert, tiptoeing over eggshells. It was hardly any way to live.

She had no idea what she would face inside. Robert was certain in one respect: his unpredictability. When she was one hundred percent certain he would act like a raging bull, he'd be calm. When she expected calm, he blindsided her with a torrent of rage. Now, she expected nothing less than his most heinous anger.

Nothing to do but get on with it, she guessed.

Feigning confidence, she took the few short steps to the front door and entered.

Inside was dim and she let her eyes adjust. With the most wicked sense of deja vu, her feet became fused to the floor; she'd been in this position before and it hadn't gone well.

It was the noise that gave her away. When nervous, her mother had a little tic that itched at the back of her throat. As children, they'd called it a frog. It was a rather gross noise that she couldn't avoid when stressed.

Robert could have risen and struck her across the face right that moment and she wouldn't have been less surprised. In fact, she'd expect that. Not this.

Mary sat back, her posture rigid and her face stern.

Robert, by comparison, had one leg crossed over the other, his hand clutching his ankle. He could have been having a conversation with a friend, so relaxed was his demeanour. Or he was a fabulous actor.

"Where are the grocery bags, Esther?" he asked.

Flummoxed, Esther checked her hands as if the bags would appear. "Grocery bags?"

"Yes, your mother tells me you went to the butcher and the grocer?"

Her bravado slipped and fear clawed at her belly.

"Oh, well it was such a lovely day out, I stopped at the park on the way and time slipped by. Antonio was playing with some other children and I realised that we still had that cut of pork I purchased yesterday. We'll have that for dinner."

Esther thought she sounded convincing and quite calm in the circumstances. But that didn't stop her armpits growing damp.

"Really?" Robert mocked. "You must think I'm stupid. Get out of my way. Go to your room."

"I beg your pardon?"

"I said," his tone sharper, impatient, "go to your room."

Despite her heart hammering in her chest, she forced normalcy.

"I'll make your dinner first."

Robert's wineglass smashed against the wall. Esther jolted and watched the red trickle seep down the wall. It would be sticky to remove.

"No dinner. You are directed to remain in your room until I say otherwise." His voice rose as he stood tall.

Esther froze. She dared a look at her mother, who had remained silent throughout the exchange.

"Your mother can't help. She's been most enlightening about you and your whereabouts. You're a liar and I do not tolerate liars and those who don't do as they're told."

Her mother's face remained impassive, blank.

For a split second, Esther deliberated about what to do. But that was foolish. She had to comply. There was no choice. To not do as she was told meant further punishment, and that would not be as easy as being banished to her room.

Silently, she turned and padded quietly across the room towards the staircase.

"Esther. The servants' quarters."

With one foot on the bottom stair, she paused, pulled in quiet breaths. When her nerves had steadied, realisation dawned—this was a reprieve. From him coming to her room later or surprising her with a push or shove from behind when she least expected it. No, this was much better. Safer. For all of them.

So instead, she made for the quarters. At the door, she paused. "Mother?"

No answer from Mary.

No answer from Robert.

Esther clicked the door shut, resisting the temptation to lock it behind her and render her mother unable to enter the rooms later.

***

Outside, Luca crouched behind the hedge. Craning over the bushy foliage, he could see one front window next to the door. Only the faintest glow emanated from within. The sun was a whisper away from meeting the horizon. Night would soon fall and he'd struggle to see.

He darted out behind the bush and headed to the side of the house. A distant memory came to him. Something Esther had said about a back garden and an entry to her part of the house—what was otherwise known as the servants' quarters. Seemed a pretty apt name, Luca thought.

Feeling his way along the left of the house, he spied the rear entrance. It seemed to be detached from the main house.

Luca crouched down again on his haunches. What to do now?

A faint cry echoed on the breeze. If Antonio was inside, surely Esther was too? Luca crept on all fours across the grass until he came to kneel below one of the windows.

He rose until his face reflected back at him in the glass.

A sharp pinch to the skin on his neck and he froze.

"Turn around real slow."

Damn it. How could he be so stupid as to get caught? He turned, his body stiff, but the sting released from his throat.

"This is what I do to peeping Toms around these parts," said a man holding a pitchfork to Luca's face.

Luca lifted his hand in peace but the man was quick to react.

"Don't do anything. You should be ashamed of yourself, peering in at people like that. Disgusting."

The man wore khaki-coloured pants and a long-sleeved work shirt. Grass stains graced the knees and his shoes were dirty, as though he'd been walking through a field. He wore a broad-brimmed hat.

"It's not what you think."

"Oh, really. A man peering inside a window where a young woman happens to be. What is it then?"

"I am a friend of Esther's."

"A friend who can't enter through the door?"

"Please, hear me out."

The man nodded.

"I am a friend of Esther's from Bruny Island. I am worried about her, but I cannot let her husband know that I am here. He might…might hurt her if he knows. She might even be in danger now. I'm not sure. But I need to see her."

The pitchfork lowered a little. "What's her son's name?" he said, testing Luca.

"Antonio."

"Her brother?" he asked.

Luca answered correctly.

"You truly are a friend and not a peeping Tom?"

"Yes."

The man looked down at his feet, contemplating. He stared back up at Luca after a few moments. "I am the gardener. If Mr Hogarth sees you, there'll be hell to pay."

"Yes, I know, but I am worried about Esther. Is she all right? Have you seen her?"

The gardener's face turned solemn. "She came home not so long ago. I could see she was nervous, patting her hands down her skirt, you know. Did a big sigh. But she went inside and I haven't heard since."

A creak sounded to their left, like the door opening. Lightning fast, they both dropped to the ground, huddled together.

"What was that?" Luca asked him.

A few seconds passed and they didn't hear the noise again. "Nothing. But you gotta get out of here. It's not safe for either of us. I'll cop a flogging too if I'm seen with you."

The blood drained from Luca's face. How could he leave Esther here? She might be in danger.

The gardener was watching him. "Look, if you are a friend, do her a favour and go. You'll only make matters worse."

Luca nodded. "Okay. But I come back tomorrow—and you can tell me she's all right?"

For a brief second, the man appeared horrified, but just as quickly his features softened.

"Not here. Meet me down the road a little, on the corner behind the bus stop." They whispered agreement on details and the man urged him to go.

Luca rose and stood at a right angle to the window. Now the room was illuminated. He let his eyes adjust. He shot his hand over his mouth when he saw her. In the far corner, standing over a cot. Antonio. They were okay. His body slackened with relief. The gardener tugged on his sleeves, again forcing him to move. Luca placed one hand to the windowpane. A physical ache shot through his chest.

Please, let her stay safe.

He wanted to go to her, sweep her into his embrace, and carry her away. Unlike last time, now he made a vow that he would return and he would ensure her safety. And take her with him. He would not accept any excuses.

The gardener grew impatient. Luca removed his hand and the misty outline of it remained on the pane for seconds before disappearing. Exactly like he needed to do.

Chapter Thirty

The next day began like any other. Antonio woke as the first glimmer of dawn penetrated the curtains. Esther smiled a sleepy smile, so happy he was the first person she saw.

"Good morning, beautiful boy."

He gurgled "mum mum" in response. Hearing her name spoken by her baby made her heart skip an extra beat. Until she took in the surroundings and the world crashed back to reality.

She'd dreamed of Bruny last night, was transported to the island. She and Luca were walking hand in hand along Lighthouse Bay beach. The surf crashed against the shores and the sand stuck between her toes. She wriggled them, checking for wet granules.

Her head crashed back against the pillow. She longed to be on that beach now. Anywhere but here. In hindsight, how idyllic their life at the lighthouse seemed. It felt like a lifetime ago.

Holding Antonio by the hand, they waddled to the small kitchenette. The cupboards were mostly bare. Today, it was necessary to pour herself a cup of coffee. It was an act of defiance against Robert and in support for Luca. The coffee was nothing like Luca would make, but it would suffice. As she inhaled the aroma, she thought of him. Finally, she loved coffee. The first sip and her situation seemed more palatable and she could face the day.

She peeled a banana for Antonio and they went back to bed. Esther sang to him and they played. Morning was her favourite time of the day. It allowed her to be a mother and focus on her son before the doldrums of a normal day began.

Dare she feel secure and safe? Was she being naïve? Robert should be asleep upstairs. He never entered the quarters so she should successfully avoid him until she had to prepare his breakfast. Another brief reprieve.

Antonio babbled and played with an old string of beads. Esther got dressed and assembled her imaginary armour. She fumbled doing up her blouse. Her sense of safety didn't last. As she slipped on her shoes, dread like a ball of chains settled in the pit of her stomach. What would the day hold?

She ventured to the other side of the cottage to locate her mother. Her bed was made and appeared unslept in. Esther poked her head in next door and Tommy snored peacefully.

Strange.

With Antonio on her hip, she turned the knob on the internal door and pulled up sharp when it didn't budge. She pulled it again. Nothing. A strange tingling began in her chest, a funny buzz that made her unsettled. This door was never locked.

She manoeuvred the knob left and right; no luck. She jiggled it and the door rattled. It didn't shift. Perhaps it was jammed?

Esther moved to the door that led directly to the back garden. She tugged it too and jerked forward, almost knocking her head against the frame when it stuck. She reeled back on the spot. Her scalp prickled.

"What's going on, Tonio baby?"

It was her mother's absence that was the strangest. Had Esther missed something? She wandered back to her mother's bedroom. A novel and a glass of water sat as usual on the nightstand. The slippers she usually wore around the house sat together in a pair under the bed.

A noise came from behind and Esther raced back to the living area. The door swung open and her mother entered with a tray. It held breakfast food: tea and toast and a dainty dish with blood-red jam. Esther had made that jam only a few days ago.

"What on earth," she muttered.

Her mother placed the tray on the small dining table in the corner.

"What's going on?" She looked behind her mother, out into the house as the door stood ajar. "Where's Robert?"

"You have never done as you've been told. Even as a tiny child, you never did as I asked. Always insisted on doing things your own way, Esther's way. All this time, you've never learned. Well, now you have no choice. Robert has tired of you and your wilful behaviour."

"I'm his wife."

"Well, you've never acted it."

"What's going on?"

"I'm doing as I am told. Mr Hogarth asked me to help him in the house and to serve you a simple breakfast. As I understand it, you are to remain here."

"Here? As in the quarters or the house? I don't understand."

Her mother gave her that disdainful look, the one Esther usually interpreted as scorn, but today she wondered if it was hatred, or at the very least, dislike. Mary turned away and shut the door behind her without another word.

Esther placed Antonio on the floor and yanked the doorknob again. It didn't open and she kicked it until her foot hurt.

"Urgh." she screeched and collapsed onto the sofa.

***

"Mr Goodwin." Esther yelled and banged against the glass pane.

The noise from the vibrating mower pierced the room so it seemed impossible that the gardener would hear her calls. She watched, waiting. She tapped the glass three more times in a half-hearted effort.

"He can't hear you," Tommy said from behind her.

"I know," she sighed. "But I'm going to stay here until he sees me. Or stops that blasted mower so he can."

The second day. She, Tommy, and Antonio remained in the servants' quarters.

The first day had felt like a treat. No work, nothing to do but play with Antonio and talk with her brother. Esther couldn't remember the last time she'd been so idle. It was so rare that she'd literally put her feet up on the coffee table and sat on the sofa.

Today, dark thoughts crept into her conscience. She had no idea what Robert was devising, and feelings of claustrophobia threatened to overwhelm her. Except she kept telling herself that it had to end. Robert would make his point, let them suffer their punishment, and then the door would fling open and the world would be set back to rights. The rights of the Hogarth household, in any event.

But patience was not one of her strengths and she slammed her body against the window in frustration. Her mother had already visited this morning. Punctual as clockwork. *Bet Robert loved that.* She'd delivered their meals—meals she had prepared. They'd reverted to their childhood with the simple minced beef dishes and over-stewed vegetables for dinner.

One thing her mother had become adept at was silence. Without a word passing her lips, she delivered those trays of food and left as abruptly as she arrived. Was she embarrassed? Esther hoped so. She should be because she'd betrayed her eldest daughter. And what of Tommy? She'd abandoned him, too.

How could her mother side with a monster? Someone so ghastly? Esther shivered when she thought of him.

Tommy made weak attempts at defending their mother. "She's only doing what she must. If she doesn't do as Mr Hogarth asks, we might all be turfed out."

What he said might be true, and Esther didn't argue with him. Deep down, she knew Tommy grappled with their mother's behaviour, the same way she did. He could reach his own conclusions. Esther knew a time would come where they'd both be forced to make a choice. For her, she knew what that choice would be. But she'd worry about that later.

The world outside went quiet. Esther stood on tiptoes to gain a better vantage. Mr Goodwin wheeled the silent mower across the back garden. Any minute he would pass the window.

With renewed vigour, she hit the pane repeatedly, her hand stinging. Mr Goodwin turned and gazed about him, even glancing up into the trees. Esther banged louder and didn't stop even though the glass might crack.

Did he see her? Yes? *No.* He kept walking. Esther slumped to the floor, her dress sat around her like a puddle. Tommy coaxed her up off the floor even though she didn't want to cooperate.

***

"I'm going to kill him." Luca roared and slammed the front door shut.

He stomped into the dining room and hissed profanities.

"Holy shit, mate," said Trevor. "Whoever you're after better look out. With that temper, you're dangerous." He chuckled in between mouthfuls of dinner.

Luca's nostrils flared and his face was mottle-red. Trevor stopped laughing and put down his fork.

"Is this about your girl?"

Luca braced his hands on the back of the chair and gripped so hard his knuckles turned white. He peered at Trevor.

"Luca. What is it?" asked Mrs Devitt as she flounced into the room, a stray of curly red hair loose around her face.

Maximillian followed behind.

"I've been back to Esther's place. I spoke with the gardener. It seems as if that bastard of a husband is playing some sort of sick game. He's locked the doors and as much as he can make out, Esther seems to be inside. It's been two days," said Luca. "He's treating her like a common dog. Her and the baby. It must be against the law. Trevor, is it against the law to keep someone against their will in Australia?"

"Mate, how would I know? But I'm guessing it would be. Against civil liberties and all that, at least."

"Yes." Luca held his fist in the air.

Mrs Devitt went to the sideboard again. The alcohol had come out many times in his honour. Tonight, she took out the near-empty bottle and poured them all a nip.

"Sit down, Luca. Let's talk about this." She ushered him into the nearest chair and Maximillian sat down alongside, rubbing his back.

Luca shrugged him off. "And turn off that stupid radio." He hung his head in his hands. "I have to get her out."

"Where are her quarters?" Maximillian asked.

"The servants' quarters out the back of the cottage. Since her, um, marriage." He hesitated. The word felt wrong. "She moved upstairs and into the proper house, if you like. Was still a servant, if you ask me, but anyway, when she was the employed housekeeper, she and her family stayed in separate quarters at the rear where the servants once lived when it was normal for people to have staff." Luca snorted.

"The gardener told you all this?" Mrs Devitt fingered her empty shot glass.

"No, Esther told me that. The gardener told me about the locked door. I needed to know Esther was safe. I would have staked out the house every day or even forced my way in, but he stopped me. The poor bloke insisted I not hang around. He was petrified to find me skulking around the place. Worried, too, about the boss finding out. He's risking a lot... I saw her."

His voice softened. He wished he'd known yesterday, at that first visit, that she was being detained. He would have stayed, broken that window, pulled her out. He would not stuff up this time. He wouldn't get this wrong and let someone else be hurt, or worse, die. And not only because he loved her. This was so much bigger than that. He needed to do this, needed to succeed because it would prove he was worthwhile, that he was a good person, that he could protect people.

"Everyone at that house is frightened. What goes on behind those closed doors?" Luca shook his head and everyone joined in, wondering the worst.

"Let's call the police. I know the local sergeant for this area," said Mrs Devitt.

"Yeah, I do too," added Trevor, "but not for the right reasons."

Luca stared him down. "This is not amusing, Trevor."

"Sorry, mate. Yes, it's a good idea. Let's telephone the coppers."

Luca slammed his flat palm on the table making them all jump.

"No. We can't. Have you not been listening?" Was he the only one taking this seriously? This man could kill her. Esther was frail. With her thin wrists and slight frame, she was no match for Hogarth's strength. She'd withered away. Where was the vibrant, vivacious woman he'd met on Bruny Island? Back then, he was the frail one.

His friends had to understand the risks.

"Esther has told me of threats. *That man*," he snarled the words, "will hurt her. And the baby."

Everyone went quiet.

Mrs Devitt rose. "We need more drink. When I return, we'll hatch a plan. Luca, we will help Esther and Antonio. We will save them."

Chapter Thirty-One

Tommy made two cups of strong, sweet tea that went cold. An uneaten sandwich sat on a plate next to the mugs of tea, its edges curling. He tried to entice her to eat with a square of her favourite chocolate. She didn't even nibble it. Antonio gripped her skirt, standing on his toes, and whined. Someone drew the curtains to cool the room from the heat of the day. Life outside the cottage continued as normal and Esther sat, motionless, on the sofa.

A door opened. It would be Mother. She didn't have anything to say to her. Silence penetrated the room. The hairs on her arms stood on end.

Robert stood in the doorframe.

Her body tensed but she didn't move, didn't acknowledge his presence. Usually, she'd jump to his attention. Esther heard Tommy's breathing become laboured, could feel the heat of his gaze.

Robert loomed over her, his ridiculous oily moustache making her stomach churn. She wanted to reach up and rip it off his smug face.

"Esther?"

"Mm?"

"Get up. We're going out."

"Out?"

"Yes." He nudged her foot with the toe of his leather shoe. "I said get up, woman."

Tommy came to her side and placed his hand on her arm. He whispered in her ear and her mind clicked into gear. She smoothed down her hair and wiped her palms down her skirt. She rose and stumbled, having sat for too long.

"Yes, Robert?"

"Come along, we're going for a drive."

"A drive?" Words of protest formed on her tongue. Feisty Esther was back. The last two days had been tough, but the fog that had been blanketing her was lifting. If Robert was going to hurt her, perhaps he could do it now and be done with it? She chanced a look at Tommy. Fear was etched across his face, his pupils dilated in saucer eyes. He shook his head, so slightly it was almost imperceptible.

She mightn't want to listen to Robert, but she paid heed to Tommy. The boy was frightened, and she didn't want him to bear witness to any more of Robert's violence.

Head down, she took a step forward. Robert grasped her elbow and steered her towards the door.

***

Robert wore his black driving beret and reflector sunglasses, like a pilot might wear in a jet plane. They looked ridiculous. In the confined space of the car, Esther smelled spirits. It explained his erratic driving and heavy foot on the accelerator. Fear gripped her insides like her hands gripped the car seat. Esther kept her face to the window.

He drove them out of town, towards Mount Wellington. The sun was hidden amongst clouds that were pink and purple. The sky seemed so beautiful to her in that moment, more stunning than usual. She paid it special attention—just in case.

The world darkened as they climbed higher. Robert took the curves too fast on the narrow road as they edged towards the summit. It usually took a leisurely half hour on a nice Sunday drive to reach the peak. Esther guessed they'd done it in less than fifteen minutes. The longest fifteen minutes of her life.

He screeched to a halt, making pebbles and gravel scatter and the tyres spin. They were at the lookout at the highest point of the mountain.

Robert turned off the ignition and reclined in the seat. Esther clung to the door handle, her eyes darting left and right and frantically planning her escape. Still thinking, he snaked his arm around the back of her neck and pulled her across the small space. Esther pulled back and attempted to wriggle out of his grip. He yanked her again, harder. She wrestled with the button until the door released and sprung open. Jerking away from his hand, she jumped out and slammed the door shut. Robert stared back for a second before he scooted across the seat and out of his side of the car. He raced around to the rear of the vehicle. Esther bolted to the front. He caught her at the bonnet in a bruising grip. Her slight frame slammed against the car. She gazed up at him, panting. His eyes were wild, darting in his head, and spittle formed at the corners of his mouth.

His hand moved to her throat. No, not again—her bruises had hardly healed from last time. The frame of the car dug into her back. Goose pimples erupted over her skin as a gentle breeze blew. It was usually about eight degrees colder on the mountain. To Esther, it felt as if a freeze washed over her.

Robert stroked her bare arms, feeling the bumps. His hand moved downwards over her stomach and to the hem of her dress. He inched his fingers inside until he reached her bare thighs.

"No, Robert. Let *go*." Esther bucked in protest.

He chuckled, leaning down into her ear. He'd love how frightened she was. How powerless.

"You are my wife and you will do as you are told." His fingers crept towards her underwear. Repulsion swept through her.

He will not do this to me again. The world grew darker yet and shadows crept behind the trees. That darkness seeped into her pores, possessed her, gave her strength and the will to do what she had to.

She swung her arm sideways and it connected with his body. With one claw-like grip, she grasped him between his legs and squeezed. He yelped—from shock or pain, she wasn't sure. His testicles fitted nicely into her palm. The saggy skin squished and it was so disgusting she wanted to drop them. She'd never touched this part of him before, and she sure didn't want to now. Esther crushed harder, thinking of his belittling comments, of the slaps to her face, his cruelty to Tommy, and the choking, so that her fingers held so tight her hand spasmed. The fabric of his trousers made it difficult to hold on, but until he crippled, she wouldn't let go.

Robert stiffened and doubled over. "You bitch," he uttered before stumbling back. He was almost out of her reach. With one last almighty tug, she yanked those balls. The effect was immediate. She let go and he bent over, catching his breath and heaving.

This was her chance. She ran.

In the few short moments they'd been fighting, stars had appeared in the sky and the world wore a deep mahogany rinse. It didn't matter what time it was or how dark the evening became, she had to get away and fast. Stepping over the stone and bypassing the rocks, she sprinted as fast as she could. The trail was not obvious to her. The ledge loomed near; she'd hide before her legs gave way. Esther jumped the few short feet and crouched. Her chest ached from the cold and she struggled to breathe. She had to be quiet, otherwise Robert would hear her.

The wind picked up and howled around her. The noise rumbled in her ears so that was all she could hear. Was that a crunch of gravel to her right? Esther ducked, her head between her knees. With the fading light, he might not spot her.

Esther, you should have run farther away.

Too late now. Yes, it was steps. It had to be him. If he found her, he'd hurt her so badly she might as well be dead. She'd squeezed his private parts. He would never forgive her.

Her leg cramped and the urge to move it was irresistible. A tingling leg would render her paralysed and that was dangerous. She inched one foot forward and it hit the edge. She was so close. The crevice was narrower than she thought. Surely this didn't give way to the rocky cliffs below?

Robert must have recovered. Did men recuperate after such a physical blow so quickly? Where was he? Esther turned. Behind her? She peeked up through her lashes and in between the last rays of sun she saw him. Not his silhouette or shadow. *Him.* His eyes glowed in the dying day. He saw her.

His face crumpled into rage, his hand shook in its balled fist and then he lunged. Robert tumbled and landed on the short ledge with her. Esther whipped her legs back in and held them close to her chest. Cigarette smoke and a pungent scent of body odour rose off him.

On his hand and knees, he grappled to secure his balance and rose for his final strike. Esther leaned back, hoping the increased distance could protect her. He stepped forward and his leg wobbled. His foot struck a rock in his path. His body swayed and he toppled. Then he was gone.

Esther listened. Nothing.

Minutes passed. Silence. Oh God, what was she going to do? What had he done? What had she done?

Gut instinct propelled her up and she climbed over the ledge. Then she ran back the way she came, guided only by the moonbeams that cast a silvery glow over the earth. She hadn't gone far at all. No wonder he'd found her so easily. But this meant the car was close.

Esther yanked open the driver's door and searched for the keys in the ignition. Empty. She checked the seat, the floor, and even her side—nothing.

"Damn it." she screamed as she slammed the door shut. She leaned against the car and took in great gulps of air. She needed to calm down. Was Robert dead? Had he fallen to the earth? The summit was almost four thousand feet high. Surely he couldn't have rolled to the bottom? He'd be dead if he had. It was all her fault. If she hadn't run, he wouldn't have chased her and fallen.

Esther waited for the dread to sink in. It arrived, but not in the measure she expected. It was not all-consuming. And it wasn't for Robert; it was for herself and the ramifications, the punishments, the shame. A blossom of hope grew. *Oh my God,* she was going to hell for such thoughts. But could she be free? Or would he be an invalid and she'd be forever caring for a disabled husband? What she did know, though, was that if he wasn't dead, and he found her, she'd be dead anyway. *Oh God, Esther, stop thinking.*

There was only one option—she had to get out of here. If he was alive, she couldn't risk it. Now the sky was black. She returned to the car and searched it again. She popped the boot, hopeful that Robert was as organised as she thought. *Bingo.* A torch. She pressed the switch and the path illuminated in front of her. Without looking back, Esther headed towards the road and ran.

***

Esther dragged her feet the last few steps to the front door and collapsed. Defeated, but home, she slumped where she lay and banged on the door. Once. Twice. Silence.

What time was it? She didn't know how long the walk from the tip to the base of Mount Wellington might take, but the moon still shone high in the sky behind it. In the shadowed light, it appeared luminous and threatening. The mountain sat in its beautiful glory, staring down at her now she'd escaped its clutches. There was no hint of the pink hues of dawn on the horizon yet.

Her arms and legs stung, the barbs deep. She shifted to place her back against the door for support and stared in awe at the peak. How did she ever find her way home? She had run until exhaustion slowed her pace, shutting her mouth against the swarms of bugs that seemed to chase her, pushing branches and bushes out of her way and stepping over logs and rocks and dry twigs on an unmarked path, always hoping that down meant safety.

Had she made it or was her mind playing tricks? Was she home? Was she safe? Was Robert waiting for her, ready to pounce and kill her this time? Something moved to her right and Esther jumped, no scream left in her. The cat. It came up to her and Esther cuddled it close, enjoying its warmth and gentle purr. Lack of sleep made her delirious and so tired. She'd simply rest for a minute.

Chapter Thirty-Two

"Esther? It *is* you. Esther, wake up."

She cracked one eye open at the gentle voice in her ear. Subtle dawn light penetrated her vision; even that muted softness made her squint. And then she felt the cold, icy fingertips of the morning grip her. Yes, it was cold, but her legs and arms shook as if something possessed her. The tremoring jerked her awake, fast.

Where was she?

"Esther. What's happened to you? Oh no."

Mr Goodwin? He stood fussing over her, his large hand on her shoulder, its warmth breaching the cotton of her dress.

"Goodness, you're freezing. Can you walk? Let's get you around the back."

The cat, who'd been curled on her lap, ran off. Esther gave in to Jeffrey's persistent requests. Assisted by his hands under her armpits, she rose, and wobbled. Each step felt like her bones were cracking back into place. Pressure on her open cuts and sores made them weep.

The short trip around the house seemed like a marathon. With each step she winced, but they made it. At the door, Mr Goodwin shouted.

"Tommy." He screamed so loudly she wanted to cover her ears.

The door opened and Tommy flung himself at her and held her tight. "Esther. I've been so worried."

"Tommy?"

"Mr Goodwin, why is she shivering like that?"

"I'm not sure, lad, but let's get her inside and warmed up. Put the kettle on, she'll need a hot drink. I think she's been out in the night air too long."

"Antonio?" she whispered as they lowered her to the couch.

"He's in the other room, I'll get him." Tommy raced away.

Mr Goodwin returned with a pile of blankets and covered her twofold. Esther savoured the immediate heat and snuggled in.

Antonio padded into the room on his still unsteady feet and rushed towards her. Tommy placed him in her lap. She inhaled his scent and wrapped her arms around him. Clarity returned.

Antonio. Her Antonio. Tears rolled down her cheeks. He was safe. He explored her face and arms and dug his little fingers into each crevice and cut. "Oh, that hurts."

"Esther, you need to have some tea." Jeffrey Goodwin, her saviour, acted like a father-figure. He removed Antonio and placed him onto the floor. The baby howled his protest. "Antonio, your mother needs to have her tea now so she can stop quivering." He spoke with authority, but still with a gentleness to his voice, and Antonio listened.

Jeffrey stood over her, ensuring she did as she was told. It was different to Robert, though. It wasn't forced or mean—it was out of concern. Esther complied without question and sipped. The warmth went straight to her core and she sipped again.

"That's wonderful, Esther. Keep drinking and I'll make you another. I understand with hypothermia it is important to get your body temperature up as soon as possible." He turned to Tommy then. "Do we have a first aid kit?"

He shrugged.

"Mr Goodwin, has Robert returned?"

"I haven't seen him this morning, Mrs." This almost made the tea come back up her throat.

"Can I make a suggestion?" Jeffrey spoke with that same authority he'd directed at Antonio and they both turned towards him. "May I run and fetch Luca?"

Esther's mouthed dropped open. "You know about him?"

"He visited here a few days ago. I found him in the back garden. I thought he was a peeping Tom. He was staring into the window all creepy-like. But he explained who he was and that he was worried about you. I sent him away at the time, frightened that we'd both be caught and there'd be hell to pay. Anyway, he came back the next day for news and we agreed I'd keep him updated. He's been distraught."

Little butterflies released in Esther's chest, making it flutter and go warm. Joy was still possible.

"What is it, man, what's happened?" Luca hadn't moved from the doorway when he'd opened it to Jeffrey. His knuckle still gripped the doorknob and his housemates gathered in a group behind him.

Mr Goodwin was panting from the rush. Sweat droplets beaded on his brow.

"Luca. Let the man come in and catch his breath." Mrs Devitt pushed Luca aside and showed Jeffrey to the living area. Max and Trevor followed suit.

Luca trailed behind, his face ashen. Why would the gardener rush to his home? They'd been so careful to meet incognito and in secluded places, and now he turned up here? This was all shades of bad.

"Luca, it's Esther."

"Go on," he urged.

"As you know, she's been in the quarters these last couple of days," he said. "Then yesterday, apparently, Robert turned up. I wasn't there, I was at the hardware store. Young Tommy said he insisted she go with him for a drive."

"Where is Esther now?" Luca said urgently.

"I assumed she returned at some later hour. But then," the room fell silent, "this morning, I went out to collect the milk bottles and she was there, on the front stoop."

That wasn't the climax for Luca. "What happened next?"

"She was cold and hurt. I don't know the full story yet, because I rushed over here, hoping you'd help. But she's returned home, alone, without Robert."

Once Luca's brain caught up, he moved quickly. "Okay, yes I come, I help. Let's go."

Jeffrey stood. "Um, Mrs Devitt, is it?"

"Yes, love. I'm the boardinghouse mistress."

"Do you have a first aid kit?"

"Yes, yes, I do. I'll fetch it. I'll come too, Luca. You'll need me. I have quite adequate nursing skills."

Luca didn't hear, didn't care. They could all come. He needed to get to Esther.

The bustle of activity woke Esther. She'd fallen asleep on the couch, the blankets strewn around her. Tommy sat next to her, rigid but alert.

She sat up.

"She's stopped shivering and had at least two more hot cups of tea. I haven't left her side," Tommy announced proudly to the group.

"Well done, Tommy," Luca said as he marched over to Esther. "Oh my God. Did he do this to you?"

Luca.

Seeing him with his creased forehead and the concern in his eyes, Esther crumbled. She hadn't cried since Robert had fallen. It had been about survival and finding her way home. The moral of her life, it seemed. But now, with all these caring faces surrounding her, she cried loud and ugly sobs.

She fell into Luca's embrace and everyone stood back.

"It will be okay, Esther. You're safe now. I will not let this happen again. I should have forced you to come with me last time. Not accepted your excuses."

Something cracked in Esther and she raised her head. Her tears dried in an instant.

"Excuses, Luca? They were valid reasons to keep me and Antonio safe. Not excuses."

"But that didn't work, did it? Look at you."

It could have been her mother talking.

"You will come with me now. I will protect you, look after you, provide for you."

She sat back farther, creating space between them as if a chasm had opened up. "Provide for me, Luca? How will you do that? You have no money, no prospects, and a job building blocks. You live in a boardinghouse."

"Oh, ah, well…" Mrs Devitt started but stopped.

"What do you mean? It's a good, solid job. The pay is okay," Luca said, his voice raising.

"Where will we live? How will we pay the rent? How will we survive?"

"We will sort it out," Luca responded, but his voice quavered.

"No, I must sort this problem out. How can I simply walk out of here? Away from my husband and this house? I am married with no independent means."

Luca interrupted. "He hurts you."

"I know that, Luca."

Jeffrey stepped forward. "There's no need to be making plans right this minute. You need to get cleaned up, Esther. Mrs Devitt has brought supplies to treat those cuts and bruises. Shall we attend to that first and then you can tell us what happened?"

Esther nodded. "Thank you. While I do that, can you please check if Mr Hogarth has returned?"

"Esther," Mrs Devitt said. "Let me help you. Let's go to your room and I can wash away the grime and see what needs fixing."

Esther agreed. She felt Luca's eyes on her back as she walked away with Mrs Devitt. Esther couldn't ignore his crestfallen face, his downcast eyes, but what? Tired, hurt, angry, and uncertain, she didn't know what to make of anything right now. A funny frisson of something passed through her chest, but she didn't have the ability to comfort her beloved right now or offer him the reassurance he wanted. And where was Robert? It seemed she had more challenges ahead of her.

***

A knock landed on the back door. Tommy raced to the curtain to peek out.

"Shit. It's the police. What do we do?" He turned to Jeffrey and Luca, as Esther remained in the bedroom.

The men searched each other's faces. "Answer it, of course, we can't pretend we aren't here," Jeffrey said.

"Are you sure?" asked Luca. "What do they want?"

Tommy shrugged and opened the door.

"Is Mrs Esther Hogarth here, please?"

Tommy nodded and ushered them inside. Two burly policemen filled up the small space. The officers regarded Jeffrey and Luca.

Jeffrey extended his hand and introduced himself. "I'm the gardener."

"Thank you. We might need to speak to you, don't go anywhere."

"What about?"

Before they answered, Esther entered the room. She wore a clean blouse and full skirt, her hair neatly tied back and her face free of grime. The only sign of her adventure last night was her pale complexion and her tentative steps. Mrs Devitt trailed behind her.

"Mrs Hogarth?

She nodded. What did they want? Her heart beat so fast she was sure it was going to explode out of her chest.

"Come and have a seat. We have some distressing news."

Esther couldn't look at anyone in the room. Didn't dare for the fear of what she might read in their faces. She hadn't revealed what happened last night to anyone, only a few tidbits to Mrs Devitt, who hadn't stop talking and asking questions the entire time she bathed her wounds. It had distracted Esther, and for that she was grateful.

"When was the last time you saw your husband?"

Esther paused. She had to think quick.

"Um, it was yesterday afternoon. Gosh, it was, oh, Tommy, what time was it when Robert spoke to me here yesterday? Late afternoon?"

Poor Tommy was stricken. She nodded to encourage him to go on.

"It was about four o'clock, I think."

"Yes, that sounds about right. I was here with my brother and son, and he came in about four o'clock," Esther said, trying to remain calm.

"What did he want?"

"What did he want?" she repeated.

The officers nodded.

"Well, um, he asked after us. How Antonio was and what we'd been doing."

"And what had you been doing?"

"I'd spent a few hours playing with my son, and Tommy played with us, too."

Ah, Esther, don't implicate Tommy.

"But then Tommy went out and ran an errand for me." Out of the corner of her eye, she saw Tommy's head shoot up, but she didn't look at him. She'd placed him in a spot of bother and didn't mean to.

"Did Mr Hogarth say he was going anywhere?"

"Not that I can recall. But he often goes out without reporting to me first. You understand, as my husband and man of the house, he isn't responsible to me." Was that overkill? She didn't know.

"Okay. Well, I'm sorry to report, Mrs Hogarth, but your husband was found dead this morning. His body was located near the base of Mount Wellington. His car was parked at the top at the summit. We are sorry to inform you."

"What? What did you say?" Her reaction was genuine. Did she hear correctly? Robert was dead? Oh no, they were here for her.

They graciously repeated the version of events and added, "We are treating it as suspicious."

"*Suspicious*?" Her body overheated.

"Yes. Can we ask, was he upset about anything?"

She tried to ascertain any meaning behind the question, but neither of their faces provided any clues.

"He has been quite upset since he lost the council election. That was a bad moment for him, and he didn't recover. I would have called it grumpy, angry, and him not being himself."

The police officers nodded and took notes. This encouraged her. Yes, that all sounded plausible, but of course, it was also true.

"Well, we cannot be certain yet, we will have to have a formal interview with you and your staff, but it appears as if it might have been a suicide."

Her hand flew to her mouth. "No."

One officer held up his hand. "As we said, we are still investigating. But we know he is a well-respected citizen, on many boards, runs a successful law practice, and as of yet, with our brief investigation, we cannot uncover anyone who would have a motive to hurt him. Even though we are keeping all possibilities open."

"Did you find a note?" Mr Goodwin asked.

"No, we didn't, but we are still searching his vehicle and the surrounds."

"Oh, deary, deary, how dreadful," Mrs Devitt exclaimed. She'd done well to keep her peace thus far.

"Well, Mrs Hogarth, it's good that you have family and friends around you at this distressing time. We will be back in touch for a formal interview, and we'll keep investigating and keep you appraised of matters as they arise. Here are our details. Call if you remember anything else that might be useful."

The officers exited, but the words left Esther's mouth in a horrified whisper the moment the door clicked shut. "Oh my God, what have I done?" She placed her head in her hands and covered her face.

"We don't know, dear, but perhaps you'll tell us now? I'll put the kettle on," said Mrs Devitt.

With hot tea in her hands, Antonio at her feet, Luca to her side, and Mrs Devitt, Jeffrey, and Tommy listening in, Esther recalled the events of the night before.

Chapter Thirty-Three

LOCAL HERO FOUND DEAD

Robert Hogarth, local lawyer, president of the South Hobart Progress Association, and hopeful one-time politician, is dead. His body was discovered by some early morning bushwalkers at the base of Mt. Wellington. Mystery surrounds the circumstances of his demise, but investigating police have revealed that he seems to have taken his own life in a tragic plunge from the summit.

"It was a distressing sight," said bushwalker Joanne Weatherby.

"His limbs were sitting at odd angles and his head was crushed. I'm sure some of his brain was spilling out," added John Weatherby. "We enjoy a brisk walk to the top of the mountain each weekend and this is the first time we've ever experienced anything like this. Such a shock."

The police reported the couple were helpful in their investigations.

But the question begs why would anyone, and more particularly a successful member of our community, choose to end their life by jumping over the rocky terrain of our most famous peak? Investigators say Hogarth's recent failure at gaining a seat in the council election is being blamed as the cause. It was apparently an ambition he'd held close to his heart for many years, and the blow of defeat was too much. He was always a positive influence in the local community, the one who found solutions to the difficult problems, raised money when it wasn't thought possible, convinced people to allow progress, and was a role model, so why would he do such a thing?

It appeared as if Robert had it all. In addition to his business success, he recently found love and married his housekeeper, the widowed Esther Anderson. He had a clean house and an immediate little family and, we are sure, plans to expand it.

Family and staff members at his home on Elboden Street refused to comment. Mr Hogarth had a sizable estate, which will now pass to his wife and son.

Everyone was silent. Trevor lowered the newspaper he'd held whilst reading out loud to the assembled group.

Max was the first to speak. "What does that mean?"

"Well," said Mrs Devitt. "The paper says Esther will own this house now that her husband is dead."

"This place?" Max's eyes widened as he looked around him. They sat in the parlour with its extravagant furnishings and plush carpet. "Hey ho. You're rich." he exclaimed. Everyone else remained silent.

Even Mrs Devitt had lost her tongue.

"I think it's advisable, Esther, to go see his partner at the law firm and get some advice. See if this is true," offered Trevor.

Esther liked Trevor. He was an adorable Aussie larrikin: bronzed, tall, and good-looking with wavy blond locks and a heart of gold. A kind soul. He'd looked after Luca in the days following the incident. Amongst his other qualities, he was sensible.

She nodded at his suggestion. "Yes, that's a good idea, thanks, Trevor. I will go there today and sort this out as quickly as possible."

The story in the paper was the first public recognition of Robert's death. Life for Esther continued in the absence of Robert. Remaining in the house was strange, but where else was she to go? Luca and his friends visited, bringing casseroles and freshly laundered clothes. Tommy had immediately perked up; he had no sense of the future and what they would do, but with the innocence of youth, he didn't care. In his view, Robert was dead so anything else that happened, quite frankly, didn't matter. He was returning to his normal boyish self.

Esther felt discombobulated. A heavy burden lifted, only to be replaced with frantic worry and uncertainty. She knew she could cope after everything life had dished up, she'd had lots of practice, but she'd prefer to know what she was dealing with. On a practical level, there'd been money left in the kitty—quite a lot—and she'd pocketed that before her mother could. Temporarily, they were okay. They had accommodation and money, but then what?

Next step was to sort out Robert's affairs. She needed answers, and perhaps Robert's business partner could give them to her. If she had nothing, she'd have to start searching for work and accommodation pronto.

She had a plan to work towards, at least.

Luca was quiet. She knew he was unclear of his role in this strange new world. In the turmoil, she hadn't had a chance to tell him how comforted she was every day by his presence. Finally, he was back in her life and it was wonderful—the small touches to her back, his hesitant smile, sage advice, that accent. She soaked it all up. One thing she couldn't talk about yet was their future. At times she wasn't even sure they actually had one.

Thank goodness Mother had kept herself scarce. She was a smart woman and knew that she wasn't a popular person. She lingered in the background, never out of sight, but not uttering a word.

What on earth would she do with her mother?

***

Esther would never tire of walking the streets of Hobart. Her meeting with the lawyer Henry Jamieson had concluded hours ago. The last thing she wanted was to rush home and share the news. She needed to ruminate and decide what it meant.

Her feet ached now in her old, threadbare shoes. Perhaps she could finally buy new shoes? And yet, she kept wandering. The people bustling past provided strange comfort. She passed Mr Pullman's butcher shop where she spied him packaging some meat for a customer. Then the grocer and baker. The waft of freshly baked bread was long gone, and in its place a sterile cleaning smell drifted towards her as the baker mopped his floor after the day's trade. Esther smiled. She liked her local shops and had become friends with these people. Would she call it home? No. She had no idea what place she could ever call home again.

Her thoughts became clearer after hours of wandering, and she knew what she had to do.

Stars were appearing in the quickly darkening sky as she walked towards *Norfolk*. Out of habit, she walked around the back. No need to now, of course, but it still felt wrong to waltz in the front entry.

Luca sat at the outdoor setting, staring at the night sky. Esther rushed at him and dropped to her knees at his feet.

He leaned down and kissed her cheek. Sweet Italian streamed from his mouth.

"Luca, will you continue to teach me Italian, and Antonio, too? Then we can all speak together. We can be one of those multicultural families. That way you can stay connected to Italy and we can enjoy the language and culture of your homeland, and all that food and history," Esther exclaimed. "Plus, when you start ranting, I'll be able to understand you."

Luca didn't respond. His stare was intense, and she had a desperate urge to explain, to comfort him, to make everything all right.

"I know I disappointed you by not running away the moment we could be together. But I'm not that rash, naïve young woman anymore. I'm no longer the woman you met on the Cape. I was young and innocent back then. I'm different now, Luca."

He nodded and let her continue.

"What I've been through, it changes you, makes you grow up too fast, and it's taken away my vulnerability, my innocence. Life has stripped me of those things. But you know what, Luca? I've survived. I know I can survive and look after myself. I need to know that I can always do that. Especially with Antonio. I've been the only parent he's had. I need to continue to survive for *him*. I can't simply rely on someone else. I refuse to rely on someone, because when it all goes wrong... well, look where that got me. It makes everything so much harder. Not now. I'm strong and capable and can care for myself."

"Si, I understand. I must get used to this new Esther."

"But it doesn't mean I don't want your love. Can you love this new me?"

"Si." He kissed her on the lips. It was tender and sweet and the best kiss she'd ever experienced.

"I've dreamed of this day since the first moment I met you," said Luca. "That crazy day when I didn't know where I was, hurt and scared, and then a vision came to me. She had blonde hair and skin like porcelain, and when she looked at me, it made me melt."

Esther's eyes welled with tears. So many tears she'd shed. She brushed them aside with her fingertips. "And me, too. My entire world changed the day you shipwrecked on Bruny Island. This dark, hairy man who spoke a strange language." She raked her fingers through his hair. "I'd never seen anyone like you before. So different, so knowledgeable, and a man who knew how to cook."

They chuckled together.

Luca fingered the tips of her hair and trailed his hands along her chin and jaw, cupping her face.

"Luca, I saw the lawyer today. There's some paperwork to complete, but the house is mine. The property inside the house is mine. Robert left a will, but it wasn't updated since we married. Henry advised that the marriage made me Robert's next of kin and I'm entitled to the estate. He doesn't have any other family and... well, it's all mine."

"You own all this, yourself?"

"Um, yes."

"Wow."

"Yes, it *is* wow, isn't it?" said Esther. "I've been thinking about this all afternoon. We can be together now, Luca. I was worried about how we were going to manage. But I don't need to worry about that now."

"What? You want me to move in here?"

"No." She shook her head so her hair swayed from side to side. "I don't want to live here. I love you and want to be with you. I've always loved you and have wanted for us to be together as a family—Antonio needs his father—but we haven't been able to do that before. Let's plan our future, together. Let's start afresh, somewhere new. Let's get our vineyard, live your dream, and live the life we should be living."

Luca pulled her to her feet and hugged her tight. She heard his intake of breath and felt his heaving chest. He sobbed and she loved him for it. These expressive Italian men. She hoped that Antonio would grow to be exactly like his father.

After they drew apart, Luca pulled a small slip of paper from his pocket. It was crumpled and tatty at the edges and he rubbed his index finger across the words she saw scribbled there. Esther thought it was his treasured photograph.

"Alessandro gave me this address. Relatives he has in Tamar Valley. It is up north, near a place called Launceston. Good wine region in Tasmania. A small community of Italian people live there. This family can help us find our own vineyard. Finally, we can be together as a family. I've been holding on to this address until I could realise my dream. Now I can be what I've wanted to be since I met you and Antonio. I can be his father and your husband. It might be tough for a while, but we are both skilled at working through the tough times, aren't we?" He thumped his balled fist against his chest. "I know that I will do everything in my power to make it work, allow us to succeed. I will give you everything: a comfortable life, beautiful things, nice clothes, after what you've experienced. I can't bear to contemplate what you've suffered. That man..." Luca's jaw clenched. "I get so angry thinking about him hurting you and Tommy. Of what he might have done to Antonio if given the opportunity. And he would have, too."

"Luca, this is our fresh start, our new beginning. Let's not talk of him ever again. He's the past, you are my future. We've both endured awful times, but we're here, together."

Their tears mingled as they held their faces close. They were happy tears. Perhaps, finally she could feel safe. And loved. It was almost too much to hope for.

Luca leaned in close, his lips close to her mouth. Esther felt his breath against her face. His soft lips touched hers and memories invaded, carried her to another place and time. *Happy* times. His kiss, his touch, were so familiar to her, it felt like coming home. Her heart swelled to double its size so that it filled the void in her chest, that empty hole that she worried would always engulf her. This was what she'd been waiting for, this was what she lived for. Him. Always.

Luca's hand cradled her neck. With closed eyes, she drew him firmly against her. She kissed him ferociously and wanted it to never end, but simultaneously couldn't wait for their life together to start.

***

Esther...

No pleasantries, Esther noticed immediately. Okay, she understood how this letter would proceed. Best brace herself.

She had deliberated long and hard about writing to her sister, but loyalty and their sibling history had once again won. Esther had always done the right thing, and it was proper, if not pleasant, to write to her only sister. She still hoped they could forge some sort of relationship into the future. She hadn't felt compelled to be honest about her whereabouts though, except that she was somewhere in Tasmania. But it seemed Margaret knew that already. Esther read on.

Scandal.

That's what you've left behind. Shame. Salacious gossip and scandal. You are all that people are talking about. I hope you are pleased with yourself.

As the only respectable member of the family remaining, I have borne the brunt of your actions. People whisper and turn their backs on me. I am not receiving as many invitations and Arthur's business is suffering.

It's all your fault, Esther.

She could hear her sister screeching those words.

How can I go on? So dramatic. *I pray every passing day that another scandal arises quickly to overshadow what you've done and people will forget about you and your appalling behaviour. You always did think you could do as you liked.*

Thanks, Margaret, just as Mother would say.

People won't forget that before poor Robert's body was even cold in the ground, you sold his house and ran off with your foreign lover. Let me assure you that you won't be welcome back here anytime soon. Or forgiven. I cannot even write about your dalliance without enormous shame coming over me and my cheeks flaming red hot. How could you not only run away like a common vagabond, but do so with a wog?

Why leave Mother behind? It's all well and good to go and buy her a place to live (rather extravagant, I say, flashing your money around like that), but she's all alone there. You took Tommy, surely you could have taken Mother with you, also? You know I am too busy to spend much time with her. That's your job, it's always been your job. I don't have time with my charity commitments, social engagements, and the proper running of this house. I am planning another gala ball to restore my tarnished position, all thanks to you. A good party can fix everything.

Perhaps Mother can join you where you are? Then there's one less thing for me to worry about.

Esther hardly thought it sounded like she was worrying about their mother at all.

However, I'm assuming because you've run away like a child that her joining you isn't an option. When she ages and cannot care for herself, Esther, I'm telling you now, she cannot live with me. It will be out of the question.

What a mess you've caused.

Oh, and by the way, I'm with child. A dastardly inconvenience, I must say. However, I will enjoy purchasing an entire new wardrobe to accommodate my ghastly growing middle.

Yours, M

With a heavy heart, Esther realised she'd most likely never meet her niece or nephew. Or ever return to Hobart. See her mother or sister again.

Perhaps that was for the best.

Chapter Thirty-Four

September 1955

Esther stretched out her legs on the picnic blanket before they started to cramp. She cradled her expanding bump and repositioned herself. It was awkward sitting on the ground now, at over six months pregnant.

Antonio chased a kite held by Luca, who ran across the green pasture. Despite being almost three years old, he ran unsteadily on his feet, not helped by the slight incline in the yard. The lawn gently sloped down and away, towards a pond.

For the briefest of moments, it felt like she was back on Bruny Island, with the sweet scent of country air and the breeze blowing. The only thing she couldn't hear was the crash of waves against the cliff face and, of course, there wasn't any salt in the air.

But she wasn't on Bruny Island, and was indeed miles from the ocean. Instead, the beautiful Tamar River flowed nearby, with its wide and murky expanse of water.

As she sat on the grass outside their modest farmhouse in Windermere, green rolling hills surrounded her and stretched up to meet the expanse of the light blue sky scattered with pillow clouds. It had been endless work, but they'd developed a self-supporting farm and their precious vineyard. To her left, safely behind the wire fence, was their small herd of dairy cows. She could hear the clack of axe against timber as Tommy chopped firewood in the shed, and the chickens clucking in their henhouse, hopefully laying fresh eggs. Nearer the house was the vegetable patch that provided more than enough for their nightly meals. Birds circled above their head and ducks roamed free near the pond.

Esther was in charge of the daily operations of the farm, while Luca had sought work outside of the farm to help them prosper. He did this with a heavy heart, but came alive each afternoon upon his return.

Tommy was learning a trade in the local area, trailing along with Luca most days. He worked tirelessly on the farm, too. Esther knew their days together were limited. She detected his enthusiasm to go out into the world and forge a life for himself. Until then, she enjoyed his company and appreciated his help. Antonio adored his uncle.

Antonio giggled. He hadn't yet rid himself of the boyish chuckle that he released at any given moment. How she loved that sound. He was a joyous child and revelled in his father's company, often asking for him when he'd left for the day or following him as he attended to chores at home. Antonio was Luca's shadow. Luckily, the boy still came to her for cuddles and comfort.

The breeze propelling the kite picked up and she drew her cardigan closer around her body. Not that she was cold. Her body temperature was elevated most days now.

Esther sat back, leaning on her flat hands and easing the ache in her back. Her younger self would be gobsmacked if she knew Esther Anderson, now Moretti, delighted in days spent working their farm, idling away the hours with Antonio, until Luca and Tommy returned from work. Young Esther would never have considered such a life for herself as she'd dreamed of exotic islands and royalty and balls and anything else that had appeared in her *Australian Women's Weekly*.

The pages of the most recent magazine flapped in the wind next to her. She still loved reading that silly magazine. No, it wasn't silly. It was the way of an Australian woman, she decided. She no longer dreamed of being part of the events in the pages, but instead, enjoyed reading about them. The book flicked open to a Fifth Avenue floral print dress. Once she would have swooned over it, dreamed of herself swishing around in it, the fabric resting against her legs. Today, she admired it and thought it pretty. She'd never wear it, would have nowhere to go in something so beautiful. Perhaps Margaret might purchase it?

The wind whipped it shut again. Yes, this was a forward-thinking magazine for and about women. Who was this Judy Barraclough who adorned the cover of the first edition of September 1955, sitting back in a chair and appearing intelligent and like she had something important to say? Reading the magazine had taught Esther a lot. She vowed to learn about why this lady was important enough to grace the nation's most prominent women's magazine.

No, Esther didn't long for more. She had everything she wanted. Finally.

Luca held Antonio's hand and led him to the plaid rug. "Let's join *Madre* for some afternoon tea."

The boy followed, would do anything his father asked. He sat with a plop and held out his hand for his cup. Esther gave it to him along with a biscuit that he immediately munched.

Luca gazed towards the rows of vines in neat precision that he had spent many hours planting.

"Beautiful weather. I'm afraid it doesn't look like any rain today," she observed.

"Yes, true. I'll have to water my precious grapes." He smiled and leaned over and kissed her on the mouth. A thrill still ran up her spine; it was something she'd never tire of. If she'd dreamed of romantic love, she could not have envisaged the feeling of fullness, of contentment and happiness that made her chest swell and life seem complete.

They'd arrived in the Valley and made straight for Windermere. Thank goodness for Alessandro's second cousin. Mr Valentino had an aging uncle with a property. He didn't live there anymore and had moved closer to family. The uncle would not return and wanted to be rid of the burden. Mr Valentino said they could have it, for a modest price.

The whole community had pitched in to make their dream come true. Finally, their own vineyard. The rambunctious Valentino family offered endless advice about the local region, known for its rich and fertile soil and already successful wineries. Luca had taken notes, considered each and every vine, tested the soil, and, of course, tasted each type of wine variety produced by their competitors. However, it didn't feel competitive; their little family was welcomed by everyone. And, too, Esther's Italian had improved fast.

It had been six months before Trevor came to visit. He remained employed at the brewery, but had met a sweetheart from Launceston, nearby to them.

"You're smitten with her," Esther had said when she listened to him. The gleam in his eye, the smirk, the inability to talk of anything else. Trevor didn't correct her.

Trevor brought news of Hobart. The four of them dined in their little cottage house with views of the Tamar River. They drank one of Luca's favourite local red wines. Trevor savoured the glass and talked with his eyes focused on the distance.

"Your sister Margaret has become the belle of Hobart."

"Really?" Esther exclaimed.

"She's prevalent in the social pages and seems to attend every event. Her husband's business has done well. By some stroke of genius, Arthur purchased a piece of discarded old furniture that was rumoured for the tip. Turned out it was an expensive and highly sought-after antique owned by a king or queen, or something of the like."

"Trevor," Esther admonished. "What's the detail? Which king or queen and what sort of antique?"

He shrugged apologetically. "Esther, I don't know those details. But I can say it was worth a mint and ever since Arthur restored it, your sister has been seen in a new flashy motor car with sparkly fine jewels and developed, might I say, if you'll forgive me, an attitude to match."

Esther glanced at Luca. "I can only imagine," she said.

"And the babe?"

"A boy named Arthur junior, and I believe there's a girl now, too."

Esther envied her sister then. She hoped she would have a daughter too, in the future.

"She goes well, then," Luca said. "What of Esther's mother?"

Antonio fell off his chair and landed with a thump. Screams erupted and Luca and Esther attended to him, soothing a bump on his head.

"Here." Trevor passed her an envelope. "Mrs Devitt writes, no doubt she'll fill you in on the gossip."

"Thank you, Trevor. I cannot wait to read her news, but you know she won't reveal any salacious tittle-tattle, that would be beneath her. Hopefully she'll give me a tidbit or two." Esther held it to her chest, buoyed by the prospect of hearing from her friend. "I miss her."

"And Maximillian?" Luca leaned in close. He hadn't had word from his old mate since they left.

"I've got him a job at the brewery. He's enjoying the free beer at the end of each day."

"That sounds like Max." They laughed.

Esther placed her hand on Luca's knee. "Luca, send a letter home with Trevor when he returns. And maybe a present. We'll invite him to visit."

Luca nodded. They had met many people since their arrival, but none had become special friends yet. Not like the ones Luca had left behind. Esther knew he felt their absence keenly.

They'd finished their meal and Esther rose to clear the table. "Coffee?"

A stillness entered the room. Esther saw a glint in Trevor's eye, a sadness that she couldn't interpret.

A knot formed in her tummy. What wasn't he telling them? Was it her mother? She hadn't heard from her since they'd left. Despite handing her the keys to her new home and helping her get settled, there'd been no thanks, no kiss good-bye, no kind words. It saddened Esther to think of it. Upon their arrival in the valley, Esther had written that they were safe and well, as she had to Margaret, but there'd been no reply. Esther wasn't surprised, but it hurt nonetheless. Charles had wished them well and even visited once, but news from him was scarce.

She busied herself with supper, an expert now at making coffee at home. It had become a shared ritual, and the bitter taste she'd once detested, she now devoured, enjoying more than she should.

Esther handed out the espresso cups and cleared her throat as she sat. "And my mother?"

Trevor paused with the small demitasse glass halfway to his mouth. He put it back down again and wrung his hands together.

Esther couldn't stand it. What on earth had happened?

"Trevor, it's okay. Whatever the news, you can tell us."

"All right. There was a fire at your mother's home. The house burned to the ground within minutes, the flames were intense. The fire brigade discovered a candle left burning. They surmise your mother had fallen asleep and it caught the curtains and the blaze quickly took hold and the house went up. Nothing could be saved.

The neighbours noticed and called for help, but it was too fast. And being such a little timber house and all…"

"And?" Esther needed him to say it.

"I'm so sorry, Esther. She didn't survive."

Trevor let the words sink in.

"And no one thought to tell me so that I could return for the funeral?"

"From all accounts, Margaret organised everything quickly and it was over before anyone found out. Mrs Devitt planned to attend, in your honour, but by the time she made enquiries, it was too late."

Bile rose up Esther's throat. It was one thing for her mother to be dead, but another not to say good-bye and for her sister to keep it from her.

She fell into a slump for the few days after Trevor left. Of course, she'd been disappointed by her family, but a small part of her would always belong to them, to the memories of the Cape and running free on the cliffs, of her father and his wisdom, of the salt and the wind and the frightening sea. Instead of dwelling on the bad memories, she'd remember the good times. Thoughts of her father always made her smile. Luckily, she was busy in their new home, their new life. She had her own family now and they were her priority.

***

And now, they sat and looked at Luca's hard work. Row after row he'd toiled and nurtured and cared for the vines. It was too early for a crop, but a crop would come and he would produce wine. Whether it was for their use only or something bigger and more successful, only time would tell.

Luca pulled an envelope out of his chest pocket.

"My family wrote."

Esther placed her palms together in front of her chest and waited, anticipating what he'd say next.

He slid the letter out and unfolded the pages. Esther could see the scribbled Italian words.

"They are proud of me, Esther." He paused, emotion overtaking him. "They are shocked that vines can grow here in Australia, but pleased that I am making wine. They realised after I left that it was what I truly wanted to do. They asked many questions about winemaking here, the climate, the type of grape, and my plans. They say one day they may come and visit."

Esther hugged him as tight as her tummy would allow. As she did, the baby within wriggled.

"My father confessed that my older brother, Lorenzo, was a terrible mistake. He was not interested in the family business, only drinking the wine. Now he's left and found another job. My other brother Raphael has taken over. They wish I'd never left and that they hadn't let me. They say also that the country is slowly rebuilding. Life is returning to our village."

It was all Luca had hoped for. Esther was grateful that Luca had revealed his pain at leaving his family, at the heartache of how he left. The unfinished business. The sadness. She knew he was happy with his new life and that they were together, but she understood old wounds were hard to heal. She knew it was those memories that drove him to work especially hard on the vineyard.

"They do not blame me for my cousin's death," Luca continued. "It was an accident. My aunt forgives me. She is happier now. She has two more babies. One is named Rose and the other, Stella. My sisters help her with their care. Her other children are doing well."

His family had forgiven him and now he could forgive himself for his past mistakes.

How far they'd come. Esther was no longer the immature, naïve girl who'd been raised on Bruny Island. She'd had experiences that she wouldn't wish on anyone. But she'd survived. Life had put her through the ringer, and she'd come out all right. Standing tall, wiser and happier for it. Now, she could truly appreciate what she had. Antonio had his father, the love of her life. They were expecting a sister or brother for their son. They had food and shelter—more than that, their own home—and would work through all of life's adversities together.

Antonio placed his hand on her belly. The baby moved as if detecting their brother was touching and listening. He giggled close to her skin. Esther placed her hand over his and took Luca's, and together they felt the baby squirming in her tummy.

The sun started its slow descent behind the nearby hills and the world was washed with light. It splayed across their bodies, making them appear golden. Esther rose her face to those rays and drank in the last dying embers of warmth for the day. When she gazed at the sun, it was full, clear, and bright.

That's exactly how she saw her future.

Of that she was certain.

ABOUT THE AUTHOR

Leanne is a lawyer and author who loves romance and reading. Her law career has caused her addiction to coffee, but provides her with countless story ideas. She lives in Brisbane, Australia with her husband and three children.

Connect with LEANNE:

website: www.leannelovegroveauthor.com
Facebook: leannelovegroveauthor
Instagram: @leannelovegroveauthor

www.BOROUGHSPUBLISHINGGROUP.com

If you enjoyed this book, please write a review. Our authors appreciate the feedback, and it helps future readers find books they love. We welcome your comments and invite you to send them to info@boroughspublishinggroup.com. Follow us on Facebook, Twitter and Instagram, and be sure to sign up for our newsletter for surprises and new releases from your favorite authors.

Are you an aspiring writer? Check out www.boroughspublishinggroup.com/submit and see if we can help you make your dreams come true.

www.ingramcontent.com/pod-product-compliance
Lightning Source LLC
Chambersburg PA
CBHW071148170626
46809CB00002B/815